Silver Bells

Book Three in the Jessica Hart Series

A novel by Jenn Brink

Look for these and other novels by Jenn Brink

The Jessica Hart Series
Black Roses: Book One
Cerulean Seas: Book Two
Silver Bells: Book Three

The characters and events in this book are fictitious. Any similarity to real persons, living or dead, is coincidental and not intended by the author.

First Edition: June 2016

Brink Books
https://www.jennbrinkauthor.com/

ISBN-13: 978-0692705414 (Brink Books)
ISBN-10: 0692705414

Library of Congress Control Number: 2016907456

Jenn Brink

For my Jessica Hart fans, keep it comin' y'all!

One

Thanksgiving is more than just a day of thanks for my mom, it's the dress rehearsal for the big show… Christmas. Tonight, mom was basking in her glory, enjoying the day before her favorite three weeks of the year. She had filled every available space with family and friends, from far and near, around a spread that could feed a small country for a month. The men brought their appetites after a day of football, hunting, and food. The children were picking at their plates after a day of uninterrupted grazing. The women, after coating the day's cooking with mom's holiday punch (which she'd had fermenting in the barn since Halloween), picked through their favorite dishes while catching up on the family gossip. Honestly, it was a bit overwhelming for a girl not trying to put on an extra thirty pounds.

That's why, against my better judgement, I found myself gathered around my parent's huge dining room table with people I barely know, that know me all too well. My family is loving, caring, cloyingly close… They're great, sometimes a little too great. Like now. Now is a bad time for me to be around others, especially my family. Fresh from my latest breakup, the house;

overflowing with mirth, music, spirits, and food; seemed to close in on me.

My name is Jessica, but only my mother and a couple of great Aunts who smell like Bengay call me that. On the surface, I'm a taller, younger, and thinner version of my mom. We have the same delicate bone structure, heart shaped face dotted with freckles, green eyes, and auburn hair. That's where the similarities end. My unruly strands are eternally fraying out of place, my makeup isn't perfect, my manicure needs redone, my skirts wrinkle unflatteringly when I sit, and my life is a terminal mess. Mom says I take after Grandma Hart, the bane of her existence. Grandma Hart says I should count my stars that I just *look* like my mother. All I know is my life needs an aspirin, most days.

Willing dinner to be over soon, I pasted a smile on my face, mentally slapping myself. "It's time to snap out of this funk you've been wallowing in. Get over yourself before you ruin mom's fun," I chastised myself.

"What?" My great Uncle Ernie turned his good ear towards me. He's almost a hundred, and looks every day of it.

"I said the food smells great!" I flashed him my biggest grin.

"No one puts out a feast like my favorite niece." Uncle Ernie beamed up the table at my mother.

Buzz ... Buzz ... Buzz ... Buzz ...

"What is that noise?" Mom looked up from her plate with a frown.

"What noise?" Dad asked, between mouthfuls of turkey.

6

"Sounds like someone's gettin' a call," Grandma Hart offered, creating a rustle around the table as people checked their cellphones.

"Uh… oh," I murmured to Barbie, knowing how mom feels about phones at the dinner table.

Straightening in her chair, mom tilted her chin in thinly suppressed anger. "I can't believe this. You brought your phones to the table, to Thanksgiving dinner!"

I had heard it so many times there was an echo in my head, *'No phones at the table, no excuses.'* Making eye contact with me, Junior wiggled his eyebrows accusingly towards our silver haired, half-conscious, great Aunt Margie. Trying to suppress a giggle, I quickly shoved an oversized forkful of mashed potatoes into my mouth. In unspoken reproach, Dad gave me a disparaging look. Rolling my eyes, I pointed toward the ceiling indicating my phone was upstairs.

With a deep breath, I tried to banish the irritation threatening to ruin my ability to enjoy the feast. They never suspected Greg of breaking the rules. Glancing down the table at my sainted older brother, I noticed family members dipping their heads in ignominy while attempting to unobtrusively slide offending electronics back into pockets and under napkins. Everyone except Grandma Hart. Grandma never followed the rules. While everyone else tried to hide their shame, Grandma held hers up high to catch the light. Grandma was texting at the table!

My Grandma Hart is short, and stocky, with long white hair. She still lives in her own home on twenty acres, rides horses, cooks all of her meals from scratch, is the local bookie, and drives her motorcycle to the nursing home to visit Grandpa Hart twice a day. I don't know how old Grandma Hart actually is. She doesn't look a day over seventy, but she's got to be pushing ninety. I only know that because Dad's oldest brother, he's the youngest of eight boys, just turned seventy-two.

Word on at the gossip mill is that she and Grandpa *had* to get married. She was promised to another man, until she went up two dress sizes. The way Grandma's sister tells it, it was quite the scandal. I look at her now, and can't imagine her ever being young. I can, however, picture her getting into trouble.

She's always doing something crazy. Like on her birthday last year, she asked me to take her skydiving. We had to go to the next county, so mom wouldn't find out. They almost didn't let her because of her age, but she shamed them into it. Sometimes, she even scares me. Like the time she broke a hip. After showing a bunch of kids at the skating rink how to do the shuffle on rollerblades, she spent three days in the hospital with a mild concussion. Rumor has it she'd hit the bottle just before putting on her skates, but I'm pretty sure she was stone cold sober. Like I said, Grandma has never cared for following the rules.

"Mama," dad admonished grandma.

"Loraine's grandson just set the turkey on fire," she replied, without apology.

"What happened?" dad's cousin Dottie asked from the other end of the table.

"He put it in one o'them fryers, without knowin' what he

8

was doing. It just plum exploded. Woulda' got the house too, but that wife o' his made him go out to the field to cook it," she replied, happy to be the one with the gossip.

"Good for her," approved Mrs. Scott, the widow from down the street. "My Herb almost blew up the kitchen once, making a sandwich. I told him, 'Herb stay out of my kitchen.' I did. Had to chase him out of the room with a frying pan. That man was a menace." Turning her face down, she added, "God rest his soul."

"Mama Hart." Mom's tone was reproachful. On her face she wore the look she usually reserved for me and Greg when we'd been particularly annoying. Lately, she's gotten in the habit of using it on Grandma.

Grandma glanced at the screen one last time before putting her phone away. I glanced at mom. She was giving dad an accusatory look. He had pointedly turned his attention back to his sweet potato pie.

Buzz ... Buzz ... Buzz ...

"For heaven's sake! We are having dinner. Thanksgiving dinner." Mom glared over the table, daring the offender to show themselves.

"Sorry mom. I've got to take this one, it's work," Greg apologized, pushing his chair away from the table.

"Of course Greg," mom smiled, forgivingly.

I couldn't help but roll my eyes. Greg is the golden child who can do no wrong in my parent's eyes. He's two years older than me, three inches taller, with bright blue eyes, and dirty blonde hair that never seems to be out of place, a respectable steady job, no police record, and a solid portfolio. In short, everything I'm not. Too bad our parents don't know him like I do.

After Greg left the room, the gossip switched to which rich and famous person would have the wherewithal to call Greg on such a sacred family day. What real estate transaction could be that important? Everyone had an opinion, everyone but me. I'm one of a select group who knows that short tempered, skirt chasing, Gregory Hart isn't what he seems.

My mouth full of gravy slathered tidbits, I struggled with myself for just a moment. "Who am I kidding? I *need* to know why *work* is calling during Thanksgiving dinner."

"What?" Uncle Ernie asked, fiddling with his hearing aid.

"I mean, what kind of little sister would I be if I didn't go check on my big brother? Right?" I continued talking to my mashed potatoes.

"I didn't catch that," Uncle Ernie said, tapping his hearing aid.

Waving him off, I stood up. "Excuse me."

My mother narrowed her eyes at me from across the table, probably worried that I would try to one-up Lorrain's grandson by setting the kitchen on fire. What she didn't know is that I did that yesterday, while making a fried egg for my breakfast. Other than some black spots on the curtain and ceiling, I think it cleaned up well. Hopefully, I'll be long gone before she notices those black spots.

"I've gotta pee," I said, in a defensive tone.

10

"Jessica." The word was filled with exasperation.

Ignoring her, I hurried through the archway, and up the stairs, toward my brother's room. Leaning my ear against the wood of the door, I heard him say, "I'm logging on now. Do I have a team?... Gotcha."

"What could be so important that he's getting called out on Thanksgiving Day?" I whispered to myself while slipping quietly down the hall to my room.

My room looks the same as it did the day I moved out, then back in, then out, then back in. Okay, I still keep some things here. I'm just not as adept at adulting as most everyone I know.

"I'm working on it," I insisted to myself, sliding behind the familiar white door. "Once I get a job... Who am I kidding?" I asked the girl in the mirror.

In silent reproach, she started back at me.

Leaning on the back of the door, I let out a sigh. "Three, two, one," I softly counted.

"Gregory! Is everything all right?" Mom's voice traveled up the stairs, clearly audible over the noise of the house.

"Fine mom. I'll be down in a minute," Greg called from his doorway.

Creak ... Creak ...

After thirty years, dad still hadn't fixed the steps. I could hear mom coming closer.

"Gregory, I'm sure that whatever you're working on can wait until after we've finished eating. After all, it is Thanksgiving, and we almost never get to see you. I spent days preparing this

11

meal. Uncle Godfrey came all the way from Houston…" She was just getting started, and Greg knew it.

I sat quietly, until I heard Greg's door click shut. I smiled, knowing that whatever national disaster had just occurred it had happened during mom's Thanksgiving dinner party. This was her shining moment. If vampires and zombies were attacking the White House, it could wait until after dessert. As soon as I heard Greg's feet on the stairs, I took a bobby pin off of my dresser and scuttled down the hall. It only took a second to jimmy the lock.

"Like riding a bike." I smiled at how quickly the skill had come back to me.

Greg's computer was up on the desk. Hurrying over, I crossed my fingers that it wouldn't be password protected. It was. He had locked me out.

"Damn!"

I'm not as good with computers as I am with doors.

"How hard can it be?" I asked the empty room.

After three tries, I was still locked out, and running short on time. With a resigned sigh, I looked around the room for clues. On a notepad, next to his wallet, were three different times and carriers written next to the words Yellowknife, Canada. It looked like someone was getting ready to book a plane ticket. I picked up his wallet, taking a moment to peruse the contents. Just a bunch of credit cards, a couple of receipts, and an unused condom. Wrinkling my nose at the thought of my brother having sex, I slid the condom back into its resting spot.

"What is he going to do in Canada?" I asked the empty

room.

"None of your business. Now, get out." It was Greg. He didn't look happy.

"I was just…"

"I'm sure you were. Mom sent me to tell you to come finish your dinner." He turned me towards the door. "Tell her I'll be down as soon as I finish up."

Buzz … Buzz …

The phone he had left lying on the computer desk began to vibrate. I got a look at the caller ID as he pushed me out the door, *Wolf.*

Anger raced through my veins. "What does HE want?"

At least he had the decency to wince. My words hung in the air between us as he yanked the brown leather wallet from my fingers. A second later, I was staring at painted wood, close up. Before I realized it, the lock 'clicked' into place. I was alone in the hall, with no answers, and too many questions.

Wolf, aka Eric, aka asshole, is my ex, well not exactly… It's complicated. He owns Wolf Inc., a company that specializes in doing things you only hear about on the news and in Jason Bourne movies. He's six foot two inches of chiseled muscle, with high cheek bones, a cute cleft in his chin, perfect mouth, eyes the color of espresso, thick dark hair that falls sensually across his forehead and curls under his ears, and a habit of appearing just when I need him, and disappearing just when I'm thinking about claiming an underwear drawer in his apartment.

Needless to say, it had been awhile since I'd set eyes on

Eric Wolf. We hadn't parted as friends. We hadn't parted as anything. The last time I saw him, he was wearing a pretty little brunette on his arm. In a raging fit, I walked out, without giving him the benefit of the doubt. Feeling like I owed him the chance to explain, I had swallowed my pride, and called him from the airport. What I wanted to hear was that I had overreacted. She was nobody, his cousin, sister, a nun raising money for local orphans...

Instead, *Veronica* had answered. I knew that voice, it was the she-devil that I'd seen wearing him, all Rambo'd up, on her arm like the latest fashion. She was gorgeous, sported a huge rock that few men could afford, answered his phone, and was all too happy to tell me to back off. She didn't even offer to tell him that I'd called before hanging up, and I didn't call back. Why bother? Eric wasn't the Rambo superhero that I'd thought he was. Eric was just one more bad decision in a long string of bad decisions. Eric had lied. Eric was taken. That was all I needed to know. I'd dated enough cheaters to last me a lifetime.

Reliving the moment tempted me to climb into my parent's hot tub with a pumpkin pie, tub of cool whip, bottle of tequila, and a fork. Instead, I put my ear to the door. I was going to have some words with Greg when he got off of the phone. He was talking to the enemy.

Greg's voice was muffled, but clear, "I need to talk to the boss about security... What do you know about it?... No, I don't have the time... Yeah, I'm at my parent's. I've got the flight schedules up. If I left now, I'd get there just in time to miss the last flight out... Looks like my only real option is a red eye out of

DFW in the morning... You are? I'd be a fool to go commercial when you're heading that way. What time?... It'll be tight, but I'll be there."

I couldn't imagine what might drag both Eric and Greg to Canada, in the middle of the night, on one of the biggest holidays of the year. "It must be big, to pull them away from their families on Thanksgiving," I whispered to the door. Blinking, I asked the empty hallway, "Does Eric *have* a family?" It hurt to realize how little I knew about his personal life. "I bet *Veronica* knows." That's the problem with eavesdropping, sometimes you learn just enough to obsess over what you don't know.

"They're calling it a kidnapping." Greg's voice interrupted my thoughts. "Uh huh... From what I hear, his wife has been less than helpful... Uh huh. The boss called it a matter of international interest... Sounds like it... Sister? Other than the Misses, I never thought of him having any family... I hadn't considered that... You may be right. It could be *that* kind of sister. You got a name?"

"Who is he talking about?" I wondered aloud to the empty hallway.

Greg's voice interrupted my thoughts, "I don't know... I read the brief. There wasn't much to it... If it wasn't the government, I'd think this was a holiday joke... You're right, the government does not have a sense of humor. Still, it's a stretch to believe... I heard. The boss said they handpicked operatives for a multi-national task-force. What they didn't tell me is why I'm on it. Not that I mind, but it's more of a CIA thing... You did? Well

15

thanks, I think... Tell me, who is your inside guy?... Right. You can't blame a guy for asking."

"I wish I could hear the other side of the conversation," I muttered grumpily to no one.

Leaning closer to the door jamb, I focused more intently, trying to catch any sounds from the other end of the line. To no avail. All I could hear was Greg moving around the room as he talked, packing his stuff.

"No one has seen him since Monday?... Everything was in place: suit, boots, sled, and reindeer?... No suspects?... No note?... Yeah, that's how I understand it. The only thing missing seems to be the big man himself... Yes, secure compound, with no sign of forced entry. No witnesses... Something's fishy."

"Gregory! Jessica! Dinner is getting COLD!" It was mom.

I rushed into the bathroom, shut the door, and called out, "Just a minute." When I didn't hear Greg's steps on the stairs, I hurried back to my position at his door.

"Yeah, she's here... I know. It came out of left field. I'd like to say it's not like her, but I'd be lying... No telling. They've been on and off for years... Last I heard, it was off." There was a long silence, then Greg said, "You didn't hear it from me... From what I hear, she set him on fire, then burned his house down... No, no charges are pending. As far as I've heard, they're calling it an accident... I told you that you didn't want to get involved with her. Sister or not, that girl is a walking disaster."

A smile slid across my face as I headed down the steps. He

asked about me. Maybe he does care. Reality had crashed down by the time I reached the bottom step. What they all said was true, when it came to relationships I should opt out, become a nun or something. It didn't matter that he was asking about me. He had someone else, someone I could never compete with, not that I wanted to. Anyway, none of that mattered. What mattered was, I was back in rural Southeastern Oklahoma, living with my parents, while I sifted through what was left of my sanity, again.

"Shit," I mumbled, wondering if I would ever get my life together.

"Jessica! Watch your mouth!" My mother sighed her displeasure, adding, "I told you not to eat all that cheese. We all know what cheese does to you." She turned her attention to Dottie before I could respond.

"What's up? Cheese?" Barbie smirked as I slid into the seat next to her.

Barbie is my mother's brother's only child. When her parents died in a plane crash, mom decided to be the mother that Barbie would never have. Not that she needed to. She may have been just ten years old, but she inherited her father's fortune, mother's looks, two super-sized life insurance policies, and a doting family. Grandma and Grandpa O'Grady sent her to the finest boarding schools, just as her parents had intended, and the whole O'Grady clan took it on themselves to give her everything that she could ever wish for, except what she wanted most – limits, making her what she is today.

As a child, I would have traded places with Barbie in a

heartbeat. Some days, I still would. She's absolutely gorgeous, has an amazing apartment, an impressive wardrobe, gets whatever she wants at the snap of her perfectly manicured finger, and the only man on this earth who doesn't absolutely adore her was taking his seat on the other side of the table, my brother Greg.

I looked up, the realization of what I'd done when I showed up two days ago on my parent's doorstep visible on my face. "I'm living with my parent's, again," I whispered in horror.

"Just figured that out didja?" Bubba smirked, causing Junior to choke on a mouthful of food.

Next to Barbie, Bubba and Junior are my two favorite cousins. They're two years older than me, wear cowboy hats, boots, and belts with big buckles, have a twisted sense of humor, and loyalty you can't buy.

"I don't know if I can do this." I stared down at my mashed potatoes, seeing only misery and failure reflected back at me.

"Have a glass of wine. It'll numb the pain," Barbie suggested, holding out her glass.

"She's gonna need somethin' stronger than that. Take a sip o' this," Bubba offered, holding out his glass.

After a slight hesitation, I took Bubba's offering, tipped it back, and drained it.

"Hang on whilst I get us another," he offered, with a knowing smile.

It felt like I had just swallowed acid as the liquid burned its way down my throat leaving behind a tingle and slight pumpkin tang, revealing it to be mom's holiday punch. "Okay," I managed to choke out after three tries.

Turning to Greg, Junior asked, "What's the four-one-one?"

Greg shrugged, "Big contract is ready to close as soon as the doors open tomorrow. I'm gonna have to catch a red-eye from DFW tonight. Give me a lift?"

Junior nodded, and answered, "Sure."

"Tonight? But, you just got here," mom protested.

"Sorry, mom. I've gotta make a living." Greg flashed her a sorrowful smile.

"Surely someone else…"

"Claire." Dad put his hand on mom's, the way he always did when he wanted to quietly tell her to stop talking.

"Charles." Mom's voice was edgy in return.

"The boy works hard to make a living. He can't just say '*no*'. Good jobs are scarce, and money's tight everywhere." Dad clasped her hand in support.

"Of course. It's just, I had hoped to spend a little more time with him." She smiled one of those smiles that didn't go all the way to her eyes, and her tones laced her words with guilt as she added, "What time do you need to leave?"

Mom is a master at making people feel guilty, even when they have nothing to be guilty for. Up and down the table forks played in half empty plates as their owners pretended not to hear the strain of her tones. Except for Barbie who, unaffected by the atmosphere, helped herself to more gravy.

"Not until after dessert," Greg answered, immune to mom's

imposed guilt. "Please, tell me you made apple pie," he added, with one eye on the dessert table.

Mom smiled, and said, "Of course. Everyone, help yourself to desert," releasing the tension.

With the impending conflict diverted, mom's guests turned their attention to the desert table, everyone but me. I couldn't get the conversation I had overheard out of my head. What was going on? It had to be important to interrupt Thanksgiving. And, why send Greg, an FBI agent, to be on an international task force in Canada?

"It just doesn't make sense," I muttered.

"Pie?" Bubba asked, staring down at the plate he had just set on the table.

"Pie makes plenty of sense. It's the amount of crap you pile on your food that boggles the brain," Barbie grimaced, at Bubba's plate. "Are you sure there's pie under all of that cool whip?"

"Yup," Bubba nodded, shoving a forkful of fluffy whiteness into his mouth.

"You're disgusting." Barbie grimaced.

"You ain't hungry?" Bubba asked me, ignoring Barbie.

"Huh?" I looked down at my plate, still full of turkey and dressing. "Oh, I guess not."

"Oh, well… Have you called him?" Bubba asked.

Barbie shot Bubba a warning look, just as Junior said, "I saw Mike over at the Wal-Mart yesterday. He didn't say nothin', but he looked good. I mean, he didn't look all burnt or nothin'."

The table shook, then Junior growled at Barbie, "Ow! Hey, woman!"

"What's going on over there?" Mom called from the other end of the table.

"Nothing Aunt Claire," Barbie answered sweetly. "This pie is delish! Can you make me one for Christmas?"

"You're coming back for Christmas?" Mom's face lit up.

"Where else would I go?" Barbie asked as if there was any question about who she would spend the holidays with.

"What's with you?" Barbie whispered in my ear.

"What?" I glanced up at Barbie.

"People are starting to talk." She motioned to the table.

"It's something I overheard," I explained. "A call to form an international team of agents. Eric is involved, too. It can't be good."

"What are you babbling about?" Barbie asked. "I can't focus with Junior Junior over there staring down my shirt. He's creeping me out." She motioned to one of my third cousins on the other side of the table.

"Yeah. He's weird all right," I agreed, still lost in my own thoughts. What had Greg said? '... *Everything was in place: suit, boots, sled, and reindeer. The only thing missing seems to be the big man himself.*'

"You'll be home for Christmas?" Mom implored Greg.

"Of course." Greg smiled like the angel mom believes he is.

"Santa's gonna give me a tractor, one I can drive all by

21

myself." Bubba's youngest beamed up at Greg.

"Patron saint of kids and bimbos," Barbie murmured into her wine. Kids don't like Barbie, the feeling is mutual.

"Santa!" I gasped in disbelief.

"No, Greg. Santa is as mythical as a good marriage," Barbie grumbled.

"If your standards included morals and love, instead of a fat bank account and big diamonds, you might have a good marriage," I quipped.

"Aren't you too old to believe in Santa?" she countered.

"I don't believe in Santa, but it sounds like the government does," I whispered.

"What are you talking about?" Barbie gave me a confused look.

"Going to Canada." Grinning, I asked, "You in?"

"Of course," she nodded.

"Excuse yourself after dinner. Pack light. We'll sneak out while everyone is distracted with cleanup. I'll fill you in on the way," I whispered conspiratorially.

"Why are we sneaking out?" She whispered back.

"Because, I'm not the golden child," I answered.

Two

Barbie was lying on my bed, a gleaming white four poster that I'd slept in since I was thirteen, watching as I shoved clothes into an overnight bag.

"Tell me again why we're running out into the cold, on Thanksgiving night, to catch a plane to someplace in Canada that even the Canadians have probably never heard of," Barbie insisted.

"I already told you. Greg got a call, and…"

"And," she mocked, "you're afraid somebody else is going to buy up all the prime igloo building spots?"

I shot her an irritated look, before admitting, "You and I both know that Greg isn't a real estate agent."

"He's not!" Barbie gave a fake gasp. "I had no idea!"

23

Tilting my head to the side, I raised one eyebrow at my melodramatic cousin.

"It's about time somebody let me in on the family secret," Barbie pouted. "I was starting to feel unloved."

"Unloved?" I questioned.

She shrugged. "So, what *does* dear cousin Greg do for a living? Let me guess. Superhero, detective, stripper…"

"Stripper?!" I exclaimed.

"No, that's all wrong. Who'd pay no-butt to take his clothes off?" She didn't even notice my look of disgust as she gleefully continued her monologue. "I know," she crowed, clapping her hands with delight, "super villain gigolo!"

Pulling a shirt out of the closet, I rolled my eyes, and said, "He's an FBI agent."

"FBI," she repeated. "What is the FBI doing sending an agent to Canada? That is definitely outside of their jurisdiction."

"That, cousin, is what we're going to find out." I smiled.

Squinting her eyes suspiciously, she asked, "Why are you suddenly so interested in what Greg is doing?"

I shrugged. "No reason."

Frowning at me, she shook her head. "I'm not buying what you're selling."

"I don't know." With a loud sigh, I put my head in my hands. "I mean, I need to get out of town, after the Mike fiasco," I admitted.

"I heard about that." She grinned. "Did you really douse him in gasoline before setting him on fire?"

"Is that what they're saying?" I asked, horror on my face.

"So, you didn't set him on fire?" she asked, disappointment in her eyes.

"It's complicated," I evaded. "Anyway, I'm pretty sure the engagement is off."

"I get that." She nodded her agreement. "What I don't get is what your kinky sex life has to do with following Greg to Canada."

"It doesn't, and my sex life is far from kinky. It's far from anything." I sighed, sinking to the floor. "I just... I don't know." I shrugged dismally. "It's like you said, why would the FBI send Greg to Canada? And," I hesitated before adding, "Wolf Inc. is involved."

Barbie's face brightened. "The Wolfman! I like him!"

Rolling my eyes, I grumbled, "Of course you do. He's a lying, cheating, scumbag. Just your type."

"So, you still don't want to talk about it?"

"There is nothing to talk about," I insisted, reaching back into my closet.

Barbie nodded, letting it drop. "Just so I've got this straight, we're going to the North Pole because you think your ex-lover is meeting up with your brother to hunt down Santa Claus, and you don't want to face your new-slash-old boyfriend after yet another really BIG fight where you may or may not have set him on fire."

Dejectedly pulling a pair of jeans off of my closet floor to put them in my bag, I nodded, and said, "It's fine if you don't want to go."

"Oh, I'm in," she said with a grin.

I looked up in surprise, and asked, "You are?"

"I always was. I just like to know what I'm getting in to." Grinning at me, she asked, "You don't think I'd let you run off half-cocked without me along to save your ass, do you?"

"I was really hoping not. Besides, you're paying," I answered, with a relieved grin.

"You have got to get a job, or a rich husband," she said. "I'd give you one of mine, but they've all come down with an incurable case of prison."

Curling up her nose at the shirt that I was shoving into my bag, she shook her head, and said, "That one makes you look fat."

"Fat?" I eyed the shirt in my hand. "I thought the stripes were flattering."

She curled her lip. "I'm sure they are, on someone else, and in a different color. Take the green one in the back. That color makes your eyes pop."

Tossing the striped shirt into the bottom of my closet, I reached for the green sweater that Barbie had pointed out. With a sigh, I slid it back into its place.

Barbie raised an eyebrow in question.

Rolling my eyes, I answered her unspoken question. "Mike gave it to me last winter, just because." With a sniff, I brushed away a tear.

"Time out." Barbie fixed me with a stare that implied I wasn't playing with a full deck. "YOU ran off to Washington with a psychotic killer you had only known about a minute, after finding Mike in bed with some skank. Jim wasn't gone half a day when YOU hooked up with the Wolfman. YOU lost everything but weight when the Wolfman left you, then happily jumped right back on that train at the first stop in Thailand. After an undisclosed altercation with the

Wolfman, YOU called cheater Mike to pick you up at the airport, let him brand you with a crappy little rock on your left hand... I could barely see it. Was it even real?"

"It wasn't a crappy little rock! And, of course you couldn't see it, from New York!" I interrupted. "Anyway, it's not like you have a great track record. Did you even have a wedding the last time you got married?"

Holding up a hand, Barbie shook her head, and said, "Jess, you're the sister I never had, but you can't keep dissing me about my choices, all while bouncing around from bad news to worse. Four months ago, you were swooning all over the Wolfman. Two months ago, you were giddily picking out curtains and flatware with Mike. Last month, you drunk called me at two am because you had run into some guy you dated a lifetime ago, and missed your chance with him to be an unfulfilled housewife with a gaggle of parasites hanging off of you. Everything was love and roses with you and Mike last week. I get here, and all you tell me is that you may have set the man on fire, moved back in with your parents, and you're *pretty sure the wedding is off*. Now, you're sniveling over a sweater that Mike bought you as you get ready to run off to the frozen tundra after the Wolfman. And, YOU want to lecture ME about my life choices?"

I wanted to say something, but she was right, and I didn't want to say that.

"At least I know what I want from life," Barbie said softly.

"Do you think this jacket will be warm enough?" I held up a brown faux leather jacket lined with green polka dotted silk.

"What happened? I *need* to know!" Barbie yanked the jacket

27

from my hands.

"It just…"

"Don't you dare tell me it just didn't work out." She glared up at me. "I invented that lame excuse."

Knowing I couldn't win, I took a deep breath, before caving in. "Fine. If you must know."

"I must," she insisted.

"He picked up the phone the other day," I shrugged, "and went psycho."

Raising a suspicious eyebrow, she asked, "Who was calling that would make an otherwise sane man go psycho? An ex-sane man?"

"Yeah." I nodded. "I told Mike, hundreds of times, I have nothing to say to Eric."

"Uh huh." Barbie pursed her lips. "And, Mike?"

"Didn't believe me. *He* accused *ME* of cheating! ME! I've never cheated on anyone." I paced the floor agitatedly.

"Technically, that's not true," Barbie interrupted.

I stopped mid-rant, mouth open, staring at my cousin in astonishment.

"Jim wasn't nearly as dead as you thought he was, when you started playing tongue hockey with the Wolfman," she argued.

"Wha… He's the one who cheated on ME. I can name names!" I raged on, not sure who I was talking about anymore.

"I see." Barbie watched as I paced. "You can't blame him, Jess. The Wolfman is super yummy hot, and loaded. You come back from Boston all distraught, and you won't talk about it. He calls, and you still won't talk about it. Now, you're running off to Canada after him. You obviously have unresolved feelings for the Wolfman."

"You've been spending too much time with your therapist." I glared across the room at Barbie.

Barbie shrugged. "I'm not seeing him anymore."

"Of course not," I conceded. "What happened in Bora Bora?"

Barbie grinned. "I found someone much more enticing, if you must know." She frowned. "But, we were talking about your man drama."

"Right." I sighed, flopping onto the floor beside my bag. With another loud sigh, I rolled onto my back, staring up at the ceiling.

"And?" Barbie prompted.

"And, we fought, and fought, and fought, for days. We fought about Mike and Traci Lee. We fought about me and Jim. We fought about Mike and Ashley. We fought about me and Eric. We fought about me and Mike. We fought about stupid stuff like what to have for dinner and what color the living room should be. We fought about my wanting to move, and live, and do something exciting with my life. When we ran out of things to fight about, we started over." I paused. "We're just so different. Mike wants to stay here, forever. And I, I want adventure, excitement…"

"If you start singing Disney songs, I'm out of here," Barbie warned.

Sighing, I said, "We were both tired of fighting when Mike said that I needed to grow up, that I was lucky to have him, that no sane man would ever consider marrying me, and that Jim had dodged a bullet."

"Oooohhhh!" Barbie cringed. "So, you gathered your stuff and moved back home?"

"Not exactly," I murmured.

"What exactly did you do?" Barbie asked suspiciously.

"It was an accident. I'm not even sure how it happened," I admitted in a small voice.

"You did set him on fire!" Barbie's eyes were wide.

"I found a matchbook, to a motel. He doesn't smoke!" I defended myself.

"Jessie?"

"He said Bubba left them there. How convenient." I frowned, reliving the moment.

"Jessie!"

"I took a match out of the matchbook, lit it, and tossed it at him, then another, and another. He was backing up, yelling that I was crazy. I followed him, throwing lit matches. About halfway through the matchbook, he tripped over a can of paint thinner. It got all over him and the floor. The match was already midair. It landed in a puddle of paint thinner. In seconds, the flames were racing up his pant leg." Guilty tears filled my eyes as I relived the moment. "I didn't expect him to catch fire. They were just matches!"

"Is he okay?" Barbie asked, stunned out of her usual flippancy.

I nodded, tears streaming from my eyes. "He kicked off his pants before the flames could hurt him. He tried to beat out the fire with them." I paused, quietly adding, "It was like those movies where you see the fire race across the accelerant. We were lucky to get out."

Barbie shook her head. "Only you would accidentally set a man on fire, right after he told you that no sane man would want you, proving his point."

Tears slid down my face as I whispered, "I know." Going back to my packing, I pulled a waist length coat from my closet.

Barbie shook her head, motioning for me to return it to the hanger.

"It's the heaviest jacket I have," I protested.

She raised an eyebrow at me in response.

"It has a hood," I offered encouragingly.

Barbie rolled onto her back, and sighed. "Someone needs to teach you Okies about winter wear. Your ski clothes would be more appropriate for this trip."

"Ski clothes! They're probably in the attic." As if on cue, a large thunk echoed through the ceiling causing our eyes to move upward.

"Sounds like they found Santa," Barbie said cheerfully. "Guess we can stay here."

"Very funny." I rolled my eyes at my cousin. "Come on!"

It didn't take long to discover the source of the noise. We just followed the thunk of footsteps to the attic. Greg, Junior, and Bubba were so busy digging through the ski clothes that they didn't notice us come in.

"What are you doing?" I demanded of Greg.

"I'm planning a ski trip. Since no one's using them, I thought I'd borrow some cold weather gear," Greg answered, without skipping a beat.

"Liar," I mouthed silently over the shoulders of my cousins.

"How old are those clothes?" Barbie asked, horror in her voice.

Greg and I exchanged shrugs. At the farm, it never snowed much or even got below freezing for more than a few days, if you didn't count the wind chill. Most of the people I knew around here didn't even own a heavy jacket. Snowsuits and other cold weather gear were loaned out on an as needed basis, like a ski trip. There was no telling in what decades our mismatched winter clothes had originally been created.

"What are *you* doing here?" Greg asked, as he went back to picking through the pile of clothes.

"I need some clothes," I said truthfully. "Barbie invited me to go skiing this weekend." Greg wasn't the only accomplished liar in the family.

"I don't know if I want to be seen with you in these clothes. You'll look like a bad eighties movie," Barbie scoffed.

"Skiing?" Greg gave me a disbelieving look. "You're broke, jobless, and sponging off mom and dad. Don't you think it's time you acted like an adult, with a job and a place of your own, instead of flitting around the slopes with the tanked-up snow bunny?" He motioned callously towards Barbie.

Thinking about what Barbie had said earlier, I sighed. "That seems to be the general consensus, but…"

But what? But nothing. Was I running away or towards something? I didn't know. It didn't matter, anyway. Greg was right, I couldn't afford to go. I groaned, trying to dispel my rising panic. I should stay here and get a job. A job would let me be independent. I needed my own space, my own life, a job, and a place of my own, not that a roommate would be bad. Living with a roommate would be a step up from living with my parents. I glanced up to see the whole room staring at me.

"She's working for me," Barbie announced.

"What?" Greg, Junior, and Bubba said at the same time.

I thought it, but no sound came from my mouth.

"I need a personal assistant. And, as Greg was so nice to point out, Jessie needs a job." Barbie's voice was so calm and matter of fact that I almost believed her.

I shook my head, hoping that I was having a nightmare. Barbie's last personal assistant, Velma, had been swiftly dismissed after shaving her head and charging enough Vanilla latte's to fill a Jacuzzi, Barbie's sparkling white Jacuzzi, to Barbie's Visa. Luckily, Barbie had returned home with her latest boyfriend, Muscles No Brain, when she found the girl slurping latte' foam, sans clothes, in her once blindingly white bathroom. It took all of the poor guy's strength to keep her from killing Velma before the cops showed up. Barbie dumped Muscles for not supporting her in her time of need. Velma went to a psycho ward. Muscles left hundreds of sobbing messages on Barbie's phone. And, I was forced to listen to Barbie fume about having to fix the stained Jacuzzi, tile, and paint for weeks.

Greg gave me a disbelieving look.

"My life has officially hit bottom," I muttered.

"She's moving in with me," Barbie announced, with a shrug.

As I said, truth spinning comes naturally to our family. At

least, I hoped she wasn't serious. I reached up to touch my thick auburn hair, willing myself not to think about what had happened to the personal assistant before Velma.

"Don't worry about the clothes, Jess." Barbie eyed the ski equipment warily. "We can get some once we get there. It'll give us a reason to shop."

"What do you need a personal assistant for?" Greg asked Barbie suspiciously. "You don't have a job. I don't think you've ever had a job."

"I am a highly sought after New York City socialite," Barbie said, as if that explained everything. "Jessie," she snapped her fingers at me, "we've got a plane to catch."

"You're leaving now?" Greg gave us an incredulous look.

Barbie nodded. "I've got a charity luncheon back in New York."

"Have you told mom and dad?" Greg demanded, stepping in front of me and blocking my path to the door.

"Ummm…" I faltered, not sure what to say.

"You do plan to tell them, don't you?" He narrowed his eyes, staring me down.

Something caught my attention causing me to turn. Junior and Barbie were standing by the door, a little too close, deep in conversation. Greg started to speak. I gave him a nudge, pointing their direction. Our personal agendas were forgotten as Greg and I watched our worst shared nightmare come true.

"Need a ride to the airport? I got room," Junior leered at Barbie.

"That is sooo sweet, Junior." She batted her eyes seductively.

Like a nineteen eighties horror movie, the scene slowly unfolded in front of us. His boastfulness and her saccharine tones were making me nauseous. I heard Greg gag beside me. I flashed back to high school. The unbidden memories I had meticulously buried swimming before my eyes.

Barbie smiled innocently, as her hand caressed Junior's arm. "I just love BIG trucks."

I threw up a little in the back of my mouth.

"They don't come any bigger than mine." Junior grinned down at Barbie.

"I'd love to go for a ride," she purred.

"Ewwwwwww!!! TMI, TMI! I need eye bleach," I gagged loudly.

"What? He's not *my* cousin." Barbie rolled her eyes.

"He's our cousin. You're our cousin. Enough said." Greg glared. "Anyway, Junior's broke. Ten months ago, Lora Lee ran up all of his credit cards, took their money out of the bank, picked up the kids from school, and ran off with some guy she worked with at the Pizza Shack."

"So?" Barbie asked Greg.

"So, you only go for rich guys, with no kids, at least none that live with them," I reminded her.

Barbie looked at Junior, "You've got custody?"

Junior nodded. "Joint custody. It was working 'til that bitch ran off with them to who knows where."

Barbie gave him a hard look, and shrugged, before saying, "I was just looking for a ride. I'm in an inexplicable place right now."

Junior nodded. "Yeah, I can't get married anyway. The divorce ain't final, on account of they can't find the bitch to serve her papers."

"No," Greg asserted.

"Off limits," I agreed.

Barbie pushed out her expertly glossed lips, crossed her arms, and narrowed her eyes. "Fine."

"Now that that's settled." Greg narrowed his eyes suspiciously, then with an accusatory tone said, "I don't know what you two are up to, but you are up to something. So, I'm only going to say this once - stay out of trouble."

Junior and Bubba stood like sentinels, nodding their agreement behind him.

Barbie glanced at me with a questioning look.

Unconcerned, I rolled my eyes, and said, "Be serious. I'm a personal assistant now." I'm proud to say, I only choked a little on the words. "I'm far too busy to get into trouble. Besides, I'd hate to get fired." I smiled sweetly at Barbie.

"Right," Barbie agreed. "Let's go."

"We're leaving in fifteen minutes, if you still want that ride to the airport," Junior offered as Barbie sashayed past him.

Turning, Barbie smiled sweetly, asking, "Can I get you boys to help me with my suitcases?"

"Sure thing!" Bubba and Junior crowed excitedly.

I watched as my cousins stumbled over themselves getting downstairs to Barbie's luggage. Men never fall over themselves to help me with my bags. Maybe I should turn into a slutty blonde? I wondered. No, I'd probably do that wrong, too. The only guys I'd attract would be retired Hell's Angels from Grandpa's nursing home.

"Luggage? I said to pack light." I eyed Barbie from my bedroom doorway.

Rolling her eyes, she said, "I packed light to get here."

"You brought four bulging suitcases and your makeup bag," I reminded her. "That is not packing light."

"You can't expect me to go without the necessities." She shrugged me off.

Bubba stood in the middle of the room, staring at Barbie's luggage. Finally he asked, "Is that them?"

I was pretty sure he'd never seen anything like it. Each suitcase was about four feet tall, bubblegum pink, with a bejeweled letter on it. When she carried the whole set, they spelled out her name. Barbie walked up to the letter 'R', unzipped and dumped it, filling my room with more clothes than I currently own. It took all I had to keep from laughing as Junior gingerly picked up a string bikini, and held it up.

"I thought we might get a chance to sunbathe," Barbie offered in explanation.

"Sunbathe?" I asked incredulously. "It's fifty-four degrees outside."

"I know it's a little chilly," Barbie acknowledged, "but the sun is out and my tan is fading."

"You brought a wardrobe full of summer clothes to Thanksgiving?" I asked, holding up a barely-there dress.

37

"In this bag. That's why I'm leaving these here. I don't think we'll need them in Can..., um New York."

"You're not going home, are you now, sweet tits?" Junior asked the question more like a statement.

"Of course we are. I'm leaving these here for Jessie, next summer. My closets are full, and we all know she will have moved back by then." Barbie tilted her head up in a defensive manner, daring anyone to disagree or question her further.

Junior and Bubba grinned at each other.

"We won't try to stop ya, if ya'll just tell us where you're really headed, just so someone knows where to look when ya don't come back," Bubba reasoned.

"Unless you want us to stop you." Junior winked at Barbie.

"That's so cute. You think you could stop us." Barbie smiled, flipped her hair, and pushed out her boobs; not that she needed to.

"Ya'll hear that. Sweet tits here thinks I'm cute," Junior grinned back at Barbie.

"Cute, in a chauvinistic backwoods hillbilly way," Barbie taunted.

Ignoring them, I placed Barbie's makeup bag and my carry-on in suitcase 'R' and zipped it up. We would need an empty suitcase for the cold weather clothes we'd have to buy soon.

When I looked up, Junior had stepped into Barbie's bubble. He was looking down into her eyes, speaking softly. "You ain't never had a real man put you in your place, have you sweet tits? Well, it's long overdue." Without waiting for her to speak, he grabbed her butt, lifted her up to eye level, and kissed her. After what seemed like an eternity, he set her down. "Now you tell Junior what's goin' on, or Bubba and Jess'll have to clear the room to give us some privacy."

Barbie looked stunned, like she'd been slapped. I saw her nod slightly as she licked her lips. No man had ever called her on her attitude before. I knew she was about to spill her guts.

"I'm gonna be sick," I announced loudly. Now that I had their attention, I needed to take their minds off of each other. "Bubba and Junior grab the 'B's." I quickly shoved a suitcase in Junior's now empty hands. "Barbie take 'A'. I've got this one."

With a shake of his head, Junior tousled my hair. "Okay little cuz, I'll see ya at Christmas. Make sure you bring that pretty little thing with you. We've got unfinished business."

Barbie's eyes widened as she followed Junior out the door, empty-handed.

"Shit," I groaned. Who was going to carry that last suitcase?

Three

"Hey woman."

I looked up to find myself staring into the bluest eyes I had ever seen.

"Lookin' good," he said, holding out a beer.

Even though I had known him my whole life, I couldn't help but check out the incredibly hot, in a redneck kind of way, guy blocking my path. He was taller than me, by a lot, with a wiry fit build, blond hair, and a mischievous twinkle in his eye. This being a holiday, I knew without looking, he would have on his good boots and nice jeans. Catching myself admiring his tight abs, visible under a t-shirt that complemented his eyes, I mentally slapped myself. We were a wrong fit, I reminded my hormones; destined to make each other miserable, crazy, or both. Just when I was ready to walk away forever, he smiled. I hated to admit it, but his boyish good looks and quick, sexy smile were a welcome sight. My heart skipped a beat, making it necessary to remind it that Mike Baine was a poor choice. A really poor choice.

"Mike." I was displeased to hear my voice raise an octave. "When did you get here?" I made an obvious effort of scanning the room for Junior and Barbie. I didn't want him to know he had my insides all aflutter. And, I needed to make sure those two weren't left alone for a minute.

"A while ago." He shrugged. "I've been lookin' for you."

"I'm sure." I was going for casual, instead my words came out sounding more than a little flustered.

"Heard you were here." He nodded conversationally, casually opening the beer bottle he had just handed me.

How does he always manage to sound so nonchalant, while my thoughts spill out in a preadolescent sounding word vomit? I wondered to myself. Life is just not fair. "I've gotta get this outside," I muttered, gesturing to the huge suitcase precariously balancing on the stair behind me.

"Got it." Without breaking a sweat, he lifted the suitcase, turned, and said, "It can't be as heavy as the one Junior brought down. That big guy looked like he was about to pop a vein. What's she got in there?"

I shook my head as I followed him down the rest of the staircase. "This one just has another suitcase and her makeup bag in it. There's a heavier one still in my room that I'm hoping some shmuck will drag down." I frowned up the stairs.

41

"Jethro," Mike called out as we reached the entryway.

A hefty teenage boy, who had the misfortune to look bored while eating half a chocolate pie covered in what appeared to be an entire tub of Cool Whip while playing a handheld game, glanced our way. I think he's a third cousin, either that or a stray.

"Ya you. There's another one o'these upstairs. Go get it." Mike motioned up the stairs.

"Name's not Jethro," the teenager responded sullenly, without glancing away from the screen.

"It belongs to the blonde in the hoochie mama skirt, boob shirt, and heels. She'll let you see her tits if you carry it out for her," Mike informed him.

The teenager paused, and glanced around. Looking back at Mike, he silently shuffled toward the stairs.

"Third door to the right," I called out, following Mike to the front door.

"Closest he's ever gonna get to first base," Mike grinned at me.

I couldn't help it. The giggle forced its way out of my throat, followed by a renegade smile.

"So, whatcha got going tonight?" He asked casually.

"Spending some quality time with Barbie," I answered evasively.

"Tomorrow?" Was that a catch in his voice?

"Busy," I sped up, hoping to avoid a confrontation.

Mike stopped walking. Blocking my path, he said, "Sunday, while everyone else is at church?"

"I can't." I looked away. "I'm sorry."

"Jess, I *told* you it wasn't mine. I meant it." His voice was sincere.

"I know." I sighed. "Bubba vouched for you."

"So?" He stood in front of me expectantly.

"Look Mike, you're a great guy, but…" Those blue eyes were mesmerizing. I shook my head to break the spell. "Anyway, I really can't. I'm heading to the airport with Barbie."

He gave me a confused look. "When your mom called, she didn't say anything about you leaving town. She said you were unhappy, that you missed me."

Mom? He was here because my mom had called and begged him to take me back? My cheeks reddened with a mixture of anger and shame. "Can't they wait at least forty-eight hours before they start interfering with my love life?"

"I hear I was their third call, but the only taker," he teased playfully. "Word got around about you setting me on fire."

"It was a little fire. Anyway, you deserved it," I defended myself.

"Deserved it?" Mike's eyes popped in anger. "You burned my house down!"

"It was an accident!" Pursing my lips, I growled, "What kind of person leaves paint thinner lying around his living room?"

"The kind who's painting his living room because his fiancé doesn't like the color," his voice cracked with the strain of not yelling.

Shaking my head, I took a deep breath and said, "Mike, I gave you the ring back."

"I know." He let out a deep breath.

Taking another deep breath, to calm myself, I asked, "Mike, why are you here?"

He shrugged. After a minute when neither of us spoke, he said, "Things are a little dull without you around. And, you're good in bed." He raised an eyebrow. "Very good."

Tilting my head to the side, I rolled my eyes. Not that I didn't appreciate the compliment, but our sex life hadn't been that great lately. He had to have noticed.

His smile faded, and his face softened. With a sigh, he admitted, "I want you to come back home."

"Mike." I blew out a frustrated breath. "You don't have a home for either of us to come back to. I burned it down two days ago, remember?"

"It was just a house. We'll get a new one, and you can paint it whatever color you want." He paused, then softly said, "I miss you."

"Mike," I paused, not sure of what I wanted to say.

"Don't say it," he warned. "Don't say anything you'll regret later."

"Mike." I shook my head softly.

Reaching up to stroke my hair, he said, "Jess, I admit, it may have been too soon to start talking forever. There's a lot of water under that bridge, but that's all it is. Water."

"Mike," I held up my hand, then said, "I'm tired of fighting."

"Right!" He grinned. "That's what I'm saying."

"You are?" I cocked my head at him.

"Jess, it doesn't matter who you've been with, or who I've

been with. That's all in the past." He paused. "Are you with me?"

Shaking my head, I said, "No."

"What I'm trying to say is, I just think, we owe ourselves, each other, we owe it to everyone to give us another shot. A fresh shot." He gave me a hopeful look, adding, "No more fighting. Just us."

Mike and I had avoided the *why do we keep getting back together* conversation for months. I, for one, wanted to keep it that way. Why? Was it Eric? Maybe. Maybe, I was afraid of what I'd learn about myself? Maybe, I already knew? Maybe, I was afraid he was full of shit? Maybe, I was afraid he wasn't. Too many maybes, and not enough answers to questions that I wasn't ready to for. Thankfully, we had reached Junior's truck. As I stepped up to the others, Bubba gave me a strange look.

"What happened to your face? You allergic?" Bubba asked me.

I could feel my face flush even more. Fortunately, Greg and Junior showed up, followed by my parents and a horde of family. Before anything else could be said, someone tossed the last of the bags in the back of the truck. I slid through the throng, closer to my two enamored cousins. Barbie is my best friend, but I couldn't let her break Junior's heart. And, I knew she would.

"I'm serious," Barbie was saying to Junior.

"Sweet tits, I've looked for them. My family's looked for them. The cops have looked for them. They even put out one o'them Amber Alerts. No one's seen hide nor hair o'those kids in months." He shook his head sadly, stopping me in my tracks. Was that a tear?

"I'll find them," Barbie assured him with a hug.

My mouth opened in shock. I'd never seen Junior cry, not even when he got bucked off that bull six years ago. He broke three ribs and a leg, and just laughed.

Catching up to me, Mike gave me an admonishing look, then said, "I'm sure jetting around the world is fun, but I'm not the only one you're walking out on. Everyone knows you and me have had our share of problems. We both know, that's just growing pains." He glanced at Junior, and said, "Some people around here have real problems. Not us. We can work through this."

I stared at him. "Mike, for most of the last ten years, *I've* been your *real problem*."

We stared at each other in silence, surrounded by my family as they continued their cheerfully loud goodbyes.

"Barbie honey, you're not leaving already?" Mom asked.

"Sorry Aunt Claire, I have an event I forgot about." She reached out and hugged mom. "I'll be back for Christmas."

"Make sure you clear your calendar this time," mom admonished Barbie while giving her a big hug. Turning to me, she said, "Jessica, don't get back too late. We have a busy morning planned. We're going to town to Black Friday shop at Wallyworld. When we get back, we'll get out the Christmas decorations. If you're wondering what to get me this year, I need new ornaments." Mom shot me an accusing look.

"Umm… You still have your silver bells," I offered.

Mom gave me a look that said she was not amused.

I'd hoped she wouldn't still be mad, but I knew better. I had dropped the heavy box full of hand blown glass last New Year's, when we were putting the Christmas decorations back in the attic. Dad had tried to catch them, but the box had bounced off of him and hit the floor. In my mind, I could still hear the eerie silence punctuated by the unnatural jingling of priceless and irreplaceable ornaments, many of which mom had owned since before either Greg or I were born. Grandma and Grandpa O'Grady's silver bells, handmade in Germany over a century ago, had been the only surviving ornaments.

"I'm sorry," I apologized.

"If silver were breakable…" Mom shook her head, "Christmas is a time for forgiving." Taking a deep breath, she forced a smile onto her face, then said, "If things go well during our Black Friday shopping, we may stop at Leroy's Pancake House. I know how much you love pancakes."

A twinge of guilt assailed me at leaving like this.

"Take it as a gift," Barbie whispered in my ear as she sashayed past me to the other side of the mob.

Barbie was right. I knew it, and normally I wouldn't feel guilty about slipping away like this, but mom was trying to be so nice about the ornaments. I knew how much they meant to her. I opened my mouth to say something, what I didn't know.

Grandma Hart beat me to it, "Claire, you know Jessie hates Black Friday shopping. I've got some things to keep her busy for a few days around my place." Grandma gave me a knowing look, adding, "That'll let you decorate your place without worrying about her breaking more of your nice things."

"I don't know Mama Hart." My mother gave me a wary look. "Jessica is… Well, you heard about Mike's house?"

"I heard on the radio, the time just before Christmas is when people are most likely to get the depression." Grandma put on a sad face. "Wouldn't that be a dandy of a Christmas if an old lady offed herself, just 'cause she was all alone, and it could have been avoided if her granddaughter had just stayed with her for a few days."

"Mama?" Daddy asked.

"I'm just saying, sometimes I get lonely. Anyway, you have so many other visitors to attend to, you'd hardly notice her not being here. It would mean so much to an old, old woman." Grandma artfully produced a single tear.

"Well of course she can stay with you, mama. Just send her home when you get tired of her," daddy agreed, giving grandma a big hug.

How about I take her for a week?" Grandma gave me a questioning look.

I nodded my agreement.

From behind my parents, Barbie held up two fingers.

"Make that two weeks." Grandma paused, then said, "I'll just bring her back at Christmas." At that, Grandma leaned in to hand me my purse whispering, "You kids go have fun, now. And, don't forget to come see me as soon as you get back. I want to be the first to hear all about your adventures."

Before mom could respond, family members were telling her how lucky she was to have such a thoughtful daughter to help take care of grandma. As Greg and my cousins piled into Junior's truck, mom shot me a suspicious look. She said something as she hugged me, but I couldn't hear over the roar of the engine, the radio, and the crowd of relatives gathered to see us off. Probably for the best.

Once Barbie had climbed up into the truck, mom was forced to release me. As I reached for the door, Mike grabbed me by the arm, spun me around, held me by the forearms, and stared deep into my eyes.

"Stay," he whispered.

"Mike." I shook my head. "I... I can't."

"Can't or won't?" he asked knowingly.

A tear slid down my cheek as I gently kissed his lips. Afraid I would change my mind, I jumped into the backseat, shutting the door. Before I could get my seatbelt fastened, Junior had fired up the engine, turned up the radio, and headed down the dirt road. Mike stood in the drive watching us leave until we were out of sight. I know, because I was watching him.

Four

"The beach? Have you lost your mind?!" I whispered incredulously to Barbie. I did not want to draw attention to our argument. I could only imagine Greg's reaction if he knew we were piggybacking onto his assignment.

"No," Barbie answered calmly.

"Everyone else is heading to the North Pole," I pointed out. "Where Santa lives and disappeared. Why would we go to the beach?"

"Isn't it obvious?" Barbie asked.

"No, no it isn't." I frowned, adding, "I mean, yes, knowing that you love the beach, it is. But, this isn't about you."

"No, it's about you showing up your brother," she flicked a perfectly manicured hand towards the front seat, "and the guy that slipped through your fingers, by retrieving a fictional fruitcake with a soft spot for reindeer, furry red suits, and black leather." Barbie gave me a stern look, then stated in a no nonsense tone, "We're going to the Caribbean, so get on your phone and buy us a couple of tickets."

"Any particular airport?" I asked, snidely.

Barbie gave me a questioningly look, then said, "You're the assistant. Assist."

Frustrated, I decided to try one last time, "Barbie, this is important. Stop insisting on heading to the land of palm trees and mango delights when you know we should be on the next flight to Christmas Town!"

"It's my card, and my card says that we're going to the Caribbean," Barbie smirked. "Anyway, you're the employee. The employee goes where they're told."

Shutting my eyes in frustration, I asked, "Why?!"

"Why? Because, you hijacked my holiday to find some fanciful fellow in seriously outdated duds, just so you can show up the most recent hottie to diddle around on you."

"Oh…" I really didn't know how to counter that.

Grabbing her phone, Barbie said, "Let's start with Aruba. I'm guessing he'll be at a tourist resort, soaking up the sand and working hard to be invisible, either that or hiding out in a palm covered hut on some long forgotten beach."

"What makes you so sure he's in the Caribbean?" I couldn't help asking.

Giving me an exasperated look, Barbie asked, "If you lived in a place where it snowed twelve months of the year, that the rest of humanity had deemed uninhabitable, where would you go?"

"In search of sun, sand, fruity drinks, and half-dressed men," I answered, awestruck that she might actually have a plan.

Barbie grinned, and said, "Exactly."

She was starting to make sense. "Uh oh!" I murmured to myself, knowing this is the part I always look back on as where things went horribly wrong.

"Make it happen," Barbie ordered, shoving her phone and a credit card at me.

"Jessie, you know once she starts making sense, it's time to run, not walk, the other way," I mumbled to myself, while steadfastly ignoring the little voice of reason inside my head. Taking a deep breath, I keyed in the number, buying our tickets to Aruba.

"Looks like this is where ya'll get off," Junior called out from the front seat, as he pulled up to the drop off lane in front of DFW. Turning in his seat, he looked at Barbie and asked, "You sure you gotta go? It just don't seem right."

Flashing him her megawatt smile, Barbie hopped out of the truck and said, "We'll see you at Christmas."

With a shake of his head, he climbed down from the truck cab. "Let us give ya'll a proper goodbye then."

Stepping down behind her, I pulled Barbie back, just as Greg stepped in front of her. We knew what Junior meant by a proper goodbye, and we were having none of it.

"No time. Our flight leaves in an hour!" I exclaimed, grabbing a luggage cart. Once the cart was loaded, Barbie and I hurried through the doors, leaving Greg behind us.

After a quick stop for our paper tickets, Barbie waved her ticket to Aruba at me, grinned and said, "I knew you'd come around,"

"Why not? I mean… we don't actually know how to find Santa's workshop," I reasoned. "No one does. People have been searching up and down the North Pole for centuries, or a long time anyway. Maybe, it doesn't even exist, right? Anyway, there's no telling where the old guy went. And, we can't just walk around asking if anyone has seen a fat man in a little red sleigh. So, Yeah, this might just work. We simply need to look for an overweight grampa, wearing a bushy white beard, with a line of children following him around like baby ducks. Do they have toy makers in Aruba? That would probably be the best place to start our search."

"Leave the sarcasm at home." Barbie shook her head at me.

"Sarcasm?" I gave her a confused look.

With a sigh, she shook her head, and asked, "You don't really believe the old man will be wandering around in candy apple swim trunks, asking snot covered midgets what they want for Christmas. Do you?"

That was exactly what I believed, but I wasn't about to admit it to Barbie. "How do you envision him?" I asked instead.

Cocking her head to the side, Barbie grinned mischievously. "Leaning back on a lounge chair, roasting his bleached fat rolls over the hot white sand, while sucking down a fruity drink, as the never ending eye candy struts along the water's edge."

"Uh… uh… but… he's married!" I stuttered, clumsily crossing myself. "Santa would never ogle some slut in a bikini!"

"Bikini, no. Banana hammock, yes." Barbie grinned.

"Banana... WHAT!" I stopped walking, staring in open mouthed horror at my tiny blonde cousin.

That was it, she had crossed the line this time. I mean, she was implying that Saint Nikolas would not just cheat, but do it with a man. There was no way God would let blaspheming one of his saints go without reprisal. With a nervous glance around the terminal, I took a step away from my cousin.

Giving me a look that said I was being dense, Barbie explained, "No way he's straight."

"What!?" Did she want a lightning bolt to strike her dead?

"Sure he has a... wife." Barbie finger quoted the word. "But, you never hear about them spending time together as a couple. It's always about him with the delivering and her in the kitchen, baking. I mean half the movies and stories don't even have her in them."

I opened my mouth to protest.

She cut me off, saying, "What straight man would coordinate his pants, suspenders, jacket, gloves, and hat? He giggles, has a fetish for black leather and white fur, and spends his time with small children and animals. It's obviously a highly fabricated ulterior lifestyle brought about by social intolerance of his sexual preferences."

Not even noticing that I was blocking the line, I stood rooted to the spot, staring at Barbie in disbelief. "Are you implying that Santa is gay?" I somehow manage to choke the words out.

"Of course he's gay!" Barbie motioned for me to catch up with the security line. "Do you really think a straight man would work selflessly, every day of the year for eternity, just to make the world's ungrateful offspring happy? I've known too many straight guys. It's not their style," she insisted.

Catching up to the line, I mumbled, "Santa is *not* gay." My words earned me a surprised look from the young mother in front of me.

"Any straight man, with mountains of cash, who could coordinate his outfits that well, and work that selflessly, would have a *much* hotter wife," Barbie reasoned, not caring who heard her.

"Huh?" Barbie's logic was making my head hurt.

"Mrs. Claus is no prize." She frowned, adding, "Always stuffing high cholesterol, fatty foods into the old man, with the goal of keeping him unattractive, in a loveless marriage, just so she can live a life of ease. She's probably hoping for a heart attack."

Enough was enough, my face turned red with anger, and I snapped. Holding up a hand to silence my cousin. I somehow managed to choke out, "Now you're insulting Mrs. Claus? I can't believe you!"

The woman in front of me turned, and said, "Do you mind?"

"*You* can't believe *me*?" Barbie ignored the woman. "*I* can't believe *you*. What does Santa's sexual preference have anything to do with him being a beloved fairytale?" Barbie glared up at me. "I have got to get you out of the Bible Belt."

"You're crushing my childhood!" I cringed, turning away from her, toward what was bound to be another unpleasant TSA experience.

"Why does everything have to be about you?" Barbie demanded, following a little too close for comfort.

Unwilling to discuss Santa's sexual orientation any longer, I busied myself by angrily shoving my belt, shoes, and purse into a gray bin. Thankfully, she let the subject drop as she placed her purse, boots, and sparkly belt into an identical container. I was busy checking my pockets for anything that might set off the metal detectors when she sashayed past me, turning on the wattage for a very accommodating TSA.

With a strained sigh, I stepped up to the metal detector, just in time to set it off. Looking down at my jeans and bare feet, I couldn't help but wonder, just how much metal is in a zipper? I had plenty of time to think about it while the TSA eyed Barbie's retreating figure.

Twenty minutes later, I was savoring a hot chocolate while meandering solo through the terminal towards my gate. Barbie hadn't waited on me. Being unwilling to get roped into another debate about Santa's sex life, I was in no hurry to find her. Enjoying the time to myself, I stopped to watch a plane slowly move away from its gate.

I was in the midst of a euphoric calm, when a familiar chill swept down my body, leaving the hairs on the back of my neck up, and my mouth dry. Closing my eyes, I willed my body to behave as pheromone saturated cologne overpowered my senses.

"I am not going away Trouble, so you might as well open your eyes," rough timbered words caressed my eardrums.

"Take a hint," I hissed, eyes stubbornly closed.

Strong hands grasped my shoulders, spinning me around to face my accoster. Opening my eyes and cocking one eyebrow, I found myself face to face with the man that I'd been avoiding for months. Crossing my arms, I eyed him with what I hoped was disdain. It must have been because he let go of my arms, folding his protectively across his chest. There we stood, in silence. The rest of the airport bustling by, in a hurry to get someplace else.

"So, how've you been?" I broke the silence.

"Terrible," Eric frowned down at me.

"Oh." I smiled. "That's nice."

"Nice?" He asked in disbelief.

Nodding, I answered, "Yes, it is."

"I heard you *were* engaged," he offered.

Refusing to show him any emotion, I shrugged. "It didn't work out."

It was his turn to raise an eyebrow.

"It's complicated," I evaded.

"I heard." He nodded. "Good thing he was insured."

Was that a smile behind his stern countenance? It was! He was secretly laughing at me. I narrowed my eyes, retorting, "It could have happened to anyone."

"Anyone who was dating you? Probably," he agreed.

"Okay, that's enough pleasantries. What are you doing here?" I asked, hands on my hips.

"That was pleasant?" He tilted his head expectantly, waiting for an answer.

Rolling my eyes, I asked, "What do you want?"

"Want?"

"You must want something," I insisted.

"You really need to work on your people skills," he said, with a grin.

Closing my eyes in irritation, I snarled, "I'll keep that in mind."

The humor left his face, as he asked, "So, this is how it's going to be?"

Glancing at my bare wrist, I mumbled, "Look at the time." Stepping around Eric, I gave him a fake smile, and said, "I'd love to catch up, but I've got a plane to catch."

Grasping my arm, he asked, "Where are you headed? I can give you a ride. Then, we can talk."

Shaking my head, I vainly attempted to separate my arm from his hand, while rambling, "It's fine. Really. I should get going. I'm sure you need to get back to… Veronica." The name tumbled out, unbidden, and I regretted it instantly.

"Veronica?" He gripped my arm tighter. "What do you know about Veronica?"

"I know enough." I twisted, jerking my arm. Managing to slide it out of his grip, I spun away from him with enough force to propel me into a passing security guard, hurtling us both down to the hard tile covering the floor.

"I've gotta go!" Somehow, I managed to untwine myself from the twenty-something. "Sorry!" I bellowed, stepping on the man's fingers in my hurry to get away. In the distance, I could hear them call my flight. Crap! I really did need to go. I took off at a run towards my gate.

"Dammit! You've got to stop letting him get to you like that. He's a cheating, lying, heartthrob. No, No, No! You are no longer attracted to him!" I chastised myself while running through the practically deserted airport. "I just wish I could have made a respectable, poised exit."

"Stop!" Someone called in the distance.

I rolled my eyes, continuing my one-sided discussion as I rounded a corner, "Who does he think he is? Showing up here? What, I'm supposed to drop everything, and swoon all over him? Could he be any more conceited? Honestly! What did I ever see in that...?"

Something hit me in the back. Seconds later a strong electric current raced through my back and into my limps. I gasped as my body convulsed, leaving my mouth tasting like I had just sucked on an old penny. I thought I heard someone yell my name, just as I experienced the unpleasant sensation of being jerked backwards and off of my feet. I must have hit my head, because everything went black. When I came to, the security guard and Eric were tensely standing over me. There was no sound, and I couldn't move my muscles.

"I'm paralyzed!" I yelled. Instead of the words that I had planned to say, it came out, "Ihhmm Pooohhmmmeffd!"

Eric glared at the security guard before leaning down to help me to a sitting position. My head lobbed to the side, resting on his shirt. He reached down to wipe the drool from my chin before glaring at the security guard again. The security guard shrugged. After an awkward minute, the security guard sheepishly handed my purse and boarding pass to Eric, then walked away.

"Are you alright?" Eric asked as the sounds of the airport slowly began to hum around me.

I tried to shake my head. Instead it flopped uselessly toward the floor, taking my body with it. *No! I'm not alright. Can't you see that?* The words came out in a strange garble, "Ngpht! Nuffloor dkoo. Ceioooot ysthhhtb?" There was no way he understood me. All I could do was fume inwardly at my useless body.

Eric ignored my grumblings, instead he carefully checked my body for obvious breaks and bumps. Once he was satisfied with my condition, he leaned me up against the wall. From my new upright position, I could see that the floor was covered with a thick brown liquid.

Is that my hot chocolate? I asked. Once again it came out in an unintelligible gobbledy gook, "Ig tgan mgn hiitooootelllph?"

I was busy trying to make my tongue work when a fuming Barbie crouched beside me, demanding, "Where have you been? We missed our flight!" Pausing to take note of the situation she asked, "What is all over you?"

All over me? "Atuo ooggg nneell?" Don't tell me I'm wearing hot chocolate all down my backside. So much for dignity.

She cocked her head, looked at me, and asked, "What happened to you?"

"Mmnnnupplleer," I tried to explain, unsuccessfully.

Not even questioning my lack of comprehensible speech, she turned her attention to Eric. Raising an eyebrow, she asked, "Flying commercial today? Don't tell me the Batplane is in the shop."

I could detect a twinge of a smile in his voice as Eric answered, "Not today, Goldie. I'm parked out back."

Barbie grinned, and asked, "So, what did you do to my cousin?"

He gave her an incredulous look before explaining, "I did

nothing. She picked on the wrong security guard. He was reading a Dear John text when she ran into him, knocking him to the floor, and spilling his coffee all over the place. Then, she stepped on his hand, broke his pinky finger, and took off running."

Barbie motioned to me before asking, "What happened to her hair, clothes, and is that drool?"

"She has a real knack for finding trouble." He shook his head in disbelief.

"Klooiuphhgc!" I protested.

Barbie wrinkled her nose at the congealing brown puddle next to my body. "Do I want to know?"

"I'm pretty sure it's hot chocolate." He pointed to the crushed Starbucks cup lying in the center of the brown liquid.

"Hot chocolate?" Barbie shook her head in exasperation. "How did she end up like this?" She gestured to my motionless form. "She's a little clumsy, but this, this is special, even for Jessie."

"Security guard chased her down calling out '*Stop*'." He gave me a pitying look. "She didn't."

"Mumnnhhhggrth!" I attempted another protest.

Barbie gave him an expectant look.

"He tasered her." Shaking his head, he added, "I can't say I blame him."

Barbie gave me an incredulous look, then said, "I can't leave you alone for a minute!" With a grimace she asked, "Have you seen yourself? You're a mess. Not your normal mess. You're a mess of epic proportions. I've never seen anything like it, and I've seen everything."

I really needed to get to a mirror. There was a bathroom across the way. Surely, I could limp over there. My leg twitched, but that was all.

"She'll be fine in a few minutes," Eric said.

"She can take her time. We've missed our flight." Barbie scowled down at me. "There isn't another one, to anywhere, until tomorrow."

"Where are you headed? Perhaps, I can help," he offered.

"Lkoiuppelld!" I attempted to protest.

Barbie, smiling mischievously, responded, "Canada. We're heading to Canada."

"Canada?" He gave her a suspicious look.

"It's ski season!" she exclaimed, clapping her hands in excitement.

There was a worried expression on Eric's face as he asked, "Trouble skis?"

Barbie cringed. "Not well, but she's great at drinks at the lodge."

"Don't let her kill herself, or anyone else." Eric picked me up, roughly throwing me over his shoulder, as he led the way down the terminal.

"Phffffkltrb!" I exclaimed, to no avail.

Unable to communicate my displeasure, all I could do was take pleasure in the idea that Eric's nice clean clothes were getting soiled with hot chocolate. It was clear that I was being carried off by the last person that I wanted to spend quality time with, against my will, and without my one piece of luggage.

Unable to speak clearly, or even move, I blinked my goodbye to my carry-on bag, hoping that someone would find it, read the tag, and mail it back home to me. We stepped onto the Wolf Inc. jet, just as red lights flashed all over the terminal, bringing the airport into a high security alert. All I could do was plan to get even with my traitorous cousin, as soon as the paralysis wore off.

Jenn Brink

Five

"What are you up to?" Greg's tone was hostile.

"Nothing," I moaned, crumpled up with my head in my hands.

"You're a terrible liar." He glared.

"You're my brother, and a federal agent. Why don't you do something useful," I groaned.

Looking perturbed, he asked, "What would you have me do?"

His snotty tones made me want to punch him. I considered it, but I'd have to let go of my head. I was pretty sure if I did that it would fall off. Instead, I replied, "You could start by arresting my kidnapper."

"Seriously?" He stared at me as if I'd just asked him to steal the Statue of Liberty.

"Seriously! I was minding my own business when Rambo," I

pointed toward the front of the cabin, "grabbed me, causing me to run into that security guard, and get tasered. As if making me miss my flight wasn't enough, he threw me over his shoulder Captain Caveman style and carried me onto to his plane, hijacking me against my will. That is kidnapping!" I insisted.

Greg sighed, and said, "Wolf didn't kidnap you."

"Yes, he did!" I motioned to the plane.

"No, he didn't." He shook his head. "You missed your flight. He offered you and Barbie a ride. Barbie accepted. That is not kidnapping."

"Except for the part where I was carried off while unable to respond," I pointed out. "I may not be an FBI agent, but the last I heard carrying someone off without their permission was against the law. As an agent and my big brother, you should be looking out for my welfare, not standing up for your delinquent friend."

Greg shrugged. "Who do you think you're kidding? We both know you only came to the airport hoping to run into him."

"N...," I started to protest.

With a stern look, he interrupted, "Up in the attic, you told us you were going skiing. In the driveway, Barbie told mom you were going to New York. Your ticket said Aruba. And, your partner in crime over there told Wolf Canada. It doesn't take an FBI agent to know you're lying."

"We're going skiing in Canada, after a quick side trip to Aruba, and then to New York. It's a whirlwind trip," I clarified, amazing myself with my ability to put all of that together so soon after having my brains scrambled.

Greg, not nearly as impressed, just glared at me.

How did he always seem to know when I was lying? "It's annoying," I mumbled to no one.

"Wolf?" Greg asked pointedly.

"I wasn't hoping to run into him. I'm over him," I insisted.

Greg gave me a disbelieving look.

"You really want to know?" I was going to regret this. I just knew it. "Fine." Lowering my voice conspiratorially, I admitted, "We came to find Santa."

Greg's mouth dropped open.

"I know!" I held up a hand to silence him. "I shouldn't eavesdrop, or snoop. But, I always wanted to meet Santa, and now he's missing, and… Well… Barbie and I want to help find him, to save Christmas. Don't try to deny it, I know that's what you're doing."

"You're telling the truth." Greg's voice was filled with surprise.

"I do that sometimes," I quipped.

"You actually believe in Santa Claus?" He gave me a pitying look. "Okay, you probably do, but not Barbie. That gold digging, cock-juggling, man bait only believes in what she can see, touch, spend, and scam away from the next loser who can't think past her double D's."

"She's got her own theories." I wasn't about to get into Barbie's thoughts about Santa's marriage stability and sexual orientation with Greg. Not while he sat badmouthing her. "Why are you being so negative? You're the one who was sent by the government to find him," I pointed out.

"This whole production, it's not what you think." He sighed.

"What is it?" I asked, genuinely curious.

"Jessie, this is a highly secretive government project. I am not authorized, or inclined, to explain the details to you, and no you cannot help," he remonstrated.

"I knew you'd say that." I nodded. "That's why we didn't tell you."

"I'll have Wolf drop you at the nearest airport. Now, I'm only going to say this once, so pay attention." Greg slid out of the seat next to me, stared me in the eyes, and commanded, "Go home."

Hunching over, I slid my head back into my hands, moaning, "Why? How do I talk myself into these messes?"

"Better yet, how do you talk me into them?" Barbie asked.

Almost imperceptibly, I nodded.

"Here, take these," she commanded.

Glancing through my fingers, I could see three little pills nestled in the palm of her outstretched hand.

"The big ones are for your head. The little one is for the nausea," she explained.

"You're a Godsend. I take back all the nasty stuff Greg said about you," I mumbled, shoving the pills into my mouth as I accepted a glass of clear fluid. Quickly, I chased the pills with the proffered drink, just to hack it back up. Burning liquid was streaming out of my mouth and nose. It was all I could do to keep the medicine from exiting with it. "What was in that glass?!" I coughed as tears streamed down my cheeks.

"Vodka." Barbie sniffed the glass. "What did you expect?"

"Water! I expected water!" I sputtered.

"I like Vodka better." Barbie shrugged.

"You don't take medicine with Vodka!" I gasped.

"You never know what chemicals water has in it. Vodka's pure." She held the glass out to me.

"Water, please," I begged.

"Fine, but only because you asked nicely," Barbie conceded.

A moment later she returned with another glass, half full of clear liquid. This time I carefully sniffed it before taking a suspicious swallow.

Paying me no attention, Barbie directed a disgusted look at Greg before shaking her head. "I overheard your little convo with our favorite secret agent. He has *got* to lighten up," Barbie grumbled.

"Give him a break, you know being around you makes him antsy," I reminded her.

"He can't still be upset about Vegas? That was three years ago, and they weren't that good of friends." Barbie half rolled her eyes at Greg's back.

I narrowed my eyes at my cousin. "It wasn't even a year ago, and they were best friends, until your ex had him gunned down at the craps table."

"How was I supposed to know he was out on bail, and obsessed with me?" She shrugged off any responsibility, just like always.

"I still have nightmares. There was so much blood." I blanched.

"Machine guns," Barbie said, as if that explained everything.

After a moment of silence, I pointed at Eric's men and wistfully said, "I just wish we knew what they know."

"Give me ten minutes." Without another word, she walked up three rows to flirt with three of Eric's men. "In the meantime, here's my tablet. Send out the emails in the save folder. Then, you'll need to make us travel plans from the next airport, and find my luggage. Honestly, I don't even have my makeup bag!"

Out of the corner of my eye, I noticed Greg tense as she sashayed past him.

"Serves him right," I mumbled to myself, "for letting me be kidnapped."

Leaning back into my seat, I shut my eyes. Focusing on breathing in and out, I willed the medicine to work quickly, before I had to deal with Greg and Barbie coexisting in the same space again.

Six

"Feeling better?" A warm voice interrupted the blackness.

"I don't know." I yawned. "How long was I asleep?"

"We're about to land in Toronto." Eric looked like he wanted to say something else.

"That long?" I asked, just to break the uncomfortable silence.

He nodded, then said, "Yes."

"Thank you… for… waking me," I stammered uncomfortably.

"No problem." He moved to leave.

"Why?" I asked, surprising us both.

"Why what?" He turned to look at me, confusion on his face.

"Why would you let me think that…," I flustered. "When all the time… Veronica." I didn't know how to put what I was feeling into words.

"Veronica?" Eric shook his head. "It's par for the course for you to blame your troubles on Veronica. When are you going to grow up?"

"What?!" I jumped up, then sat down, grasping my head in my hands. "Ooooh," I murmured in pain.

"Tell me one thing. Were you engaged at Phuket, or did you wait until after you ran out of my office without so much as a see you later?" Hurt seeped through his words.

A familiar face peered over the seat in front of us. "Sir, they need you up top."

Eric nodded, his lips a taut line. Not making eye contact with me, he growled, "Later."

I didn't have long to think about his words before a dragon tattoo slid into the seat beside me. Laughing eyes met mine, while callused fingers pulled jet black hair into a small pony tail at the nape of a naturally bronzed neck. That smile was infectious, I couldn't help but return it.

"Hey," he greeted me. "Things have been dull around the office, since you left."

"Hi Angel." I couldn't help but grin. "How's Isabella?"

"Pregnant!" He exclaimed.

"What!" My mouth fell open.

"I'm gonna be a papa, with a little bambino!" He made a rocking motion with his arms. "We're getting hitched next month, before she gets too fat for her dress."

Grinning, I exclaimed, "That's great!"

"Yeah." He gave me a goofy grin. "I still can't believe it. You coming with Wolf to the wedding? You'll love Isabella."

"That might be… awkward." I cringed.

"Nah!" He waved the thought away. "You're with Wolf. That makes you like, the boss's girl. You oughta make a honest man outta him, like Isabella with me. Yeah?"

I blinked. The boss's girl. An honest man. What would *Veronica* have to say about that? Visions of his perfect little girlfriend, wait fiancé, sporting a big shiny rock on her left hand swam before my eyes. I needed some air! The walls of the small plane were closing in on me! Frantically, I clawed at my seatbelt, trying to unfasten it.

"You okay?" Angel's voice was full of concern.

"I have to get out of here," I shrieked.

"They're landing the plan as fast as they can," he reasoned.

I leaned forward, desperately trying to avoid a scene.

Angel gave me a concerned look. "Should I call Wolf?"

"No! I mean, I'll be fine. Just give me a minute." I closed my eyes, concentrating on breathing slowly, in and out.

"It's not a problem," Angel insisted. "It's not like he's landing the plane or… uh oh."

"Uh oh? What is uh oh?" I asked, momentarily forgetting my panic.

"Nothing." Angel pursed his lips together, keeping his eyes toward the front of the plane.

Pulling myself up to strain against the seatbelt, I could just see some activity centered on what appeared to be an unconscious man. It was hard to tell just what was going on with all the big guys in black cargos huddled in the aisle. It was like staring into a black hole.

"Who is that?" I leaned forward against the seat in front of me.

"The pilot," Angel answered, sweat trickling down his forehead.

Turning my head towards my seatmate, I repeated, "The pilot!" Taking a deep breath to calm myself, I asked, "There is a co-pilot, right?" The longer it took him to answer, the more I felt myself losing the battle to not panic. "There has to be a co-pilot. Isn't it a law or something that you have to have a co-pilot?"

"You probly wanna sit down, unless you can fly a plane," Angel cautioned, fastening his own seatbelt.

"Barbie!" I exclaimed loudly while lowering myself back to my seat. Not waiting for her to answer, I grabbed the two ends of my belt and shoved them together. "Barbie!" I called out again.

"The blonde?" Angel asked.

"A couple of years ago, Barbie dated an airline mogul. She dumped him, but not before getting her pilot's license. If he hadn't gotten himself arrested for drug trafficking, she probably could have gotten a plane out of him." I raised up, yelling louder than I'd intended, "Barbie! *Oomph!*" My seatbelt pulled at my insides.

"The blonde?" Angel asked again.

"She's smarter than she looks," I defended my cousin.

"What?" Barbie stuck her head over the seat in front of me, obviously annoyed at the interruption. "Did you get those emails sent? What about our reservations? The car service? Have you tracked down my luggage, yet?"

"No," I responded in disbelief.

"Seriously?" Exasperation colored her words. "A trained

73

monkey could do this job. Wha…,"

"Barbie!" I interrupted. "Do you still remember how to fly a plane?"

"Of course, I borrow my friend's Cessna every so often, to keep from getting rusty." She paused suspiciously, then asked, "Why?"

I pointed to the black hole, and exclaimed, "That's the pilot!"

Barbie's eyes widened. Taking a deep breath, she said, "Don't worry, I'm sure the co-pilot has it under control."

"Co-pilot?" Someone asked.

"There is a co-pilot?" She asked the man seated next to her.

"Technically," he evaded.

"Well, where is he?" She was using the no nonsense voice she saved for telemarketers, ex-husbands, and personal assistants. Not giving him a chance to answer, she ordered, "Jessie, find the co-pilot, and tell him to get his ass up there."

The plane dipped alarmingly to the left, as if to accentuate her words. I sat debating between leaving the safety of my seatbelt, and the wisdom of her words. Tightening the belts as far as they would go, I pointed at Angel, indicating that he should go and find the co-pilot. It made sense to me. I didn't even know who to look for.

"He's already up there," Angel offered instead.

"What's the problem then?' Barbie asked, as the plane dipped erratically to the right.

Paling, the man seated next to Barbie cringed. "It's Wolf."

"Wolf?" Barbie and I asked at the same time.

Angel nodded, adding, "He can probly land the plane. He's

been taking lessons."

The plane made a sudden dip in response to his words, sending the black hole scattering to their seats.

Forcing back the contents of my mostly empty stomach, I squeaked out, "Barbie!"

"On it!" She called behind her, already halfway to the front of the plane.

Fighting down a wave of panic, I tried to remember a prayer, any prayer. "Hail Mary…" The plane jerked. "Angel of God…" It was still shuddering, making me thankful that I hadn't eaten breakfast yet.

Hearing a masculine voice join mine in the long forgotten prayer, I startled. It was Angel. A second later, I recognized my brother's voice adding to ours. It wasn't long before the small plane was full of voices repeating the prayer together. God, if you get us through this, I promise to go to church, I silently added.

Minutes later, the plane evened out. Knowing my life depended on Barbie and Eric, it was a harrowing ride as the plane made an emergency stop at the nearest airport. It was only after we taxied into a smooth stop, that I could bring myself to unfasten my seatbelt. Looking around, I realized that I hadn't been alone in my quiet panic. Faces beamed at each other from all corners of the plane as, one by one, we realized that we weren't just alive, we had landed safely.

Half an hour later, the pilot was secured in the back of an ambulance on his way to a local hospital. Barbie and I were finishing breakfast in the terminal, while Greg and Eric searched out a replacement pilot. I had hoped to catch some gossip illuminating the details of this trip and what could be expected once we reached our destination, but it seemed Eric's men only gossiped about each other. No one was talking about anything other than the pilot's poorly timed heart attack.

"This sucks." I sighed, dragging my fork through the sugar congealing on top of the Cinnabon in front of me.

"Tell me about it. I spent hours flirting with the Wolfman's merry men. All I got was propositioned," Barbie grumbled into her coffee.

"Well, that shirt is a little…" I waved my hands in the air, not wanting to annoy her further.

"A little what?" Barbie's voice dared me to finish the thought.

Raising an eyebrow, I answered, "You have to admit, you're a little…" I gestured toward her chest, adding, "Don't you think?"

"What is that supposed to mean?" Her voice dripped with animosity.

"Come on! You're busting out of it." I motioned to the bulging seams that seemed to defy physics.

Barbie held her tongue as Greg and Eric sauntered up to our table, each with a steaming cup in his hand. Glaring across the table at me, she shot me a look that said our conversation wasn't over. As Eric slid into a chair next to Barbie, Greg seated himself next to me. Sullenly, Greg focused his attention on dumping tiny packages of milk and sugar into his coffee until it was a milky tan color. Once he had finished doctoring his coffee, he helped himself to what was left of the Cinnabon lounging indolently on the plate in front of me.

76

Grateful to be spared the calories, I shoved my plate his way. Anxious in the unnatural quiet, I glanced up at Eric, curious that he hadn't so much as looked at me. He hadn't seemed to have noticed me at all. Instead, he was carefully studying Barbie.

Barbie matched his stare without blinking.

I was about to ask what was going on when Eric took a drink of his coffee, then casually asked Barbie, "You have a license?"

"For a lot of things," she answered glibly.

"This is a bad idea," Greg interjected.

Eric nodded his agreement, then said, "I need a pilot. Can I count on you?"

Grinning, Barbie winked. "I thought you'd never ask."

"Alright then." Eric nodded. "Time to go."

Greg's lips were a disapproving straight line, not that anyone was paying him any attention. Anyone but Barbie.

Still grinning, Barbie winked at Greg as she stood up from the table.

I rose to follow, just to have Greg push me back into my chair. "Not you." He dropped a handful of hundred dollar bills on the table. "You're catching the next flight home."

What? He couldn't do this to me! Knowing it would be no use arguing with my brother, I turned to Eric. He avoided my gaze.

Without a word, Barbie sat back down. Casually, she picked up her almost empty coffee cup. Once she had everyone's attention, she calmly stated, "We're a package deal."

"We don't need her," Greg protested to Eric.

"We can't afford the delay," Eric reasoned.

"It's not worth the risk of having her along," Greg argued. "She's worse than Jessie." He gave Barbie a pointed look, then said, "She gets people killed."

"That was one time, and it wasn't exactly my fault," Barbie rolled her eyes. "Let it go already."

"Let it go!" Greg exclaimed.

"I'm sure there are hordes of trustworthy pilots, waiting around the airport to drop what they're doing and run you and your men up north, that won't ask questions or tell what they overhear or see," Barbie said knowingly, ignoring Greg.

"Fine," Eric overrode Greg's objection. Looking at me he said, "At least we'll know where she is, and what she's up to."

Giving Greg a sly smile, I whispered, "Better luck next time," as I slid past him.

Seven

Stifling a yawn, I watched snowbanks rush by as we raced down an abandoned runway towards a barely discernible tower that stood, as if abandoned, against a surreal background. I was excited to end what could only be described as the most uneventful, and truly mind numbing flight of my life. Barbie had spent the entire trip in the cockpit with Eric. I had spent it with Greg, who had made no effort to hide his displeasure at having me onboard.

Looking out the window at the snow covered wasteland, I turned to ask where we were. The only person near me was Greg. I already knew how that conversation would go. I glanced around for a friendly face, but everyone else was busy pulling on their winter gear in anticipation of exiting the plane.

Watching them, I was reminded of mine and Barbie's lack of preparation. What were we thinking? We were in Canada, northern

Canada. We were far north of the home of Eskimos and sled dogs, without winter gear, or even a change of clothes to layer against the weather. White speckled wind caressed the side of the plane, mocking the thin faux leather jacket on my arms. Somehow, I doubted its ability to keep me from freezing to death in this wasteland. Suspiciously, I touched a gloveless palm to the window beside me.

"Brrrrrr... I'd hate to be out there in just jeans and a crappy jacket." Greg grinned while sliding on a heavy ski jacket and pants combo that I was pretty sure had starred in the movie 'Hot Tub Time Machine'.

Unable to think of anything brilliant to say, I shot him an unamused look.

Tugging a pair of colorless boots over matching pants, one of Eric's army of toy soldiers advised, "Yous girls'll wanta gear up. It's colder than the hinges of hell out there, and twice as deadly."

Biting my lip at the cold beginning to seep into my imagination, I frowned, before softly saying, "Thanks, but we didn't bring any."

"Any?" The guy gave me a confused look.

"Gear. We didn't bring any winter gear, to gear up in," I floundered, feeling like a simpleton.

"What?" Angel asked, disbelief etched into his features.

"We weren't really planning on coming so far north," I explained lamely, to what felt like a crowd of judging faces. "We thought there would be," I looked out the window at the mounds of snow blanketing the horizon, "someplace to shop."

"Oh," Angel shifted an awkward look from me to Greg.

80

"The girls aren't going to be getting off of the plane," Greg offered, a little too glibly. "Try to have some sandwiches ready for us when we return." Grinning at our misfortune, he winked as he hopped off of the plane.

I stood silently fuming, thinking about all of the horrible things that I wanted to happen to my older brother just then.

"Adios." Angel gave me a discomfited glance as he followed Greg towards the now open exit.

I was still fantasizing about Greg getting buried so deep in a snow drift that his neon jacket couldn't be found, when I felt espresso eyes watching me from across the plane. I looked up to see Eric frowning at me. Well, maybe it wasn't at me. Maybe he was frowning at the men in front of me. No. He was speaking to the men, but his focus was definitely on me.

Color flooded my face as anger surged through my veins, warming me. How dare he frown at me? He was the kidnapping two timer. I was the innocent here!

As his men filed out the door, Eric made his way over to me. Giving me a confused look, he asked, "Are you alright?"

"I'm fine," I murmured through thinly veiled hostility.

"Alright," he said with a nod, turning to go.

"What is wrong with you?" Barbie asked, appearing at my side.

I blinked, focusing my eyes. I had been in my own little world and hadn't noticed her walk up.

She gave me an expectant look.

I answered with a shrug.

Rolling her eyes, she said, "Acting like a bitch is not going to win him."

"I'm not trying to 'win' him, or anyone else for that matter," I protested.

"Obviously," she agreed. Sitting beside me, she asked, "Are you going to tell me about it?"

"There's nothing to tell," I insisted.

Rolling her eyes, she gave me a look that called me on my BS.

With a sigh, I said, "There's someone else."

"Mike?" She sneered.

With an over exaggerated eye roll, I explained, "*Eric* has someone else... and then there's Mike."

"Oh!" Surprise registered on her face, as she asked, "Are you sure?"

"Yes, no, maybe..." I struggled to put my feelings into words. "I mean he came to my parent's, even after I falsely accused him of cheating, set him on fire, and burned his house down. He begged me to come back, but I left him hanging. I couldn't blame him for finding someone else. He should, right? I don't know. I mean, I love Mike. I do. But, do I LOVE Mike?"

Barbie rolled her eyes skyward, and growled, "The Wolfman! Focus!"

"Oh, right." I nodded. "I saw them together."

"Together?" Barbie asked, putting an emphasis on the word that left an unwelcome vision of sweaty limbs fused into one.

"Not that kind of together!" I sighed, explaining, "They came out of the elevator at his office. She was wearing a ring, and him."

She shook her head in disagreement. "No. He's into you."
She headed to the bar.

"It doesn't matter." I waved the thoughts away, hoping to change the conversation.

"Are you sure it wasn't his sister?" She quickly filled two glasses with amber liquid, adding just a touch of coke.

"She was somebody's sister, but not his," I disagreed. "She made it *very* clear on the phone that he was taken."

"You called her?" Her voice was startled.

"I called him, and Veronica answered the phone. Can we change the subject?" I asked, accepting a proffered glass.

"Does he know he's taken?" Barbie asked.

"What?" I stared dumbly at her.

"I once dated this guy, except he's the only one who knew that we were dating," she explained.

"You have GOT to stop sleeping around." I rolled my eyes.

"I didn't sleep with him! I didn't even kiss him. Well once, but the rest of the time it was completely platonic." She waved the thought away. "Anyway, I found out six months later that we had been dating."

I gave her an incredulous look. "That is crazy."

"You're telling me! I couldn't convince his girlfriend that we were never an item. It took a restraining order to get rid of her! Anyway, I can see where he got confused. I mean who wouldn't want a piece of this?" She gestured to herself.

"You're kidding, right?" I couldn't help but ask.

"I wish I was." Digging through the bar, she explained, "We

hung out, talked on the phone, everything that couples do, except the physical stuff. I guess he just thought I wasn't that kind of girl."

Accepting the drink she held out to me, I said, "I thought you said you spent time with him?"

"He was a nice guy!" She exclaimed.

"Oh, that's why you didn't date him." I nodded my understanding.

"Well, Yes. That, and he was short," she admitted, with a cringe.

"Short? You're short," I reminded her.

"He was my height, in heels." She paused. "I like to look up at a guy when I kiss him."

A gust of wind raced along the plane, interrupting our conversation.

Ignoring the cold seeping into my skin, I said, "Anyway, you think that Veronica is just some delusional friend of Eric's who just happened to answer his phone when he wasn't around?" Disbelief rang through my tones as the question slid from my lips.

"There is no way he looks at you the way he does, and he's hooking up with some floozy." She shook her head.

"What if I'm the floozy?" I asked.

"What?" Barbie gave me a look that implied I had gone off the deep end.

"She had a rock." I pointed to my left hand ring finger. "A BIG one."

"Oh..." Barbie thought a moment. "Did you ask him about her?"

"Yes." I nodded.

"And," she prompted.

With a shrug of my shoulders, I shook my head. "You've talked to him. Having a conversation with Eric is like having a talk with a brick wall."

"Ask him again," she insisted.

"What? No," I declined.

She nodded her insistence. "Make him tell you about her. He owes you that much."

The conversation stopped as we listened to the wind howl through the swirling ice.

Finally I asked, "Why didn't I think of that? I'll just trudge through the blizzard to wherever he is and, with my last frost laden breath, demand to know who Veronica is. If I hurry, I'll bet I can avoid too much frostbite, where it matters."

Barbie shrugged her delicate shoulders.

We sat in silence as the cold seeped into the metal around us. As I watched my breath crystalize in front of my face, the direness of our situation hit me. It was cold, getting colder. There were some blankets and such that we could use to keep warm enough, if the men didn't stay gone too long. Not knowing if they planned to come back today or next week, that didn't seem like a good idea. I stared out the window. We could try to find a better place to weather the storm, but the blizzard looked too thick. We had no idea how to find shelter and nothing to protect us from the intense cold. Leaving our dubious refuge wasn't an option, unless we wanted to be human icicles. Things weren't working out as well as I'd planned. I had to admit that could be the problem? I hadn't actually planned anything.

"I've gotta start planning these things," I mumbled to myself.

"Yes, you do," Barbie agreed, heading to the back of the plane.

"Where are you going?" I asked.

"Exploring," she called over her shoulder.

"Are you insane? It's freezing out there. Literally," I reminded her.

Barbie opened a door next to the lavatory. Turning to look at me she said, "We'll never find out what happened to Santa sitting in this plane. Besides, I'm cold and this," she put down a half empty bottle, "will only do so much to warm me up."

Before I could think up a retort, she disappeared behind the door, leaving me alone with my thoughts. "She's right. This isn't getting us anywhere," I said to the empty seat next to me.

With a sigh, I took another swallow from the bottle Barbie had left, and headed toward the back of the plane. It wasn't hard to find my cousin. She was kneeling in the cavernous belly of the black beast, digging through other people's luggage.

"Another combination lock!" Barbie snarled.

Pushing the suitcase into a pile of locked bags, I glanced around. We had only been at it for a few minutes, but we had already gone through most of the luggage, only finding a couple of unhinged locks, one of which was half full of condoms and pictures of large women in unflattering stances. As awkward as it was to know that someone we were traveling with had a fat fetish, it was entertaining to listen to Barbie debate which of the merry men the case might belong to, and who he was expecting to use all those condoms with. She was hoping it was a quiet guy named Tank. I just hoped it didn't belong to Greg.

"I'm sensing a lack of trust," I said, tossing another suitcase into the locked pile. "Face it, we're stuck here in this flying icicle." My face lit up with a new idea. "Do you have the keys?"

Barbie tilted her head in irritation. "If I had the keys, do you think we'd be digging through unwashed underwear in the cargo hold?"

"Maybe," I shrugged. "Sometimes you're unpredictable."

"Well, I don't," she grouched. "The Wolfman took them with him. It's almost like he doesn't trust me or something."

"Asshole," I grumbled.

"Yeah." She slumped next to me.

"I don't suppose you know how to hotwire a plane," I asked conversationally.

"I've never tried," Barbie admitted.

"How hard can it be?" I wondered aloud.

Barbie grinned. "Cousin, I like how you think."

Once we entered the cockpit, Barbie pulled out a pocketknife and stepped up to the control panel with a gleam in her eye.

"Where did you get that?" I asked.

"Found it in one of the bags." She shrugged.

With a nod of acceptance, I took a minute to look around. After checking under the dash and seat cushions, I let out a deep sigh, announcing, "No hidden keys."

"They couldn't make it easy, just once," Barbie muttered.

She was just beginning to unscrew a small section of the panel when we heard a noise, followed by a louder noise.

"What now?" Barbie grumbled.

"I think someone's here," I answered.

"So glad you're here to share your powers of perception," she quipped.

"Don't be a bitch. I'm your only friend here," I reminded her.

"Lucky me." She lingered under the control panel, fingering the pocketknife.

Ignoring her, I stood up. "It's about time they came back for us," I grumbled, making my way to the exit. "Come on."

Barbie stood unmoving, pocketknife poised over the control panel. "I've never hotwired a plane before."

"You may still get to," I offered.

"You think so?" Her voice was excited.

"Maybe." I shrugged. "But first, we need to find out who's here."

Eight

My heart skipped a beat at the thought of Eric's scowling face looking down at me. I had it all planned out. I'd pretend to be annoyed, which wouldn't take much pretending, seeing as he'd left me to freeze to death in his planesicle.

Reaching for the door handle, doubt assaulted me. What if it wasn't Eric? It wasn't like him to leave, just to turn around and come back. No, it wouldn't be Eric. He would have sent one of his henchmen to fetch us. Thrusting away my disappointment, I pasted a smile on my face. No need to appear ungrateful. My hand barely touched the door handle when a stylish brunette slunk unbidden from my memories. Doubt carelessly tossed my confidence out into the icy mush. *She* was waiting for him in Boston, which meant that he had no reason to come back for me. Taking a deep breath, I reminded myself that I had enough man troubles, without getting all googly eyed about one who was unavailable. Experience warned where that would get me, heartbroken.

Shaking off displaced feelings, I braced myself to deal with what could only be my brother's scowling face on the other side of the door. With a deep breath, I closed my fingers on the handle. Greg had made it very clear how he felt about us being here. He would be even pissyier than usual at having to come back for us. I rolled my eyes at the childishness of it all.

"He'd let us freeze to death, just to prove a point, if he didn't know he'd have to deal with mom and dad," I grumbled under my breath.

"What?" Barbie asked. She was still messing with the control panel, oblivious to my internal struggle.

"Put that down, and let's go see who's here," I snapped. Arranging a calculated scowl on my face, I calmly stepped into the cabin area to deal with my big brother.

An eerie quiet met me on the other side of the door. Greg was nowhere to be seen. A chill ran down my spine as I watched an ethereal form wrestle the exit door closed. She was even tinier than Barbie, with violet eyes and a pert nose. Her feet were nestled into a pair of snow white, fur lined boots. Tucked into those child sized boots were silvery white snow pants, half covered by a matching jacket. Pushing back the hood, she revealed shimmering black hair tucked into the back of her coat. Actually, she sparkled all over. Was she wearing glitter? Smiling warmly, the surreal form gracefully slid a pair of alabaster ear muffs to her neck.

I opened my mouth to ask who she was and what she was

doing here, then thought better of it. Sure, she had brazenly broken into our, I mean Eric's, plane. That deserved some direct questioning, but her appearance had me flustered. All I could think of was that she must have come from somewhere that wasn't covered in snow and ice. If we were nice to her, she might invite us to go back with her. Imagining a warm fire, I rubbed my hands together.

The elfin form smiled warmly, as she explained, "The Missus sent me to fetch you."

"The Missus?" I blinked.

"Mrs. Claus," she explained, "wanted me to give her apologizes for not fetching you herself. She's occupied finding accommodations for all of our visitors. We don't usually get so many all at once. To be honest, we weren't expecting two more. She hopes that you'll understand."

"Of course." Awkward silence hung between us. "And you are?" I asked, just to have something to say.

"The hospitality Elf here at Santa's workshop," the iridescent figure replied.

"You're fucking kidding me." Hearing the words bypass my filter made me second guess the Jack that Barbie and I had been drinking to 'keep warm'.

With a dismissive snort, she replied, "It's my job to welcome visitors. So, welcome." Turning her back to me, she began digging through a bag at her feet.

Did she say ELF! Discombobulated thoughts swirled through my brain, trying to make sense of what I was hearing. Was this shiny child/adult/person...? I closed my eyes. She obviously wasn't a child.

Could I be staring at a real, live, elf?"

Ignoring me, the girl concentrated on her task.

An elf that had stepped out of a full on, white-out blizzard looking like she was on her way to après ski? She was dressed more stylish than Barbie. And, look at her hair! Even though she had been wearing a hood, her hair was perfect! And, she shimmered. She was tiny, and beautiful, and she actually shimmered. I started to second guess everything that I knew about the world.

"If she's an elf, does that mean that there really is a Santa Claus?" I whispered to no one. Fighting the urge to inspect her head for pointy ears. I said, "Ummm..." What do you call an elf?

She turned her head sharply, causing her hair to cascade around her, revealing delicate pointy ears!

Blinking my disbelief, I tried to wrap my brain around what my eyes were seeing. Sure, I had been willing to play along, hedge my bets, but this, this was an elf, standing in front of me, welcoming me to the North Pole, to Santa's Workshop.

"A real live Elf." I heard myself say.

"Who did you expect, the Prime Minister?" Sarcasm dripped from her lips, making it clear that she was less enthralled by her elfishness than I was.

Stepping through the doorway, Barbie shot me a strange look. Realizing that I was incapacitated, she turned her attention to our visitor.

"Who the F...!" I slapped a hand over Barbie's mouth.

Santa's elf had been nonplussed with my reaction, and I didn't want to upset her any more than I already had. Anyway, I wasn't sure if it was okay to curse in front of an elf. I mean, are they adults, kids, somewhere in between? What if she repeated it to Santa? I bet Santa wouldn't want a bunch of foul mouthed elves running around saying 'F' this and 'F' that. That might upset his gentle nature. I really didn't want to upset Santa, especially now that it was looking like he might actually exist. I silently sifted through a million questions in my head, like how to get on the good list. I REALLY needed a new car. I'd settle for an old one. Barbie bit me, interrupting my internal freak out.

"Ow!" I jerked my hand back. "What was that about?"

"You slapped me!" Barbie retorted.

Sure enough, there was a red handprint across her mouth. I cringed, "Sorry, I was... You were about to say the 'F' word in front of the... uh... ummm..." I gave the wraithlike girl at my feet a helpless look.

With a humorless look, the girl in front of me said, "Elf."

"What?" Barbie wore a look of disbelief.

"Elf. You know, Santa's helpers. We make the toys, compile the lists, load the sled, feed the reindeer, do the cooking, and occasionally," she sighed loudly, "rescue unprepared tourists."

"I thought you preferred to be called little people," Barbie responded, not missing a beat.

"Sure, every organization has a few who like to be all PC about things, but according to the job description, we're elves. Personally, I prefer to be called Amanda." The elf shrugged.

Barbie and Amanda sized each other up. After a moment, Barbie shrugged, and said, "Okay. I'll play along, Amanda. I'm Barbie."

"Of course you are," Amanda responded drily.

Barbie motioned towards me. "This is my cousin, Jessie."

I nodded dumbly, somehow managing to ask, "So, Santa, elves, the North Pole... It's all," I paused, feeling a little foolish for saying it, "real?"

"Would I be out hiking in the middle of this godforsaken winter wonderland if it wasn't?" She answered my question with a question.

"I should hope not!" Barbie responded, kicking away the snow that had oozed in through the now closed door. "By the way, great boots!"

"Then you'll love these." Amanda smiled, shoving a pile of glimmering fabrics into Barbie's arms.

Barbie eagerly inspected the winter gear that Amanda thrust at her. Forcing myself to let go of the idea that I was in the presence of an actual elf, I smiled. I could really use a change of clothes. Neither of us had any luggage on us, and I was eager to exchange my soiled travel clothes for whatever warmness our well-heeled visitor had in her bag.

Amanda turned her attention to me. Obviously uncomfortable, she explained, "Elves don't really come in your... err... size. I searched the whole complex, that's why it took me so long. Anyway, these will keep you warm enough, until we get you inside." She shoved a half-full bag of mismatched fabrics into my arms. "It's the best I could do," she winced, holding out a pair of black Santa Claus boots that looked like they could fit my dad.

"Ummm...." I moved my eyes from my feet to the boots, not

wanting to be rude. "I have boots." I gestured to my feet, which were currently nestled in my favorite red cowboy boots.

"Those won't keep your feet warm out there," Barbie and Amanda spoke in unison.

"They're boots." I shrugged.

"It's not the same." Barbie shook her head, adding, "The snow will dump down the top of those things in a frostbite minute. And, there is no way those things are waterproof."

"Leather!" I pointed to my red boot tips. "If it keeps the cows dry, it's good enough for my feet."

"We had better hurry. The ground crew is on its way," Amanda interrupted, pulling open the door.

"Ground crew?" Barbie asked.

"They'll get the plane in a hanger, give it a good de-icing, and fill up the tank," she explained. "It would have already been done, but they were waiting on me to fetch you."

"They might want to take a look at the control panel," Barbie suggested.

"Why?" Amanda asked.

"Squirrels," she offered.

"Squirrels?" Amanda asked.

"We must have picked them up along the way," I backed my cousin up.

Amanda shrugged, speaking quietly into her headset, she ordered, "Check the control panel for squirrel damage. That's right, squirrel."

Nine

At my request, Amanda took us to clean up. It seemed like weeks since I'd showered. She even brought us clean clothes, since we were without. Stepping out of the bathroom, I turned to my cousin. She looked just as you'd expect, if you expected a genuine, living, breathing elf. Which I hadn't, not even for a minute. I shook my head to clear it. Was Barbie an elf? It would explain her small stature. But, no. Elves were described as jolly. Barbie had been called a lot of things in her life. Jolly wasn't one of them.

Noticing my presence, my diminutive cousin looked up from smoothing the bright pink hose on her legs. Her mouth gaped open as she took in my ensemble. With a barely suppressed laugh, Barbie asked, "What are you supposed to be?"

Closing my eyes in shame, I took a deep breath.

Before I could answer, Amanda hurriedly declared, "It's

temporary. We'll have your things back to you as soon as they get dry. Then you can both change into more fitting clothes. Follow me," She added, leading us out the door.

"Both of us?" Barbie asked. "What's wrong with my outfit?"

Amanda looked surprised. "Most of the elves aren't so…" She motioned to Barbie's breasts, which were currently defying the laws of gravity in a tiny purple blouse that was never meant to show that much cleavage.

Barbie gave her a clueless look.

Amanda tried again, "Don't you think it's a little, tight?" She motioned again, adding, "In the top."

"No," Barbie answered, with a wicked smile.

I shook my head, explaining, "She's always wanted to be a slutty elf."

"A what?" Amanda blinked her surprise.

That's me, always saying the wrong thing. I could practically hear my daddy saying, 'Even a fish wouldn't get in trouble, if he kept his mouth shut'. Once again, he was right. Determined not to say anything else, I looked helplessly at Barbie, silently praying that the nice elf wouldn't kick us back out into the cold, taking her clean clothes with her.

"What? You don't have any sluts here?" Now, Barbie was the one who looked surprised.

"Santa's Workshop is a Christian organization. You have to sign a morality Claus to work here," Amanda explained.

"Trust me, they're here," Barbie insisted.

A male elf walked by, took one look at Barbie, and crashed

into a nearby wall.

"I bet he could tell me who the easy elves are," she said loudly, as he stumbled away.

"Um… Are you sure you'll be comfortable here?" Amanda winced.

"I'm comfortable with myself." Barbie grinned.

"Not the cold, God. Please, don't send us back into the cold." Softly praying, I snuggled deeper into my warm robes.

"What?" Amanda looked confused.

Barbie shook her head sadly, and said, "She's been through a lot. I think she could use an adult beverage. I know I could."

"Hot cocoa right this way!" Amanda brightened.

"Hot cocoa?" Barbie frowned at Amanda's retreating form. Loud enough for the whole workshop to hear, she said, "If that's what she calls an adult beverage, then it had better be spiked with Rumple Minze."

Amanda was either deaf or ignoring us, because she kept walking with no sign of hearing Barbie's rant.

With a snort of disgust, Barbie stage whispered, "Brightly clothed midgets, spreading wholesome holiday cheer like a stripper on dollar beer night, make me vomitus."

"You might want to consider a twelve step program," I offered.

"A what?" Barbie turned to follow the multi-colored form in front of us.

"Alcoholics Anonymous, Betty Ford, Hazelden, cold turkey," I listed off options.

"You're kidding right?" Barbie gave me a depreciatory glare.

"Well, no." I met her gaze.

"You're the third person this month to suggest that." Barbie frowned. "I probably should cut back."

"Good idea," I agreed.

"We'll quit together." She smiled innocently. "It'll be fun, like summer camp, except with more irritability, sweating, nausea, and cursing. Instead of canoeing, we can hold each other's hair, and do needlepoint. Do you think lemonade is too strong? You're right, it's strictly water for us from here on out," she finished in a high pitched voice, batting her eyelashes sarcastically.

"I should know better than to have fallen for that," I grumbled.

"Yes, you should," she agreed. "Now, mind your own damn business before you get fired."

"Fired?" I exclaimed. "You can't fire me. I don't work for you!"

"Sure you do. Remember, you're my new personal assistant." Barbie's words dripped with cloying sweetness.

My eyes popped in surprised annoyance. "You're delusional!"

"Watch it! I've fired help for less," she warned.

"I am not your assistant," I stated, staring her in the eye.

"Whatever you need to tell yourself." Barbie waved off my objections. "Payday is the first day of the month, insurance after three months. Please, use the dental."

"What is that supposed to mean?" I demanded.

"Remember Richard?" She gave me a knowing look.

"Richard who ate whole onions?" I asked.

"He didn't use the dental, floss, or even brush regularly." She shuddered. "His breath was horrible."

I nodded in agreement. "It was the onions."

"So," she paused, "use the dental."

"Okay," I agreed. "Just one thing."

"What?" She turned to look at me.

"I don't work for you!" It came out louder than I'd meant for it to.

Amanda scurried to put some distance between herself and us. I didn't blame her. I wanted to join her.

"Finally! Good job getting us some space," Barbie whispered.

"You have got to work on your people skills," I reprimanded Barbie.

"Me?" Barbie smiled. "You're the one yelling."

"You asked one of Santa's elf where to find the slutty elves and booze," I reminded her.

"Yes, that was me." Barbie giggled.

"The poor thing's gonna give Santa a bad report," I said. "We'll end up on the naughty list."

Barbie's laughter rang through the underground halls like a crystal bell. "Oh Cousin! I've been on the naughty list for years." With a wink, she added, "It's more fun than the other one."

"Barbie!" I chastised.

"Relax, you need a drink. While you're at it, I could use one too," she admitted.

Crossing my arms in front of my chest, I fixed her with my most judging stare.

"You're not buying all of this Santa crap?" Barbie asked, amusement coloring her words.

Turning down yet another hallway that suspiciously resembled the decorating style of my second cousin Angie's five year old, I shrugged, offering, "It seems legit."

Barbie gave me an incredulous look.

"I know it's hard to believe, but here we are, following a self-described elf, through festively decorated hallways, deep under the frozen tundra in… Where exactly are we?" I looked around as if the walls would tell me.

"Borden Island," Barbie responded.

I gave her a blank look.

"Think of what you know of Canada, then think north. Waaaaaayyyyyy North. We're on a completely uninhabitable island at the northernmost edge of Canada," Barbie explained.

I stared blankly at Barbie, trying to picture our location on a map.

"Think of it this way. If you were to go outside without the proper clothing, they'd never find your frozen body under all the swirling snow. This is basically the coldest, most miserable area of the earth, and there's not a drop of liqueur to warm us up." Barbie shuddered.

"Uninhabitable?" I asked. "Knowing that, you're asking if I believe that we're strolling through the halls of Santa's underground fortress." I gestured to the ceiling painted to look like blue skies. "None of this passes any logic test. At this point, I'd place my bets on the Easter Bunny being real too." I laughed, adding, "And, the Tooth

Fairy. Maybe a few of those old Twilight Zone episodes."

Barbie gave me a startled look.

"Like the one where each second is built in, and sometimes the builders forget to add in your car keys, and that's why you can look for something over and over again, and then it just appears, right where you've been looking for it." I paused, "That's probably real, too."

Stopping at an open doorway where brightly clothed adults, who were roughly as tall as my midsection, diligently wrapped toy after toy, Barbie shrugged. "Fine. Elves are real. Santa and Mrs. Claus are real. They all live in a huge underground fortress, at the northernmost edge of the world. But," she pointed a perfectly manicured finger at me, "I draw the line at the Twilight Zone." After watching the elves work a moment longer, she turned to me, and said, "If all of this is real, then that means that Santa Claus really is missing, and we are witnessing a genuine Christmas catastrophe."

"I guess it does," I agreed.

Turning her attention back to the elves toiling busily, she asked, "Do you still want to find him?"

"I think we're obligated," I answered, motioning from our clothing to the building around us. "Besides, someone has to save Christmas."

"Save Christmas?" Barbie asked. "I'm not sure how much Christmas relies on Santa."

"What is that supposed to mean?" I gave her a confused look.

Barbie shrugged, explaining, "If the whole world thinks that Santa is a myth, and parents buy the gifts their kids want, how much does Santa really have to do with Christmas, as we know it? I mean, would we even notice if there were no Santa Claus, seeing as only small children and the certifiably insane believe in him anyway?"

"You can't possibly be this jaded." I frowned.

"Do you even know me?" Barbie asked.

Rolling my eyes, I took a deep breath, stating, "Yes. I still want to find Santa Claus."

"Like that?" Barbie motioned to me.

"What?" I looked around, thinking I'd missed something.

Barbie looked me up and down in silent judgment.

I frowned down at my too big, mismatched wardrobe. "Yes. Fine, like this!" I glanced around me. Were the narrow halls closing in on us?

"It's a good thing you haven't seen yourself in a mirror." Barbie shrugged condescendingly.

"Why?" I took a deep breath. I knew it was just my imagination, but I could swear the halls were tighter than they had been a moment ago. A solitary bead of sweat slid down my hairline.

With a smile she said, "You might change your mind."

Biting my lip to keep from saying something I might regret later, I growled, "You heard Amanda, it's temporary."

Barbie gave my outfit a harsh look. Curling up her nose, she said, "I would have put back on my dirty clothes before wearing that, anywhere."

Forgetting my growing panic, I followed the vision in pink and purple beside me. "You forget that I was covered in hot chocolate after my run in with the Rambo Lothario in DFW."

"Right." She turned a corner, keeping Amanda in site.

103

"I was also wearing almost a whole soda, compliments of Angel, from right after you went to help fly the plane. By the way, thank you for not letting us all die," I added sincerely.

"No problem." She waved off my words.

"And, I sat in something in the Toronto airport. There was sticky goo all over my backside. It was as if I'd made a snow angel with my butt, but instead of snow I used tar." I grimaced at the thought.

"TMI cousin." Barbie held up a hand to silence me.

"Not to mention the smell," I continued, ignoring her.

"You do sweat when you're nervous." Barbie grimaced.

"It's not my fault. It's my dad's fault," I pouted.

"Uncle Charles is a sweater." Barbie frowned in acknowledgement.

"Same dad, same mom, but does Greg get all sweaty when he's nervous? No, because Greg is Mr. Perfect with Mr. Perfect genes," I groused, stepping through a large entryway. "Not me. I had to inherit dad's sweat genes."

"We can't all be perfect," Barbie agreed, twirling on her toes in perfect ballerina form.

"Give me a gun," I demanded, passing a well-placed mirror.

"Why?" Barbie gave me a startled look.

"I'm gonna shoot myself," I replied calmly, eyes fixed on the figure in the mirror. "And then, I'm gonna shoot her."

"Let's get you some food. You're cranky when you're hungry," Barbie said, steering me away from the mirror.

"I'm hideous!" I craned my neck toward my reflection.

"Yes," Barbie agreed. "We can fix that."

A sharp whistle pierced the air.

"Do you have to do that?" I exclaimed.

Nervously, I glanced around as the earth rumbled ominously. It would be just like my life to cause a cave in at Santa's Workshop. Headlines flashed through my brain. *'Santa's Elves killed in avalanche.' 'Christmas cancelled.' 'Mrs. Claus airlifted to local Emergency Room.' 'New York debutante among multinational task force killed in North Pole avalanche'.* I sighed. At least I wouldn't have to face Eric again.

Amanda appeared at our side, asking, "Did you make that noise?"

"It was nothing." Barbie shrugged. "Everyone in New York knows how to give a loud whistle."

"Can you teach me?" she asked.

"Sure." Barbie nodded her agreement. "But first, we have to do something about my cousin."

"What?" Amanda asked.

"She saw herself in the mirror. Now, she's threatening to shoot herself," Barbie explained.

"I'll call the team," Amanda agreed, pulling down her headset.

"Team?" Barbie and I asked in unison.

"We have a team designated for just such an emergency, ever since the massacre of Nineteen thirteen." Blank looks greeted her explanation, prompting Amanda to expound. "The winter of Nineteen thirteen was a particularly cold winter. Kris Kringle X didn't handle stress well. Everyone knows that. The job was almost too much for

105

him, most years." She paused, explaining, "It wasn't just him. It was a lot harder to be Santa back then. There were so many more believers, and the kids were so much better, which meant more toys to deliver, which meant more toys to invent and make. And they didn't have the technology that we have today. Most of the toys were made by hand," she explained.

Barbie and I exchanged glances. Neither of us was expecting a history lesson.

"Due to a clerical error, the workshop was short supplies," Amanda continued. "The elves and Kris had worked triple shifts for weeks to complete the list. Finally, Christmas Eve came, and disaster struck. Kris lost his compass while delivering toys. Then, he got caught in a snowstorm outside of Leningrad, taking hours longer than he should have to complete the night's job."

Barbie opened her mouth to speak. A quick elbow in her ribs kept her quiet. I wanted to hear the story.

"It was well past the breakfast hour when Kris finally returned from his run, missing a reindeer, and suffering from severe frostbite. When the news that Rudolph VIII had been shot by hunters and turned into deer burgers somewhere in Texas got back to Kris, he lost it. He loaded the German Luger that had been gifted to him by Kaiser Wilhelm II, grabbed the sword that King Alfonso XIII had presented him years before, and went on the bloodiest rampage in history, stopping only when the lives of elves and reindeer alike seeped along with the snow into his boots." Amanda paused, adding, "The few survivors were left to pick through the dead, and send them home for burial."

"He got away?" I asked in horror.

Amanda nodded sadly. "He escaped into the night, taking his grisly rampage to Russia, Germany, and finally Austria where he murdered Archduke Franz Ferdinand, setting off a global chain of events that no elf could have foreseen."

"That is not the way I learned it in school," Barbie scoffed.

"Of course not." Amanda explained, "We couldn't let the world know that its beloved toymaker had gone on a brutal killing spree. An international team of public affairs agents was called in to cover the whole thing up, with the help of an unsuspecting Sarajevo nationalist."

"Are you telling us that Santa Claus started World War One?" I asked, with disbelief.

"No, Kris Kringle X did," Amanda clarified.

"Keep up," Barbie snarked. "What happened to the North Pole? Everyone was dead, right? Was it a frozen world without a Kringle, or did mama Kringle take over the operation?"

"Mrs. Kringle disappeared, in the height of the confusion, taking the only heir, Santa Claus XIV with her." Amanda frowned. "The missing heir was declared a global situation, setting precedent for today's gathering of international elite forces. Amidst the crisis of WWI, the world's leaders assigned a small group of specially trained men to find the heir."

"That's a version I didn't get in history class," Barbie snickered, nudging me.

Ignoring Barbie, Amanda continued, "It was months before the elite forces tracked them down, by then the world was firmly

107

ensconced in combat. In the grips of constant battle, the nations had forgotten humanity, love, and hope. Without a leader, the North Pole had shut down. Christmas spirit was lost in the animosity of war." Amanda shook her head, sprinkling glitter into the air. "It was truly a dark time in the history of mankind."

"What happened to them? I mean, where did they go?" I asked, entranced by the story.

"Hollywood," Amanda replied.

"Hollywood?" Barbie and I repeated in unison.

Nodding, Amanda explained, "Her plan was to sell her story to filmmakers, star as herself, and make millions. Unfortunately, negotiations with her publicist were permanently put on hold when she was locked up in a mental ward for claiming to be the wife of Kris Kringle and matriarch of the North Pole. By the time she was located, and her release secured, it was too late. She had been given a full frontal lobotomy. They say she was never the same." Amanda shook her head sadly.

"Hard luck." Barbie winced.

"What about Santa, Kringle... the kid?" I asked, enthralled with the story. "What happened to the heir?"

"When the men in white coats showed up for his mother, the heir escaped to the streets. Too young to fight in the war, he fell in with a group of homeless boys who taught him how to survive. They became a sort of family to him," Amanda explained.

"Santa was in a gang!" Barbie chuckled.

I shot her a warning look.

Amanda nodded sadly. "Those were tough times. Alone and

afraid to tell anyone who he was, in case he was labeled insane, he lived on the streets. It took almost two years for the task force to find him."

"I thought ya'll knew everything about kids, and where to find them," I said.

"You have to remember, there wasn't anyone except Santa's right hand elf, Gerard, left to track him," Amanda reminded me. "With no access to the workshop bank accounts, supplies couldn't be delivered. The elves had been sent home, the reindeer set free, and the workshop abandoned. Only Gerard had stayed behind. They say he was too old, and too stubborn, to leave."

"So, Gerard used the naughty and nice tracker to find him?" Barbie asked.

Amanda shook her head. "Back then, we didn't have the quality of gadgets and tracking devices we have today. The workshop relied on letters from parents to know if kids had been naughty or nice, and to find them. Even now, we have a harder time with those who don't have a stable residence. We were dependent on the task force. They knew he was somewhere near Hollywood, so they did a clean sweep of all the schools, hospitals, orphanages, and jails. They finally got a break when the heir was picked up and placed in juvenile hall. The task force was able to get the charges dropped, and bring him back home, averting a worldwide crisis, but the rest of the world was still at war. He became our youngest and greatest leader."

"At least there's a happy ending," I offered.

"Yes. But, things were far from functional. The workshop was devastated." She paused before adding, "Our greatest learning happens when we completely mess things up."

"What is she talking about?" I looked at Barbie in confusion.

"History." Barbie nodded her understanding.

"One of the first decisions Santa Claus XIV made was to select a group of elves to study under the finest Psychotherapists in the country. When they returned, they formed a very important part of our community," Amanda said pointedly.

"The team?" Barbie asked.

"The team." Amanda nodded.

"I'm fine." I held up my hands in surrender. "I'm not going postal on anyone, especially not after that story."

"She just hates her clothes," Barbie backed me up.

"Her clothes?" Amanda asked.

"They're horrible, mismatched, unflattering," Barbie waved her hands in my direction. "Just look at her! She looks like an anorexic, second hand, Santa."

"It was all I could find," Amanda defended the outfit.

"Surely, someone has something," Barbie reasoned. "There's a guy."

"A guy?" Amanda asked.

"A Rambo hottie," Barbie nodded.

"I saw those guys." Amanda paused. "Let me ask around."

Ten

"It's a little tight." I gasped.

"It's a lot tight." Amanda winced.

"It's perfect. Really makes your girls stand up proud," Barbie insisted.

"You couldn't find a size larger?" I pleaded.

"I'm sorry. You're just so tall. You're Amazon Woman tall," Amanda babbled, while attempting to tug a bright yellow skirt down low enough to cover my cheeks.

"At least the hose stretch," I said, gratefully smoothing the thick silky green material.

"Invented right here in the workshop." Amanda smiled.

"Really?" Barbie asked.

"Yes." Amanda glowed with pride. "I wanted to be an inventor, but my aptitude test put me as a greeter.

"Inventor, is that an elf job?" I asked.

"Someone has to make all the complicated electronic and

sciency toys," Barbie said sarcastically.

"Exactly! Barbie, you could almost be one of us," Amanda crowed.

"Except, I'm not an elf," Barbie stated, motioning for me to turn in a circle. "Much better."

"I don't know, I mean, you do sparkle and shine like Amanda here," I teased Barbie.

"So do you," Barbie fingered my hair.

"It's because of our shampoo and body wash," Amanda explained. "The inventors were originally looking to create a shiny bubble bath for kids. Santa liked it so much that he kept it just for us elves."

"That's not very neighborly of you," Barbie quipped.

"You think so?" Amanda questioned. "We share most of our patents with the world," she rationalized, turning troubled features to Barbie.

"What do you mean, you share most of the patents?" Barbie perked up with interest.

"The inventors create things. If it's feasible, we sell the patent to the world's countries to generate revenue. Everything from radios and televisions, to drones and lasers were invented right here." Amanda lifted her hands in gesture.

"Really?" I asked, surreptitiously glancing around for an elf in a white lab coat.

"How do you think we finance this operation? It costs tons of money to run a city out here in the middle of nowhere. Sharing our patents with the nations of the world has the added benefit of keeping the world's governments friendly, so that Santa doesn't have to worry about getting blown up on his run," Amanda added.

"And, explains why the world powers would create a task-force to find a missing Santa." Barbie nodded her understanding.

"So, you invent high tech stuff, and sell it to other countries, to buy food and clothes?" I clarified.

"Yes and no. The inventors aren't limited to high tech. It's their job to create anything that could be on a wish list. Sometimes the ideas come from the kids' letters. Once we've invented it, there's no reason not to share with the rest of the world." Amanda paused, waiting for us to process the information, before continuing. "We aren't dependent on other nations for food, clothing, or any necessities. We buy some raw goods, but most of our food is produced here in our greenhouses. Meat is from the sea or the non-flying reindeer herds."

"You eat the reindeer!" I exclaimed.

"Not the sled pullers," Amanda reassured me.

"That's like eating the family dog," I gagged.

"No, it's like eating ranch grown beef," Amanda refuted.

I gave her a suspicious look.

I've been out there, out of curiosity. It's not any different than the way my parents run their ranch. Honest," Amanda insisted.

"Your parents have a ranch here?" I asked.

Amanda laughed. "No! They live in Wyoming. They think I'm crazy to live way up here."

"So, the elves aren't born here?" I asked.

Amanda stopped in the middle of the hall, giving me a strange look. "You do know that elves are regular people, just shorter? Don't

113

you?"

I traded surprised looks with Barbie.

"We choose to be elves," she explained.

"Wait." Barbie held up a hand. "Your parents weren't elves?"

"No." Amanda gave a nervous laugh. "They don't understand this." She waved a hand around her. "They're normal sized."

"Really?" I asked.

"I was born with a genetic mutation," Amanda explained.

"Oh!" Making eye contact with Barbie, I widened my eyes, and raised an eyebrow, trying to communicate that we should let the issue drop. I searched my brain for a topic, any topic, to change the subject to, not knowing how sensitive Amanda might be about it.

"Dwarfism?" Barbie asked, effectively shutting down my change of subject.

I narrowed my eyes, staring her down. Barbie just ignored me.

"It's more common than you think. I know that now." Amanda made a sweeping gesture. "Growing up, it was harder to see," she admitted.

"So, how did you end up here?" Barbie asked.

Amanda shrugged, then said, "This one time at dwarf camp, I met a girl whose grandfather used to tell her stories about his time as an elf. It sounded great, so I decided to do it."

"Dwarf camp?" I asked.

"Yeah." Amanda frowned. "My parents sent me EVERY year, so that I could meet others like myself."

"Why?" Barbie and I asked together.

"Apparently, I wasn't fitting in." Amanda rolled her eyes.

"So, you like being up here in the middle of nowhere?" I asked.

"I've gotta live somewhere," Amanda stated, matter of factly. "Out there, I'm a minority. Sinks are too tall. Cars are too big. I have to wear children's clothes, and keep a step ladder in the kitchen just to reach the top shelves in the fridge. All anybody ever sees is a little person, midget, dwarf, shorty... People call me names, point, and stare." She paused, adding, "I didn't want to spend my life as a reality TV show. Here, I'm average. Everything is made to fit someone like me, and no one judges me based on how tall I'm not. Santa pays us well. We have some of the best medical care in the world, few expenses, and generous leave packages. All he asks is that we dress the part, where the ears," Amanda pointed to her ears, "and make him look good. It's a good gig."

Barbie looked Amanda up and down, then said, "I am NOT a little person."

"No, but you could almost pass." Amanda smiled.

"So, without Santa...?" I changed the subject.

"There is no without Santa. He's the CEO, Mayor, President, and King of Santa's Workshop all rolled into one. He was born into this position. In the past, there have been a few Santas that didn't want the job. The bylaws state that he may abdicate to a younger brother, nephew, or other male relative of direct lineage if there is such a person. Otherwise, he must be Santa until someone of equal qualification comes along," Amanda explained.

"And this Santa...," I ventured.

"Doesn't have an heir." Amanda's words floated between us.

"If we don't find Santa, the workshop will shut down."

"Then who will invent the next DVD?" Barbie asked mockingly.

"Exactly." Amanda nodded.

"Can't you just find another one?" I asked.

"We've tried to grow one." Amanda cringed. "The cloning process isn't perfected. There is always a problem. An extra limb, no nose, or they look perfect, but come out a little crazy."

My mouth dropped open. "You grew Santa monsters?"

"Don't worry. That project was terminated until it can be perfected. I just wish we had known about the issues before we sold cloning to the rest of the world," Amanda lamented. "Not that they haven't worked out some of the kinks, but we really do try to sell a well-developed product. Don't think there weren't some eyebrows raised at R and D when word got out."

Barbie and I traded glances.

Barbie interrupted, "So, no babies for the current Santa and Mrs. Claus?"

"Early in their marriage, they had a few miscarriages. No live births." Amanda shook her head sadly. "We gave up hope years ago."

"Gave up? Are they really old or something?" I asked.

"Abraham and Sarah were in their nineties when they had Isaac," Barbie interjected. "Surely, the Santas aren't that old."

"I think they're in their fifties," Amanda paused, adding, "or sixties."

"So, there is still time," Barbie reasoned mockingly, earning herself another jab in the ribs from me.

"I guess." Amanda shrugged.

"Except?" Barbie pressed.

With a sigh, Amanda said, "Except, they hate each other."

"What?!" I exclaimed.

"Everyone knows," Amanda offered. "She carries around a coffee cup, but she's not drinking coffee, if you know what I mean. They barely speak to each other. Just to convey information. And a few years ago, Santa all but moved into the workshop. He has a little apartment set up above his office. And...," Amanda stopped herself.

"And?" Barbie asked.

Amanda hesitated. "Nothing just, rumors."

"Of?" Barbie pressed.

"I shouldn't gossip." Amanda shook her head.

"It's not gossip. It's pertinent information that could help lead us to the missing Santa," Barbie rationalized.

"I guess that makes sense." Amanda squirmed under Barbie's stare.

"So?" I questioned, curiosity getting the best of me.

"So?" Amanda asked.

Wearing a grin to rival that of the Cheshire Cat, Barbie asked, "Is Santa getting a little extra turn down service? Tangling with a new tiger? Playing a grownup version of Duck, Duck, Goose? Riding the..."

"We get the picture. A very unsettling picture." I grimaced.

"There's been talk," Amanda hesitantly confirmed.

"Anyone in particular?" Barbie asked.

"Just rumors. I never believed them." She paused, conflicted emotions playing across her face. "And…"

"And?" Barbie and I spoke in unison.

"A friend of mine said she saw Mary Anne Guffin sneaking out of the workshop late one night." Amanda quickly added, "He was never anything but nice to me."

"How nice?" Barbie leered.

Giving Barbie a warning look, I said, "We should talk to Mary Anne Guffin, before anyone jumps to conclusions."

"She works in wrapping," Amanda agreed.

"I'll bet," Barbie sneered.

"Don't worry Amanda, we'll be *nice*. Won't we Barbie?" I glared at my cousin.

"I'm always nice." Barbie smiled sweetly.

Eleven

Once you've seen the elves at Santa's Workshop in action, you'll never take wrapping for granted again. They make those department store wrappers look like amateurs. The place was huge and there must have been a hundred wrappers working at full speed.

Fortunately, the elves were all very accommodating, probably because of the YouTube mix of my tazing in the airport. Apparently, I was the newest hit. Every elf we passed seemed to have seen it.

"If I hear, *'Don't taze me bro'* one more time, I may crack," I announced, passing another table full of rapturous YouTubers.

"She's over here," Amanda offered. "I'm pretty sure she doesn't watch YouTube. Honestly, she's a little weird."

Mary Anne Guffin was a lot weird, for an elf. She was taller than Amanda, heavier too. Her clothes were a mixture of gothic black and indigo, her long black hair had the lackluster shine of needing a

119

good wash, and her makeup consisted of heavy blue eyeliner, thick mascara, and blood red lipstick.

"Mary Anne!" Amanda crowed falsely.

Dead eyes raised briefly from their work. Mary Anne Guffin appeared to be missing the sparkles and happy glow that we had come to expect from Santa's elves.

"We met a couple of times at Crystal's. I'm Kyle's girlfriend, Amanda." Amanda gave Mary Anne an expectant look.

"Amanda." The girl in front of us responded with dead tones lacking Amanda's enthusiasm.

"This is Barbie and Jessie. They wanted to ask you some questions," Amanda continued, unfazed.

"Uh huh," Mary Anne drawled, continuing her wrapping.

"They're here to help find Santa." Amanda's voice took on that same irritated tone she'd had when she came to fetch us from the airplane. "The Missus has asked that everyone help, in whatever way you can."

Mary Anne put down her wrapping, turning to look at us for the first time. After a moment, she dubiously asked, "They're going to find Santa?"

Amanda gave her a no nonsense look, looking purposefully at the clock over our heads, she asked, "Isn't it about lunchtime?"

Mary Anne shrugged.

"Why don't we talk about it over lunch at Wanda's?" Amanda offered, with an overly friendly smile.

"I need to let Steve know," Mary Anne answered.

"I've already cleared it with Steve. Come on." Amanda took

Mary Anne's hand, leading her away from her work table.

Wanda's turned out to be a burger joint straight out of the movie 'Grease'. The staff wore big smiles, poodle skirts, and rolled up white t-shirts with jeans. There was a jukebox in the corner, and the walls were covered with pictures of small American towns in the fifties.

"Can we get Santa's table?" Amanda asked an elderly woman at the front door.

Looking us up and down, the woman gave Barbie and me a disapproving look.

Glancing down, I frowned. The borrowed skirt had pushed into my soft midriff, creating a muffin top. Hastily, I tried to shove the extra skin inside my waistband. With a sigh of relief, I smiled. It was gone, all I had to do was keep it pulled tight over that awful spot, without showing all of my southern goods to the entire elfin population.

The elderly woman reached out, roughly jerking the hem of my skirt down, and undoing all of my hard work.

I looked down at her, confusion preventing me from speaking.

"Nice girls don't walk around with all of their jewels hanging out for everyone to see," the woman admonished, giving me a harsh look. "At least, not in my restaurant they don't."

Blushing, I attempted to pull the tiny skirt up and down at the same time.

"It's not her fault Ms. Wanda, her clothes are at the cleaners and this is all I could find for her," Amanda explained.

The older woman held us all in her stare, just long enough to make both me and Amanda uncomfortable. Neither Barbie nor Mary Ann Guffin seemed to notice. After what felt like an eternity, she finally nodded, looked me in the eye, and said, "Okay then. Next time I see you, I'll expect you to have on more suitable clothes. You look like the happy hooker of the North Pole. It's disgraceful!"

Suitably chastised, I mumbled, "Yes, ma'am."

Tentatively, Amanda asked, "Santa's table?"

"I'm sorry. It's reserved," Wanda frowned. "She'll have to make due with a booth."

I was starting to understand what it felt like to stand out, in a bad way. Everywhere we went, people stopped and stared. At first, I had thought it was Barbie. I mean, I could barely not look at her in that top. I kept waiting for her to blow a button!

After overhearing some reactions as we wandered the halls, I realized that they were staring at the 'Amazon'. I'd never really thought of myself as that tall. But, if I stayed here much longer, I might develop a complex. The child sized tables and chairs didn't help.

"The milkshakes here are just amazing! You've got to try one!" Amanda beamed, sliding into a corner booth.

I stared at the booth, unsure how I was going to fit, finally I said, "Maybe we should go somewhere else. There is no way I'll fit in there. My knees will be in my face and there is zero chance of my skirt coving what it was meant to cover."

Amanda shook her head. "I'm sorry. There aren't very many places to go in the workshop, and the table situation will be the same at all of them. Can you make it work?"

"It'll be fine," Barbie answered for me. "Could you order us cheeseburgers, fries, and chocolate milkshakes? We need to find the restroom."

"Make mine strawberry," I added, thinking it was easy for Barbie to say it'll be fine. She was half a foot shorter than me.

"It's back there." Amanda pointed past the jukebox.

Once she checked that there was no one else in the bathroom, Barbie burst out laughing. "You should see your face!" She giggled. "And those chairs! It's like seeing my mom sit in my desk chair back in fourth grade." She was almost laughing hard enough convince me it was funny, almost.

"You brought me in here for this?" I asked, unamused.

"Yes," Barbie grinned. "That and the combination of Ms. Sunshine and Lollipops with Ms. Gloom and Doom was really getting to me."

"Do you think she was…?" I trailed off, not wanting to finish the thought.

"I don't know. I'd expect the jolly old elf to be banging someone like hot Eduardo, or even Amanda. Maybe he likes them rotund and depressing."

"She's an easy target: low self-esteem, few friends, a negative in a positive world," I reasoned.

"Makes you wonder why she stays here" Barbie nodded her agreement.

"Let's go find out," I suggested.

Stepping out of the bathroom, we all too quickly discovered who had reserved Santa's table. Inwardly cringing, I forced a

123

nonchalant smile onto my face. Maybe, he wouldn't see me. I looked down at my overly tight top and skirt, giving it another quick tug to cover something, anything. Still feeling under-clothed, I tried to convince myself that he wouldn't notice that my chest was popping out of the too tight top, or the Band-Aid skirt. Not likely. He noticed everything. The best I could hope for was that he wouldn't say anything.

I turned to the side, letting Barbie pass while I vainly attempted to shove my breasts deeper into the stretchy fabric, and tuck in the muffin top that wearing clothes two sizes too small had created. Managing only to uncover parts that public decency laws require to be covered, I readjusted. The only good thing about this outfit was the tights. When I turned around, the hallway was empty, except for the man in Black blocking my path.

"Is it Christmas already?" Eric grinned down at my boobs hanging out of the low cut top.

Closing my eyes in humiliation, I tried to step around him. It would have been easier if he'd made room in the narrow hall. Of course, he didn't even try.

Stepping into my bubble, he backed me against the wall, and said, "We never got a chance to talk."

My head was ringing from his proximity. Closing my eyes, I whispered, "No."

The world ceased to exist, as the silence stretched out between us. He lowered his head. Was he going to kiss me? Did I want him to kiss me? I held my breath, unwilling to break the spell. I could feel his hot breath wash over me as his lips brushed my ear.

"Later." Wearing a self-satisfied grin, he lifted his right arm, releasing me.

Later? I took a deep breath. *Later?* Why did I let him get to me? Why couldn't I, just once, get to him? Then I could be the one to walk away, unfazed. Instead, I was scrabbling like an inexperienced adolescent after a run in with the high school quarterback. Attempting to regain my dignity, I edged around him.

Following me, he fingered the hem of my micro-mini skirt. "Cute," he declared. His dark eyes laughing at my discomfort.

"It's on loan." I blushed, attempting to ignore the heat pulsating through my body where his fingers brushed my leg.

"Pity," he said. Fingering the material again.

I reached down to slap his hand away, just as it edged past the material. Taking my hand in his, he leaned his body against mine. Trapped against the wall, I could feel his warm breath on my neck, as his fingers gently raced up my thigh. Quickly, I caught my breath, banging my head into the wall behind me. Looking up, I could see the hunger in his eyes. My breath grew ragged, responding to the heat flooding my veins.

Mentally, I slapped myself upside the head. Jessie, he has a fiancé! You need to get out of here, away from him! Damn my traitorous hormones! Going around him wasn't working. Did the hallway just grow? It seemed like it. I didn't want him leering at my barely covered backside all the way back to the dining area. Where was Barbie when I needed her?

Pushing him off of me, I meekly motioned towards the dining area. "You go ahead."

"I insist." He motioned to the hallway. "It's the gentlemanly thing to do."

"Gentlemanly?" I questioned, while physically removing his hand from under my skirt. "Not if you're just looking at my ass."

"Your ass looked at me first." He winked.

Taking a deep breath, I headed for my table. If Barbie could do the walk of shame with no visible effects, so could I. When I saw that Barbie had stopped to talk with a couple of Eric's men, I realized that she wasn't embarrassed by the fact that her clothes were designed with a much smaller woman in mind. No, she was practically shoving her buoyant chesticles in their faces.

"No shame." I shook my head. "That's okay," I said to myself. "I've got enough shame for the both of us."

It took everything I had to walk, not run, across the quickly filling up restaurant. I could feel eyes on me with every step. Was that my imagination?

"Of course it is," I rationalized. "He was just having some fun. You don't mean anything to him. He's focused on his lunch by now."

Halfway to the security of our table, the jukebox blared to life. The singer was going on about walking away. Was that a coincidence? Or a statement? I had to know.

"Be casual. Pretend you're flicking your hair. Just barely peak, then eyes forward," I coached myself. Glancing toward the offending machine, my eyes were held hostage by a too familiar pair of espresso ones. "What is he playing at?" I asked the air. "He knows I know about Veronica, but he's still flirting, as if I didn't know, and he didn't know that I know." Closing my eyes to break the spell, I turned away. I could still feel his eyes on me. When I glanced back, Eric lifted his hand in salute to my retreating form. "God hates me," I muttered to no one, as I crossed the room to the beat of the song.

By the time Barbie joined us, our food was on the table. Amanda was right, the milkshakes were amazing.

Twelve

Having been called to Mrs. Claus' office, Amanda had taken her burger to go, leaving us alone with Mary Anne, after promising to catch up to us later. For a moment, we sat in silence, pretending not to feel Eric's eyes on us as we ate our lunch. Halfway through her milkshake, Mary Anne cracked.

"I hate her," Mary Anne growled.

"Who?" I asked.

"Miss Perfect," Mary Anne grunted. "Look at me. My hair is so sparkling. My boyfriend is so perfect. My boss is Satan's mistress."

"Don't you mean Santa?" Barbie asked.

"I thought SHE was Santa's mistress,' I whispered to Barbie. "How many mistresses does the old man have?"

Barbie shrugged, turning her attention to Mary Ann.

"The Missus. She is evil," Mary Anne sneered. "I can't believe this. Santa is missing and you two bimbos are the best they could come up with?"

"Bimbos!" I exclaimed. "We are not bimbos."

"You look like bimbos." Mary Ann gestured to our too tight in all the right places outfits.

I opened my mouth to protest, caught a glimpse of myself in the window, and thought better of it. Shrugging my shoulders, I looked at Barbie.

"Own it," Barbie advised.

Mary Ann had stopped paying attention to us. Instead she was picking through her burger, removing all of the vegetables. Brushing a solitary tear away, she softly whispered, "You want to know something?"

"What?" Barbie leaned forward, eager for the word vomit that she knew was coming.

"Her boyfriend has slept with half the girls here, even some of the married ones." Mary Anne nodded.

"Really?" Barbie asked.

"Uh huh," Mary Anne confirmed. "Everyone knows. Everyone except Miss Everything About My Life Is Perfect. Rumor has it, he's the reason Felicity had to move back home last month." Nodding, Mary Anne made a rounded belly gesture.

"Tell us something else," Barbie insisted, a little too eagerly.

"I could. I know all of their dirty little secrets," Mary Anne claimed. "They want everyone to think they're so morally upright. They're not. This place is just like everywhere else, just colder. I hate this place."

"What about you? Are you just like everyone else?" Barbie asked.

"No," Mary Anne denied.

Barbie raised an eyebrow in disbelief.

"Whatever she told you. It's a lie," Mary Anne maintained.

"What do you think she told us," Barbie asked.

"I know what she said. They don't think I hear them gossiping. But, I know what they say about me," Mary Anne grumbled.

"So, is it true? You and Santa?" Barbie wiggled her eyebrows.

"It's not like that," Mary Anne insisted.

"What is it like?" Barbie asked.

"I was his assistant." Mary Ann paused, adding, "We became friends. He's the only one in this godforsaken wasteland with any intelligence."

"Except you," Barbie added.

Nodding, Mary Ann said, "One night, he asked me to stay late and help him with some things. We got to talking… He told me all about how horrible she was to him. I mean, I guess I already knew. It's not like they even try to hide how much they hate each other. Everyone knows he pretty much lives in his office. Then, there were the rumors."

"Rumors?" I asked.

"Every now and then, someone would say they saw a girl leaving the workshop at odd hours, or one would transfer to a different department, or suddenly go home. People talk." Mary Anne shrugged.

"I never thought much of it."

"So, he came on to you?" Barbie asked.

"No, he's not like that," Mary Ann declined.

Barbie gave her a knowing look.

"What about the rumors?" I asked.

"I don't know if they're true or not." Mary Ann shook her head.

"Yes, you do," Barbie insisted.

Mary Ann shrugged. "It was my fault."

"Did you jump him?" Barbie asked.

"NO! I mean, I must have done something, stood too close, or something," she rationalized. "I was flattered that he noticed me at all. No one notices me." She turned her attention to her milkshake, adding, "I didn't even mind when he asked me not to wear my clothes so baggy and long. I mean, I am supposed to be an elf. They don't wear long baggy dresses like this." Mary Anne gestured to her obviously too large clothing.

Barbie and I nodded our understanding.

"I started dressing more like everyone else. And, finding reasons to go to his office." Mary Anne brushed another tear away, adding, "He always had time for me."

"He's married!" I interjected, earning a harsh glare from Barbie.

"I know. I was just so lonely. I don't have any friends. I pretend I do, but..." Mary Anne slumped further into her chair.

"So, you came onto him?" Barbie asked, digging for the dirt.

"I don't know. He asked me to stay late one night, to help him with some paperwork. One thing led to another… I honestly don't know who came on to who," Mary Anne admitted. "Does it really matter?"

"No." I shook my head.

"So, how long have you two been hooking up?" Barbie asked.

"It was mostly over by time the rumors started. He said he couldn't let her find out," Mary Anne said tearfully. "He was worried about what would happen to me. So, he transferred me to wrapping. I hate wrapping."

"Mostly over?" Barbie asked.

"He calls me every now and then, to come over. But, it's not what you think," Mary Anne insisted.

"A booty call?" Barbie suggested.

"We're in love," Mary Ann whispered.

"Love?" Barbie's voice betrayed her disgust.

"I know he's married, but he's a nice guy." Mary Anne stared off into the distance, as if we weren't there. "He doesn't deserve to be with someone like her. She's so horrible to him. Always harping on him. You'd think he couldn't do anything right. And, since they found out she can't have kids, she won't have sex with him. Not that he wants to. He doesn't love her."

"And, he loves you?" I asked.

"I know how it looks, but…." Tears streamed down Mary Anne's face, taking the heavy mascara with it. "He was nice to me. No one has ever been that nice to me." Mary Anne was sobbing uncontrollably now, drawing attention to our table.

I gave Barbie an uncomfortable look.

Ignoring my silent plea to end the interview, Barbie asked,
"When was the last time you heard from him?"

Blue mascara smeared across Mary Anne's cheeks as she
wiped at her eyes. Sniffling, she answered, "The night before last."

"Two nights ago?" Barbie offered.

Mary Anne nodded. "I left around four. I always leave before
the early shifters start their day. We didn't want it getting back to
HER."

"Of course not," I heard myself say.

"You don't understand." Mary Anne explained, "He was
going to leave her. But, first he had to make sure that she couldn't try
to claim any part of the workshop."

"Could she do that?" I asked.

Mary Anne nodded. "He was going to divorce her years ago.
She threatened to ruin him, and take everything."

"But, Amanda told us that Santa's Workshop has to have a
Santa. How could she expect to take over?" Barbie asked.

"She was trying to impregnate herself with some sperm
samples they had frozen back when they were trying to have a baby.
Once she had a baby boy, she was going to get rid of Santa." Mary
Anne explained. "He found out about it from one of her aides."

"Do you think she was successful?" I asked.

Mary Anne nodded, not even bothering to wipe her eyes. "I'm
afraid she's done something terrible to him. That's why I called the
task-force."

"You called them?" I asked, surprise evident in my voice.

Mary Anne nodded morosely, adding, "I found the number in

his rolodex under workshop emergencies. I didn't know what else to do."

"Are you sure Santa didn't just leave?" Barbie asked.

Mary Anne wiped away another tear. "He wouldn't do that."

"He wouldn't be the first man to walk away from it all," Barbie suggested.

"No. He wouldn't have left without me," Mary Anne insisted. "He loved me. Once he was free of her, we were going to go public and get married. He's the only reason I haven't gone back home."

"Did he tell you that?" Barbie asked.

Wiping at her tear stained cheeks, Mary Anne mumbled, "Not in so many words. But, he made it clear."

"You weren't the first girl he had a relationship with. I mean, other than his wife," I pointed out.

Mary Anne peered at me through her bangs. With a shrug of her shoulders, she asked, "What does that matter?"

"It matters," Barbie insisted.

Her face flushed with anger, she wiped away a mascara stained tear, stood up, and growled, "You don't understand. How could you? Why are you sitting here, eating, and asking me these dumb questions? Your job is to find him. So, go find him!"

Barbie and I watched Mary Anne stomp out of the restaurant.

After a moment of stunned silence, Barbie offered, "That went well."

"As well as the rest of this trip," I agreed. "So, what do you think?"

"I think she's right," Barbie admitted.

"You think the Missus offed Santa?" I asked.

"I don't know about that." She shrugged. "But, we came to find him, so let's get to it."

"Let's go!" I agreed, heading for the door, milkshake in hand.

"The Wolfman is motioning for us," Barbie pointed across the room.

"I see him," I admitted, heading for the door. It was easier to focus on Santa Claus and his troubles than my own, so that was what I was going to do. I could feel irritated eyes following me out the door. "He'll make me pay for ignoring him, but…"

"But what?" Barbie asked.

"But nothing. He can take his petty, attention seeking, childish, temper tantrum out on Veronica. I don't care anymore," I fumed.

"Just keep telling yourself that," Barbie said, leading the way out the door.

Thirteen

Amanda had warned us that people might be reluctant to talk about Santa with outsiders. Thanks to YouTube, it wasn't a problem. Everyone at Santa's workshop seemed to know who I was, and each one had an opinion, fact, or piece of gossip to share about Santa's disappearance. We traded a selfie and a smile for everything from information to chocolate covered pretzels. By the end of the day, Barbie and I were yelling, *'Don't taze me bro'* with my YouTube fans. We had just found our way back to the business side of Santa's Workshop when Amanda caught up to us.

"I've been looking everywhere for you!" She cried.

"We're right here," Barbie offered.

"We were looking for some dinner," I admitted. "We had a few offers, but the price was too steep."

"Some days, it pays to dress like a slutty elf. But, not with those guys," Barbie agreed. "Where are all the hot elves?"

"Huh?" Amanda asked.

"Do you take them in during the day or something?" Barbie asked, confusing Amanda even more.

"Um... No," Amanda answered. "There are hot guys," she looked up and down the street, "around. They're probably at the gym or dinner."

"Great! I'm starved!" Barbie beamed.

I elbowed Barbie. "Tone it down. You're scaring Amanda."

"It's been a couple of days." Barbie shrugged, asking, "Where do we go for food?"

"What are you in the mood for?" Amanda asked.

"Brandy," Barbie responded, "with a side of beef."

"I'm sorry," Amanda apologized, "Santa's Workshop is a dry city."

"Dry? As in not wet?" Barbie asked.

"Dry, as in no liquor," Amanda clarified.

"Why?" Barbie asked.

Amanda shrugged, "It's always been that way."

"No wonder Santa went missing," Barbie muttered.

"What?" Amanda asked, shock on her face.

"Don't mind her. She's just going through a much needed drying out," I expounded.

"I thought you said Mrs. Santa drinks," Barbie reminded Amanda.

Amanda shrugged, offering, "Santa isn't that strict. They are old laws, just followed in public really. The restaurants and stores aren't allowed to stock it, so those who really want it pay to have their booze shipped in."

"You should get those laws changed," Barbie advised. Glaring at me, she complained, "If I can't have a drink, I want a big juicy steak, and sex. Lots of sex."

"I can get you a steak," Amanda offered.

"Good enough. I can find my own sex," Barbie announced, a little too loudly.

"Let's get her off of the street," I suggested to Amanda.

Amanda led us to what promised to be a nice steak restaurant. The hostess led us to a large round booth in the back. We hadn't even sat down, when a familiar face rounded the corner heading our way.

"You have GOT to be kidding me!" I exclaimed, not even trying to hide my irritation.

"I saw you talking to him at Wanda's. Is he your boss?" Amanda asked, following as I turned back toward the door.

"No!" I exclaimed. "He's my..."

"Your what?" Sensual tones whispered, as warm breath embraced the back of my neck.

"My... nothing." I turned, staring into Eric's eyes.

"Oh... Hi! I'm Amanda." Amanda swooned at Eric.

"Wolf," Eric said, not taking his eyes from mine. "Really, Trouble?" He grinned. "I thought we meant more to each other than nothimg."

"Don't you have someplace else to be?" I asked querulously.

"Nope." Eric grinned annoyingly, gesturing for me to sit down.

Knowing he would just follow me if I left, I slid into the booth. I took a deep breath then pointedly turned my head away from him. I hoped that he would get the message.

"I should go," Amanda offered uncomfortably.

"Just ignore Batman and Skipper," Barbie suggested, sliding into the other side of the booth. "They just need a good fucking."

"Are they always like this?" Amanda asked, joining her.

"Most of the time." Barbie nodded.

I shot Barbie a look.

She was too busy perusing the menu to notice. "This place doesn't serve booze!" She announced, loudly.

"I told you. This is a dry city." Amanda shook her head at Barbie.

"I never thought of Santa's Workshop as having individual restaurants." I attempted to change the subject, and put some space between myself and Eric.

Amanda smiled, explaining, "Decades ago, there were none. Everyone just ate cafeteria style. Then, about fifty years ago, Father Noel VI allowed the first restaurant to open. It did well, so he let more in."

"You would think Santa would put in a Taco Crack." I frowned.

"You won't find any chain restaurants," Amanda stated. "They're against the town charter."

"I understand what Santa has against chains, but what's his problem with booze?" Barbie complained.

Amanda shrugged in response.

"I'm sure they'd do just as well as his other restaurants," I offered, trying to ignore the black clad leg that no matter how I sat seemed to touch mine.

Amanda shook her head, explaining, "Santa doesn't own the restaurants. They're owned and managed by individuals, just like in any other city."

"But, I thought this was Santa's city." I frowned.

"Think of him like the Mayor," Amanda offered.

"There are people here, at the workshop, that don't work for Santa?" Barbie asked.

Amanda nodded, explaining, "Some people decide they want to stay up here, but they don't want to work in the workshop anymore. We have a fully staffed office to work with potential business owners. They help them complete the required background checks, business plans, and file business applications. Once they've turned everything in, the same office reviews the applications before sending them up to Santa for approval. Santa is pretty strict about quality, but if someone can get approved, a space is found for them. People can stay as long as they have income, and follow the rules."

"We've seen a couple of stores, and restaurants, what other businesses are here?" I asked, trying to ignore Eric who seemed to be sitting just close enough to notice.

"We have just about anything you would want. There is a bowling alley, skating rink, movie theatre, beauty salons, barber shops, doctors, dentists, schools, churches, gym, of course the restaurants. And, my favorite," Amanda grinned, "shopping at The Island of Misfit Toys."

"The what?" I looked up in surprise.

"It's a mall, and it has *everything*: toys, electronics, furniture, paper goods, trinkets, cell phones, clothes, grocery, an indoor play land for the kids, laser tag....," Amanda gushed. "It is my absolute favorite place!"

"And, all of this is underground?" I asked in awe.

Amanda nodded. "I can't think of anyplace I'd rather live."

"How many people live here?" Barbie asked.

Amanda thought for a moment before answering, "The Williams family moved back to South Dakota last week, so five thousand, eight hundred, and eighty two. It's a pretty tight community."

"This place is bigger than I thought," I mused. "Have ya'll searched for Santa here?"

Amanda gave me a surprised look.

"I mean everywhere?" I expanded, gesturing with my arms.

"Santa's team did a thorough search," Amanda confirmed.

"House to house?" I pressed.

Amanda squirmed. "I'm not sure."

I looked at Eric.

"We're working with Santa's team," he answered my unasked question. "They've been very methodical in their search."

I opened my mouth just to have a finger placed over my lips.

"There will be plenty of time for that later. Right now, you can let me buy you dinner." Eric gave me a smile poised to turn my insides to butter.

Fine, I'd drop it, but I was not going to melt into his arms, no matter how much he turned up the heat. I couldn't say the same for Amanda. The look on her face said that she'd dump her boyfriend for a one night stand with Eric. I shook my head, rolling my eyes, and causing Barbie to laugh, and Amanda to blush. Eric, of course, was clueless.

Fourteen

Greg and a sprinkling of guys from some of the other teams joined us just as the waiter came to take our orders. With the added company to divert our attention, dinner ended up being pleasant. Greg had finally accepted that I was here, and there was nothing that he could do about it. Eric and I called a truce. With all the man candy around, Barbie had even snapped out of her funk. Anyway, there was no use fighting amongst ourselves when there was a Santa snatcher on the loose.

Yawning, I asked Barbie, "Do you remember how to get back to our rooms?"

"No. I'm good with staying right here." Barbie snuggled into the agent beside her.

Glancing around the closing restaurant, I frowned. "We should have asked Amanda, for directions before she left."

"I'll take you to bed," Eric offered, causing me to choke on the water I was in the process of swallowing.

Greg's head snapped out of the conversation he was having with Brian, one of the CIA team. Brian was medium height, not fat, not skinny. He had thinning sandy blonde hair, hazel eyes, was soft spoken, and completely forgettable. I could see why he was in the CIA.

Eric held his hands up, explaining, "I meant, I can show you to the room that you're sharing with Barbie. It's down the hall from mine."

"Right," Greg muttered, returning to his conversation.

"Unless you liked my first offer better," Eric whispered into my ear.

A shiver raced down my spine. Shaking it off, I whispered back, "What would Veronica think?"

Eric leaned back, looking at me. "Just who do you think Veronica is?"

His sudden willingness to discuss Veronica caught me off guard. The words were there, but I couldn't bring myself to speak them. Instead, I looked at him blankly.

"Well?" He prompted me.

"Well, she's your, um…" The words stumbled over each other as they tumbled out of my mouth.

"She's my…?" He left the sentence hanging.

Was he really going to make me say it? "You're such an ass!" I exclaimed.

Eric lifted an eyebrow at my outburst.

All other conversation stopped. Everyone's eyes turned to us. All ears perked up to hear what we were saying.

My cheeks were flaming. "This isn't the right time," I mumbled.

"It's the perfect time," Eric disagreed.

"Your fiancé, okay?" It wasn't so bad, now that I said it out loud. "I know that Veronica is your fiancé. Happy?" I shouted.

Eric's mouth dropped open. The room was silent, except for the low jazz coming through the speakers. I wanted to run and hide. Just my luck, I was in the back of the booth, unable to get away, and surrounded by questioning glances.

"I know. You know. Now, everyone knows," I growled. "So, can we quit with all of the nonsense?"

"Boss?" Angel looked hurt. "You an' Steve's wife?"

Eric closed his eyes, sighed loudly, and said, "No."

Surprised by his answer, I turned questioning eyes on Eric.

"I do NOT have a fiancé." His words were quiet but clear. "If I did, it wouldn't be Veronica."

Once he finished speaking, the rest of the table went back to their conversations, leaving us to sit in uncomfortable silence. I wanted to believe him, but I kept seeing her with that ginormous diamond glinting off of her left hand as she clutched Eric close to her, like a priceless mink stole. Attempting to make sense of what he'd said, and very aware of the fact that Eric and I were sitting uncomfortably close, I turned to him. Sound seemed terminally stuck in the back of my throat. I needed a drink, of anything. Reaching for the nearest water glass, I hoped that the owner didn't have any incurable diseases as I gulped it dry.

I glanced up.

He was still looking at me, waiting for me to say something.

I wanted to say something, to ask him about her, but the words wouldn't come. Instead, I busied myself with my plate.

Finally, he asked, "Where do you come up with these ideas?"

I shrugged. "I saw her with you."

"In Boston," he finished my sentence.

I nodded.

He shook his head. "I wanted to introduce you two. When I turned around, you were gone."

I closed my eyes, and explained, "I saw you with her, and... I may have overreacted." Feeling my face warm with hot shame, I paused. "I wanted to give you a chance to explain, so I called you from the airport." Taking a deep breathe, I continued, "Veronica answered your phone."

"She did?" He asked, in obvious surprise.

I nodded. "She told me that you were taken, and that I shouldn't call back, ever."

"What?" It was Eric's turn to be at a loss for words.

I shrugged. "She had a great big shiny rock on her left hand. She was with you. She answered your phone. What was I supposed to think?"

"Veronica and I are friends, and business partners, not anything else," he assured me. "She's like family."

I bit my lip. I wanted to believe him, but I kept hearing Veronica's voice in my head, *'He's taken.'*

"She is… was Steve's wife, my business partner," his words were filled with suppressed sentiment.

"Oh." I frowned, suddenly feeling like a horrible person. He had told me about Steve. They were like brothers. When he died on a mission, it had been Eric's job to tell Steve's wife and child that he wasn't ever coming home. And, Veronica was Steve's wife. Like a piece in a puzzle, it all suddenly made sense.

"When Steve died, I promised him that I would take care of Veronica and little Steve. She owns half of the company. We get together for lunch, when I'm in town. I take little Steve out for ice cream, and go over there for dinner occasionally. Like I said, they're family." He looked so sad, I had to believe him.

"I'm sorry." It was all I could think to say. I felt horrible that my words caused him such obvious pain.

"Is that why you avoided my calls. Why you were with him? Because of Veronica?" The pain behind his words stung. He was always so strong, so together. I never thought that he could be hurt.

"That's why I left," I evaded.

"Why you left," his words pointed out what I had left unsaid.

"Mike and I, we have history. We've known each other, well… forever. I know his family, his third grade teacher, I know his dog, and his favorite movie. I know everything about him. The good and the bad," I stammered, trying to put my feelings into words.

He sat stone faced, staring at me as if I'd just grown a third head.

"Let me try again." I paused. Taking a deep breath, I attempted to explain what I was feeling, "I hardly know anything about you. I don't know your middle name, or if you have a sister. I didn't even know there was a Veronica."

He opened his mouth to speak.

Cutting him off, I explained, "You say she's this big part of your family. But, you've never mentioned her by name. You haven't mentioned anyone. Do you have a dad, mom, cousin, a dog? I don't know. All I know, all you've let me know, is this." I motioned to his body. "You know everything about me. You haven't shared ANYTHING about you."

"That's it? I'm not good at sharing?" He asked incredulously.

All of that, and that's what he got out of it? I sighed, shaking my head, I said, "Never mind." I got up to leave.

"What do you want?" He grabbed my arm, preventing me from leaving.

"I'm tired, you're tired. Let's just call it a night," I suggested, pulling away from him.

Barbie was right. I needed to think things through. I looked across the table for my cousin. She was gone. It didn't take much thought to figure out where. She had been flirting with a guy from the Australian team all night.

Fifteen

I lay in the dark, watching as my mind replayed the conversation with Eric, again. After I had walked out of the restaurant, he caught up to me. In silence he had walked me to my room, surprising me with a tender kiss at the door, and then again inside my room. What did it all mean? *Goodbye, I'm sorry, let's start over?* After he'd left, I had tossed and turned in the dark, replaying it over and over again.

After hours of useless agonizing, I had closed my eyes, determined to get some sleep. I had just drifted off when the door slowly squeaked open, waking me. I wasn't worried. Whoever it was, they were covered in Barbie's perfume.

"Jess, get up!" Barbie hissed in my ear.

"What time is it," I asked, yawning. I looked toward what should have been a window, but was just wall. Remembering that I was deep under the frozen tundra, I sighed. The sun wasn't going to help me tell time today.

"Almost two." Barbie flipped on the light, blinding me. "Get up."

"Two o'clock!" I groaned. "Wake me in the morning. I'm tired."

Barbie ripped the covers off of me. "Morning is too late. The whole town is asleep now."

"That's because they are normal people. Normal people sleep at night." I reached for the blankets.

"Those same normal people are all over the place during the day, preventing us from going anywhere they don't want us," she reminded me. "Grab your clothes, we have a job to do."

"Clothes!" I exclaimed. "I didn't get my clothes back."

"Lucky for you Batman loaned you his shirt to sleep in," Barbie stated, eyeing the too big shirt covering my body. "I'm gonna need details. But first, get dressed."

A pair of well-aimed, brightly colored tights hit me in the face, followed by the rest of my borrowed elf outfit. I was looking for my shoes when Barbie came back from the bathroom, looking glamorous in her borrowed clothes. I glanced at myself in the mirror. I didn't look nearly as good. It made me hate her, just a little.

"Where are we going?" I yawned my displeasure.

"To find Santa," Barbie hissed. "Isn't that why we came here?"

"Yes, but we looked for him all day. I don't think he's here," I admitted.

"Darran gave me some interesting information I want to check out," Barbie explained.

"Darran?" I asked, pulling on my other shoe. "Is that who you've been with?"

"Yes." Barbie's voice held a smile. "I'm ready for those details. Are you and the Wolfman back together or did you just take a break from the fighting?"

Did we get back together? I wasn't sure. Shrugging, I said, "It's complicated. But, I found out who Veronica is."

"I bet I know who she's not," Barbie offered.

"Who?"

"The future Mrs. Wolfman," Barbie said smugly.

"No." I shook my head, adding, "She's his partner's widow."

"Widow?"

"Widow. He promised his partner, when he died, that he'd take care of her and their son," I explained.

"Sounds like you've got competition. I hope you gave him a little something to keep you at the top of the list, because your attitude towards him this trip has been shit." Barbie grabbed her purse. "Are you ready?"

"Yeah." I tripped over the bed. "Ouch. No! Didn't you hear me? They aren't engaged. They aren't even dating. They're like family, sister and brother."

"Then why did she tell you he was taken?" Barbie asked.

I didn't have an answer for that. Why couldn't things be easy, just once? "So, where are we going?" I asked instead, following her out the door.

"Do you remember Amanda telling us that the Claus' couldn't have kids?" Barbie asked as I slid out the door behind her.

"Yes," I nodded, wondering if it ever got fully dark here.

"What about the Santa monsters?" Barbie's whispered voice seemed to carry in the stillness.

"Santa monsters," I shuddered at the thought.

"Mrs. Claus told Darran that she would have an heir soon." She paused, turning to give me an expectant look.

"How soon?" My skin crawled with fear, as the eerily lit halls suddenly seemed ominous.

"Soon, very soon," Barbie's voice was unnervingly quiet.

"Shit!" I exclaimed, earning a shushing from Barbie. Dropping my voice to a whisper, I asked, "Are you telling me that crazy woman grew a Santa monster?"

"I think it's time we checked out the lab, where they're growing the next Santa." Barbie nodded.

"How do we find it?" I asked.

"I have a map." Barbie beamed, holding up a partially folded piece of paper.

"I'm not even going to ask how you got that." I shook my head.

"That's probably for the best," Barbie acknowledged.

Barbie led the way, quietly. That was fine with me. I had plenty to keep my mind occupied, without being distracted with idle prattle. We seemed to be wondering aimlessly through the underground city, when Barbie stopped suddenly around a dark corner. I was so absorbed with my thoughts that I almost ran over her.

152

Giving me a knowing look, Barbie said, "Either get over him, or sleep with him."

Instead of acknowledging her opinion, I asked, "Is this it?" My voice betrayed my lack of faith.

"Uh huh," Barbie muttered. "Now, back to your man drama."

"I don't have any man drama," I denied.

"He's not engaged, and he's all over you," Barbie pointed out, taking off her wristwatch.

"Your answer is always to sleep with him." I rolled my eyes in the dark.

"I like to stick with what works." Barbie pursed her lips in silent concentration, allowing me to mull over her words. Pulling me deeper into the shadows of the dark hall, she whispered, "Be ready."

Curiosity got the best of me as I watched my cousin expertly open the key code box, pulling two wires loose. Taking wire cutters from her pocket, she quickly severed the filament, stripped half an inch of the plastic protectors off, and attached her watch to the now exposed metal tips.

"Did you get that from Darren, too?" I asked, pointing to the watch.

"Focus and be ready," Barbie whispered, ignoring my question as the door silently slid open.

Motioning me inside, Barbie retrieved her watch before following me through the ominous entryway. Once the doors slid closed behind us, I realized that it was dark, not the dark where you can't see your hand in front of your face, but the creepy dark where there is a light coming from somewhere illuminating things just well enough to make you wonder what else might be in there with you. I was waiting for my eyes to adjust to the darkness when a bright light burst forth from Barbie's wrist. Temporarily blinded, I cried out, tripping over my left foot. Barbie grabbed my arm, steadying me.

"Don't break anything," she whispered.

"Seriously, where did you get that thing?" I demanded, pointing to the metal band encircling her wrist.

Barbie shrugged. "It was a gift."

"Can you get me one?" I asked.

"No." Barbie walked off to look at something.

I shrugged. It was probably for the best. I'd be more likely to blind myself or sear off a finger than find a good use for it, like telling time or breaking into spooky labs.

"We're looking for lab number three," Barbie whispered.

I nodded, wondering how we would know which door led to lab number three.

Pointing the light away from us, Barbie turned down the narrow hall, leaving me to follow. Each time we passed a door or new hallway, she would flash her light up, reading the solitary number that had been placed in the middle of the luminous entry. By the time the tiny light illuminated the number three, my pulse was racing, and my scalp tingled with fear.

We both held our breath as Barbie turned the knob. Nothing happened.

I looked at Barbie, and whispered, "Now what?"

Barbie held a finger to her lips. Not that she needed to. The echo from my quiet words had been enough to startle me back to silence.

Barbie squatted down, examining the door. Nodding to herself, she pulled something from her pocket. Pushing me behind her, she shielded her eyes. A minuscule red laser shot from her hand to the doorjamb. Seconds later, Barbie pulled the door open, ushering me in.

We stood side by side at the front of a huge space faintly illuminated by the same spooky light from before, peering through the half-light at a laboratory straight out of a bad movie. There were strange science experiments everywhere. Some bubbled. Others dripped, or sat encased in glass containers like a 1950's horror movie come to life. I peered towards the back of the room. It, and the strange experiments, appeared to be endless.

"We found lab number three. Now, what are we looking for?" I whispered, trying to keep myself from backing out of the menacing lab, and away from the creepy building.

"We'll know it when we see it," Barbie whispered back.

Without another word, we drifted to opposite sides of the vast space. Barbie's watch illuminating things just well enough to throw shadows that played havoc with my imagination, and made me regret every scene of Freddy and his bloodthirsty friends that I had ever watched. I cursed myself for being nervous, ready to jump out of my skin.

"Is that anyway for a grown woman to act?" I whispered to no one, while trying to get my heart to stop racing.

Turning a corner, I noticed a soft glow that didn't belong to Barbie or the creepy hidden half-lights that followed us throughout the building. Curiosity overcame my fear, forcing me to follow the source into a darkened corner.

"This is why in a zombie apocalypse you'd die first," I cautioned myself. "You can't leave well enough alone, and you're never armed when you need to be."

Shaking off the thought, I turned the corner. A soft blue light radiated from inside a glass windowed room. Pressing my face to the glass, I vied for a better look. Inside the room, were rows and rows of thick tubes, some big enough to hold a small adult. Each tube was filled with a cloudy blue liquid emitting a faint glow into the room. Pressing closer, I focused on a large tube to the left. I watched as the weird blue liquid swirled, revealing a deformed face staring back at me.

"Aiiieeee!" The sound had come from me. I slapped a hand over my mouth, hoping no one had heard it. Envisioning hordes of special ops elves pouring into the lab, I carefully backed away from the window.

Something sharp poked me behind my kneecap. "Shit!" I whispered. I hate getting shot. Slowly, I raised both of my arms in surrender.

"What are you doing?" Barbie's voice came from over my left shoulder.

"Surrendering." I was surprised to hear how calm my words were.

"To who?" Barbie glanced around the room.

I shrugged, asking, "An elf?"

"A table," Barbie's voice held mirth.

Taking a deep breath, I peered over my shoulder. There were

no special ops elves. Just the same tables full of science projects gone wrong that I had recently walked past. I had backed into a table. At least no one but Barbie was there to see me surrender to it.

"What has you so jumpy?" Barbie asked.

Exhaling slowly, I pointed through the window at the Santa monsters.

Barbie leaned in closer. Jumping back, she turned in open mouthed horror. "They did it. Those bastards really did it." She shook her head in a mixture of disbelief and respect.

"What do we do?" I asked, staring into the room. If I focused, I could see distorted faces and seemingly unattached limbs floating in the other tubes. The effect was spine chilling.

"We can't allow this," Barbie echoed my thoughts. "We're going to have to kill them."

"Kill?" I stared at my cousin. "But…"

"Jessie, they're vicious monsters," Barbie reasoned.

"We don't know that," I argued.

"We do," Barbie countered. "Amanda told me all about it, while you were getting your flirt on with the Wolfman. The others, the ones that grew to adulthood, they had to be put down. They got out of the lab, into the town. Jessie, people died. Innocent people. We can't let that happen again."

At her words, the creature nearest us began thrashing violently, knocking over his tube, and unplugging it from the others. We stood speechless as cracks raced through the container, allowing the weird blue liquid to seep out. Horrified, we watched it kick its way out of its tiny prison, until it was finally free, then lunge itself at the window between us. Startled we jumped back. The grotesque creature threw itself at us a couple more times, before sinking to the floor. Cautiously, we stepped up to the window. Eyes wide, we stared down at the creature as he struggled to breathe the air around him.

"Okay," I stammered my agreement with Barbie's assessment of the situation. "But, what's to stop her from making more?"

"You saw that. They can't breathe on their own, yet. If we shut off the power, it will eliminate all of them." She motioned to the remaining Santa monsters. "It will also shut down the refrigeration system, ruining the DNA, sperm, eggs, everything. Then, she can't make more." Barbie had her tiny camera pressed to the window in front of us.

"Pictures? Like we could ever forget this?" I asked.

"We may need them to prove that we weren't conducting terrorism," Barbie said, nonchalantly.

"We... what!" I exclaimed.

"It happens," Barbie said matter of factly.

I stared in horror at the Santa monsters. "Why don't we make it public? Then, the people can decide."

"And while we're trying to convince them of the danger, Mrs. Claus sets these creatures loose on the community," Barbie reasoned.

I stared at the Santa monsters, floating in their tubes. Before this night, I would never have believed that such a sweet old lady could do something so completely evil. It just didn't fit with the stories in my head. But, like it or not, all of the evidence pointed to Mrs. Claus.

Barbie turned somber eyes toward me, and said, "There are two kinds of evil in this world, cousin. The kind that does bad things, and the kind that doesn't stop bad things from happening."

"When did you develop a moral compass?" I asked.

"I've always had one. Frankly, it's more developed than yours." Barbie smiled.

"You've been under the florescent bulbs too long," I argued.

Motioning to her map, Barbie pointed to a spot in the center of the paper. "The central power station is here, in the middle of the Workshop. We need to get there, and shut it down."

"Don't lose that gadget on your wrist." I motioned to Barbie's watch, turning toward the front of the lab. "I have a feeling we're gonna need it."

My heart raced as we slipped out of the lab and through the darkened halls of Santa's Workshop. In my mind, I imagined dark clothed little men and women, armed with Uzis, racing towards us from all directions. What was that? Were those footsteps? Beads of perspiration dripped into my hair. I felt like Pac Man trying to avoid the ghosts as he makes his way around turn after turn of identical looking walls. I looked over at Barbie. Her breathing was even and slow, and she didn't have as much as a hair out of place. How could she be so calm at a time like this?

By some miracle, we made it to the central power station unobserved. Okay, it was probably less of a miracle and more of it being two o'clock in the morning, in a town with no crime, and no nightlife. Barbie had her watch off again. This time I knew what to do, keep a watchful eye out for anything suspicious. I couldn't see anything. I peered into the darkness. Someone or something, was out there. I could swear I heard muffled footsteps echo through the still air.

Backing further into the shadow of the door, I whispered, "Someone's coming!"

"Just... a... second..." Barbie's words betrayed her calm exterior.

"What was that?" I hissed.

My body was pinging with dread, and the surety of being discovered. What would they do to us, knowing what we knew? Image after image flashed through my mind, each worse than the last. My anxiety continued to rise, paranoia had taken root. Wait. Is it paranoia if you're right? Sweat poured down my face. Unsure of what to do, I braced myself to run. A hand grabbed my arm from behind, causing me to jump back and hit my head on the wall behind me.

Pulling me through the now open door, Barbie commanded, "Get a grip!"

A grip. Right. I took a slow deep breath. Barbie was right, I needed to get a grip on my imagination. After a few more deep breaths, I went to find Barbie, and hopefully redeem myself. Fortunately for me, I just had to follow the glow from her watch.

It didn't take long for us to find the power room. It was clearly marked, exactly where the map said. I loved the efficiency of the elves!

"Um, Barbie..." I hesitated, almost afraid to speak after my mini freak out.

"What?" I could tell from her voice, she was still peeved.

"If we flip the breakers, shutting down all of the power," I made a downward motion with my hands, "won't they just run over here and flip them back on?"

"That's why we have to blow the breakers," she explained calmly.

"Blow?" She couldn't mean what I thought she meant.

"Blow up, to be precise," Barbie confirmed my suspicions.

"We can't blow up the workshop's power source!" I protested.

"Why not?" Barbie looked me in the eye, waiting for my response.

"If we do that," I grabbed her by the shoulders, "then the whole town will lose power, for who knows how long!"

"Collateral damage," Barbie shrugged my hands off of her shoulders.

"But, it'll get cold. And, it'll be dark, really dark," I insisted. "There has to be another way."

"There's not. Anyway, it won't get cold and dark," Barbie countered.

"It won't?" I asked, my voice skeptical.

"We're underground. The earth helps to heat everything down here. As for light, the walls, streets, everything is made of a type of rock that basically glows in the dark," she explained.

"Are you sure?" I touched the wall in front of me, wondering if she might be right.

"Didn't you notice how dark it wasn't on our way here?" Barbie motioned to the walls around us, adding, "How dark it isn't right now?"

"Not really." I searched my memories of how dark it actually was on our way here.

"It was dark, but we could see, right?" Barbie prompted.

"Now that you mention it, I guess it wasn't exactly pitch black," I conceded. "But, are you sure everyone will be okay?"

"Everyone except the Santa monsters," she assured me.

I wanted to ask how she knew. Knowing that I wouldn't like the answer, at least the version that she would tell, I decided to take this one on blind faith. "Okay, let's do this, and get back to our room before the elves realize what we're doing."

Barbie shook her head. "We can't go back. They'll know it was one of their visitors, and we're the only ones not on a government payroll. It won't take them long to figure out who's responsible." She reached into her purse, pulled out something sticky, and began attaching it to the inside of the control box.

"Wait!" I protested.

Focusing on cutting the plastic protectors off of two wires she had freed from the box, Barbie pretended to ignore me.

"If we can't go back to our rooms, where do we go? There aren't exactly many places to hide down here under the frozen ground." I gestured to the walls and ceiling surrounding us.

"That's why we have to leave," Barbie rationalized.

I blinked, asking, "Did you forget about the monster blizzard howling outside? Even if we had the proper clothes, which we don't..."

"What are you trying to say?" Barbie asked.

"We'll die out there!" I exclaimed.

"You don't know that," she retorted.

Sparks flew from between Barbie's fingers, convincing me to

give her another foot of space. She gently blew on the sparks, coaxing them into a small fire. Satisfied with the small flame, she stood back, admiring her work. I stood transfixed, mesmerized by the sizzling sound coming from the breaker box as the flames spread. I was wrestling with my conscience about whether or not to put the fire out when Barbie grabbed my arm, pulling me away from my thoughts.

"We have exactly fifteen minutes to get out of here," she informed me. "MOVE!"

"What have you done?" I demanded, running for the door.

"We. We're in this together," she corrected.

"Shit!" I exclaimed.

We practically tripped over each other as we rushed through the door and down the hall, like uncoordinated Olympic athletes. Reaching the entrance, I ran right over a little old man on his way in. The old man and I rolled down the steps, with Barbie hot on our heels. Untangling myself from his beard, I opened my mouth to ask if he was hurt, just as Barbie zapped him with the smallest stun gun I have ever seen. His eyes glazed over and his body became limp.

I turned to Barbie, the horror of what she'd done all over my face. "You killed him! Why?"

"He's not dead. Just sleeping," she assured me.

"Are you sure?" I asked, feeling for the man's pulse. It was there, steady and strong.

"Help me get him out of the way," Barbie demanded, grabbing the little man's legs.

Barbie's idea of out of the way was a conveniently located broom closet around the corner.

"I don't feel right about this," I protested, checking the man's pulse again.

The old man was snuggled into a mop bucket. His legs stuck up in the air, and he was drooling. He looked like one of those life sized dolls toy stores like to sell at the holidays.

Barbie rolled her eyes, shoving a package of washrags under his head. "Better?" she asked.

"Actually, yes." I nodded.

"Good! Let's move," Barbie barked.

We raced across the workshop. Having no idea where we were going, or how to get there, I blindly followed my cousin, hoping we wouldn't get caught. Rounding a corner, she stopped so quickly that I bumped into her, jolting the map from her fingers.

"A key lock?!" She exclaimed, staring at a door.

"I've got this one," I replied, happy to pull my own weight.

I fished a bobby pin out of my hair and, seconds later, the door swung open. I'm not sure what I expected, but it wasn't a nondescript flight of stairs. Barbie rushed past me, leaving me to shut and lock the door behind us. Racing up the stairs, I cursed myself for not keeping up my exercise routine. Barbie, of course, flew up them without so much as a muscle twinge. By the time I reached the top, Barbie was pushing steps up to the door to Eric's plane.

"Wait! Wait! Wait!" I yelled, out of breath.

"We have two minutes!" She yelled down from the top of the steps. "Get the doors open!"

My eyes followed her fingers to two huge bay doors. Glancing back at the black plane, I winced. Eric was going to be pissed!

164

Shaking my head, I rushed through a door labeled *office*. Locating a power grid, I flicked the switch labeled *doors* and stuck my head out of the room. The doors were opening! Racing up to the waiting plane, I reached the top of the steps just as the plane started to move. Grabbing the open door, I half leapt, half fell into the plane, somehow managing to close the door on my knee. After securing the door, I limped into the cockpit. Barbie was confidently steering past glistening snow mounds. Collapsing into the empty seat next to her, I quickly fastened my seatbelt.

"I don't suppose you asked permission to borrow Eric's plane?" I asked hopefully, knowing the answer.

"Batman and his group of merry thugs will get over it," Barbie reasoned.

"Where'd you get the keys?" I asked, noting that she hadn't hot-wired the console.

"I found them," she evaded.

"Where?" I pressed the issue. I wasn't sure why it mattered, but it did.

"In the Wolfman's pocket, while he was busy sexing you up in the hallway of that burger place." She grinned, pointing the plane towards the East.

Sixteen

After a long night of flying, we landed at a small airport, just outside of New York City. Stepping off of the plane, I reached into my purse to get my phone. Closing my eyes in trepidation, I fidgeted with the device, debating with myself whether or not I should turn it back on.

Not that the time mattered as much as the messages that surely awaited my attention. There was no getting around it. We had slipped out, without forewarning, blown up the city's power source, and stolen Eric's plane. There was no way my phone had been spared the anger of my brother or Eric. I didn't have to look to know that whatever they had to say, it would be unpleasant.

Fingering the power button, I reminded myself that I hadn't had much opportunity to sleep over the past two nights. And, although the sun was high in the sky, my internal clock was disorientated from traveling in and out of so many time zones. Basically, I was tired, too tired to deal with what waited on the other side of the power switch.

Deciding that whatever messages were waiting could wait a few hours longer, I slid the device back into my purse.

"Seriously? What are you afraid of?" Barbie admonished, leading the way to the entrance and hopefully a waiting taxi.

"We just stole a plane, from mercenaries! How can you be so calm?" Sure, Eric and I had made up, kind of, hadn't we? Anyway, I wasn't sure if whatever we had between us was enough to keep us on Eric's good side. I mean, he seemed to be pretty attached to his routine and his stuff, and here we were messing with both.

"What's he gonna do about it? He's on ice. Besides, you two made up." Barbie shrugged away my fears.

"Umm... Right," I mumbled.

"You didn't make up?" Barbie asked. "Why the hell not?"

"Well, umm... You see..." I stammered.

"Ms. O'Grady, Ms. Hart, please come with us," a deep voice spoke in my ear, just as a gigantic hand wrapped itself around my forearm.

"Fuck!" Barbie exclaimed as a giant hand gripped her just above the elbow.

Our new friend led us to a black Escalade, waiting at the curb. I didn't recognize the man in Rambo brown who opened the door for us. I didn't need to. I knew who had sent him, and I knew why. Barbie was right, I should have given him a good reason to think kindly of me. Looking at the two armed men escorting us to an unknown location, made me reconsider the chasteness of our parting kiss.

"You were saying?" I asked Barbie.

"How was I supposed to know he'd send Thor and his brother from another mother after us?" Barbie groused. "What do you think he wants?"

"Let me think… His plane, an apology, our heads on a platter?" Now that Eric had made his move, and it wasn't having us shot on sight, I was surprised to realize that I was feeling calmer.

"We don't have time for this," Barbie grumbled.

"I don't think we have much choice," I sighed.

Turning on my phone was worse than I'd expected. There were twenty-three missed calls, my voicemail was full, and too many text messages to bother reading them all. Deciding to tackle texts first, I breezed past the ones from friends and relatives who had no idea that I'd just committed a felony.

"Little Abby's having a baby!" I exclaimed.

"Isn't she twelve or something?" Barbie asked.

"Twenty. Remember, she married that off-off-off Broadway actor last year," I reminded her. "You hooked up with the groom's cousin during the ceremony," I added.

"That sounds like something I would do." Shrugging, she added, "Good for her, I guess," Changing the subject, she asked, "What's the Wolfman got to say?"

"Let's see… *'You stole my plane!' 'Bring back my plane!' 'Where is my plane?'*" I scrolled through the texts. "I think he's upset."

Barbie rolled her eyes, and snarked, "One of these days he's going to learn to string together multi-syllable words and make a complex sentence."

"Too bad we won't live to see it." I glanced meaningfully towards Thor.

"Excuse me," Barbie spoke sweetly, leaning toward the front seat. "Your boss lost these. Would you mind giving them back to him?"

Hands the size of two of mine closed around the keys.

"Thank you." Barbie flashed a mega what smile at Thor.

Giving Barbie a confused look, Thor mutely dangled the plane keys from his hand.

Barbie turned her attention to me, and said, "Now, you can tell the Wolfman that we delivered his plane, and keys, to his henchmen. Then, have him tell them to let us go."

Out of any better ideas, and not wanting to end up a prisoner in Wolf Inc. headquarters, I texted Eric.

Seconds later, I received my answer, "Like Hell."

"I think that means no." Looking at the text message, I sighed.

I wasn't worried that Eric would hurt us. I just didn't like the idea of being locked up, until he showed up to let me out, and lecture me like I was a small child. I could see it in my mind, of course Greg was there too, both of them fuming and being annoyingly loud and cranky. No, I did not want to deal with that.

The Escalade slowed, then completely stopped. Traffic was a mess, and we were being rerouted. Curiosity pulled me out of my musings. My eyes widened. I blinked, then shook my head. The vision was still there.

"I must have spent too much time thinking about Santa," I mumbled.

Everywhere I looked people were decked out in red and white coats, white beards, and black boots. There was even a healthy sprinkle of brightly colored elfin costumes. Looking closer, that was exactly what it was, costume. The streets were covered, as far as the eye could see, with hundreds of people dressed like Santa, Mrs. Claus, and their elves. I even spotted a few reindeer.

"What the hell is that?" Thor's brother asked.

Smiling at the scene in the street, Barbie explained, "That, boys, is Santa Con."

As the car slowly edged around the crowd, Barbie leaned back, kicking the door with both feet. Grabbing my arm, she pulled me through the now open door. On the way out, my hand brushed a sticky chunk of what looked suspiciously like chewed gum shoved into the locking mechanism. It was still wet.

"Gross!" I cringed.

"Sorry fellas, but I have other plans tonight," Barbie called, blowing a kiss toward the car, as we raced through the festive crowd.

I glanced back. Thor was already out of the car, chasing after us. His buddy was right behind him, leaving the car in the middle of a no-parking zone.

"Eric is not going to be happy with them." I shook my head at the men's misfortune.

Barbie and I took advantage of the fact that we were still dressed as Santa's elves to merge into the Santa Con swell. Between our brightly colored elf clothes and much smaller stature, it was easier for us to slide through the crowd than the two bullgoons following us. Sure, we had a head start, but with their longer legs and superior stamina it was only a matter of time before they overtook us. Looking for a hiding place, we jumped on a float at the head of the parade, joining several hundred of our newest friends dancing and singing to jingle bell rock.

From the front of our float, we could easily watch Eric's goons, pacing us, waiting for their chance to snatch us from the crowd and avoid the wrath of Rambo. Not in any hurry to help them out, we quietly slipped off of the float and down a back street, each of us in an oversized Santa coat and hat bought with illicit kisses and promises that we didn't intend to keep.

Seventeen

"Book us on a one way to Aruba," Barbie commanded. "We'll need clothes. And, tell them that we were originally heading there and we'll claim our bags at the airport. If they try to tell you they sent them back, make a fuss."

"It's been two days," I reminded her. "Do you really think our bags are still there?"

"I'll blame you if they aren't," Barbie responded.

"Me? You're the one who rerouted us to the North Pole via Eric," I reminded her.

"Yes, but you're forgetting one very crucial fact. I'm the boss, and trust me rank does have its privileges. Mainly, we do things my way. Capisce?" Her treacly sweet smile, warned of an impending meltdown.

"Our bags are full of winter clothes," I reminded her, hoping to avoid a scene.

"I don't care how you do it. You're my assistant, work some magic," she growled.

"You're forgetting, I'm not free to walk around the city," I reminded her.

"This would be easier if your boyfriend hadn't left his goons to guard my apartment," Barbie fumed.

"He's not my boyfriend," I reminded her.

"What you do with Batman is your business, but he and I are through!" Barbie's eyes threw unseen daggers at an invisible target.

We were one floor beneath Barbie's apartment, in her on-again-off-again's, Muscles No Brains, apartment. It was as close as we could get to her place. Eric had a guy in the lobby, and another at Barbie's door, waiting for us.

Muscles wasn't very bright, but even he couldn't miss Eric's men. They stood out like two sore thumbs on Fifth Avenue. He had gotten a message through to Barbie, through the doorman, in time for our cabby to drop us off by the back door. Knowing who was waiting for us, and where, we had entered the building through the service entrance, then used the service elevator to get to Muscles' apartment. Now, he was preparing roasted asparagus in hollandaise sauce, and something else that I couldn't pronounce but smelled mouthwatering, while I worked out travel plans and Barbie paced the floor irritably. I probably should have questioned a few things, but it was Barbie.

"Try this." The dark haired Adonis shoved something pink into Barbie's open mouth.

"I don't want…" Barbie's eyes widened, then she said, "Just one more."

Muscles' brain cell showed through his grin as he went to fetch her another bite. "Jessie," he asked, "Would you like to try one?"

"Yes, thank you." I smiled, trying not to drool.

It wasn't my fault. The man had his perfect body clothed in

173

just low rise jeans and a waist apron that said, *'Kiss the Cook.'* Every time he came out of the kitchen it seemed like a better idea.

"Careful, it's hot," he warned, racing back to the kitchen.

"You never told me he was a chef," I whispered to Barbie.

"He's not. I mean, he doesn't work as a chef. He's a model. He just likes to cook," Barbie explained.

"Did he go to chef school?" I asked.

Barbie tilted her head, watching him stretch to reach a top shelf. Shrugging, she said, "I can't imagine any school graduating him. To be honest, I'm not sure how he manages to live unassisted."

"He can't be that dumb," I protested.

"He once spray painted a Fendi sweatshirt, because he wanted it in yellow." She grimaced at the thought. "I asked him why he didn't just buy it in yellow. You know what he said?"

"No," I answered, unsure what a Fendi was but pretty sure it was expensive.

"They were out of yellow," Muscles said, reentering the room.

I knew I was going to regret asking, but the words were already coming out, "Why didn't you just dye it?"

Barbie winced.

Muscles gave me a disgusted look, and said, "Because, I'm pro-life."

My mouth opened.

Barbie shot me a warning look.

Taking a deep breath, I floundered for something to say. "I didn't know that."

Muscles nodded. "I care deeply about letting things be alive."

"That's great," I offered, wondering again what Barbie and Muscles could possibly have in common, outside of the bedroom.

"Don't judge," Barbie warned.

"I wouldn't dare," I assured her.

"Dinner," Muscles announced cheerily. "It's a beautiful night. We'll eat on the patio."

"So, how did you two meet?" I asked, desperate for dinner conversation.

"I dropped something off of my balcony," Barbie offered.

"Panties, pink panties," Muscles finished.

"He brought them to you?" I asked, swooning at the romance in the story.

Barbie winced, shook her head, and said, "No."

Muscles frowned. "I threw them to her. They kept coming back. Like a boomerang." He pretended to throw something up in the air.

"By the time I got to his apartment, they were long gone." Barbie sighed.

"I thought they were going to make it, then they sailed past my balcony, down into the alley. They landed in a homeless guy's shopping cart," Muscles added. "I think he really needed them, because he roared really loud when he saw them."

It was all I could do to not choke on my asparagus at the mental picture of some poor homeless guy being hit with Barbie's hot pink panties. Blinking away threatening laughter, I looked up towards Barbie's dark apartment. "I guess it's not really that far up."

Barbie's gaze followed mine. "It's not, is it?"

175

"No," I agreed, turning my attention to Barbie.

Barbie smiled, tilting her head toward the balcony.

I looked back at the balcony. Was Barbie suggesting what I thought she was suggesting? Each balcony was spaced ten feet from the last, and surrounded by a glass railing. I glanced at the walls. Too smooth to climb. I must have misread her intentions.

"Do you still have your climbing ropes?" She asked Muscles.

"Yes," Muscles answered.

Still staring up at her apartment, she asked, "Can we borrow them?"

Muscles gave her a confused look. "Do you want to go to the climbing gym?"

"Something like that." Barbie smiled.

"It's been awhile since I've used them. Let me look in the closet." Muscles disappeared inside.

"If you're thinking what I think you're thinking, the answer is no," I protested.

"You said it yourself, it's not that far," Barbie reasoned.

"To fall," I protested.

"We won't fall," Barbie reassured me.

"I am not climbing a building," I stated, hands on my hips.

"Of course not," Barbie agreed. "The building is much too smooth to climb. That's why we need ropes."

"We're twelve stories up!" I protested.

Muscles came back in with a pile of ropes.

"Can you do something with the ropes so they protect us from falling?" Barbie asked Muscles.

"What are you climbing?" He asked, still clueless.

"That." Barbie pointed up the wall to her balcony.

"No. No we are not!" I protested.

"A Prusik would work," Muscles said, ignoring my protests.

"Prusik? What is that? It sounds bad," I said nervously.

"It's a knot." Muscles began twisting the ropes. After a couple of minutes of intense concentration, he held up a knotted configuration. "Simple, but sturdy."

"Smarter than he looks, isn't he?" Barbie grinned at my disbelief.

"He's an idiot savant," I whispered back.

"I'll just secure the ropes, like so...." Muscles threw the end of a rope over the balcony. "Almost ready. This will be an easy climb. Just remember to hold on."

"Hold on?" I repeated, still unsure about rappelling up a building in the middle of the night.

"Don't fall." Barbie smiled, stepping into the open harness that Muscles held out to her.

"You're kidding." I took a deep breath, silently telling myself that this was one of the more dangerous stunts we've pulled together.

"YOU can let the Wolfman dictate where you don't go, but not me. I'm going to my apartment," Barbie said, sliding her purse over her shoulder.

That was cheating. Barbie knew that I couldn't stand to be told what not to do. I took a deep breath. I wasn't going to let her goad me into acting rashly. I watched nervously as she tossed a hook over the glass balcony above us. It landed perfectly, as if she'd done this sort of thing a hundred times.

"Thanks for dinner," she said, giving Muscles a long kiss.

With a tug on the rope, she stepped onto the edge of the railing. Hoisting herself onto the wall, she quickly walked up the side of the building to her apartment. It looked easy enough. I glanced at Muscles. With a sigh, I stepped into the remaining harness, allowing Muscles to strap me in tight.

Once Barbie was over the edge of the balcony above us, she called down, "Coming?"

"You know I am," I grumbled, wishing that I had my purse on me, then I would at least have ID to help them identify my body, but it was still in the Escalade where I had thoughtlessly left it earlier today. "I couldn't grab my bag? That would have taken all of what? Half a second?" I muttered to myself, as I yanked on my straps. "If you die, they'll put you on a slab and write *'Barbie's cousin'* on your toe tag. All because you couldn't grab your purse."

"Should I make a drink and come back when you're done complaining?" Barbie asked impatiently.

"No, I'm coming." I sighed, wondering once again how I let her talk me into these things.

Eighteen

"You'll break something. No, you'll land looking like a runway model on vacation. I'll break something." I was staring down into the alley next to Barbie's apartment building.

"It's perfectly safe," Barbie insisted.

"The door is perfectly safe." I pointed behind me. "This is crazy."

"We can't use the door. It's still being guarded by thing one and thing two," Barbie reasoned. "Don't you want to find Santa?"

"You know I do." I looked down again. "Are you sure he's not at Santa Con? There were a lot of Santas out there." I was willing to try anything to keep from tumbling down the side of the building while attached to a rope. I could already picture the rope burns in places where rope burns shouldn't happen.

"You and I searched the city yesterday. He wasn't there.

Anyway, the Santas have legit lives outside of the Con," Barbie responded.

"Legit? I bet those Santas still live in their parent's basements," I challenged.

Barbie shrugged. "I know for a fact that one of them is CEO of a major cooperation."

"How could you possibly know that?" I asked.

With a grin, she admitted, "We hooked up after last year's Santa Con."

"Is there anyone in this city you haven't slept with?" I asked.

"New people come here every day," she offered without shame.

"Okay, some of them have real jobs. That doesn't mean he's not here," I insisted.

"I made some calls last night. He's not here. But, we have a lead in the Caribbean. Our flight leaves in two hours," she reminded me. "It's time to get moving."

I sighed, looked toward the door one last time, and shouldered the gym bag full of borrowed clothes Barbie thrust at me. "This is insane!" I grumbled, stepping into my harness. "If I die, I'm coming back to haunt you," I threatened, stepping onto the balcony railing.

"I may just look him up when we get back," Barbie mused.

I looked around, but it was early. There wasn't anyone else moving around out there. "Who?"

"The CEO." With a smile, she added, "I like a CEO with a Santa complex," then pushed me off the railing.

"Whaaaaaaa!!! I wasn't ready!" I yelled up at her.

"Push off with your feet and hold on," Barbie called as I unceremoniously licked the wall.

Righting myself, I pushed off, sliding down the rope. It was over in a flash. I'm proud to say that I only kissed the wall once on the way down. I was fighting off a rush of exhilaration when two of New York's finest walked up. They silently took in my obviously borrowed athletic gear and the gym bag flung over my shoulder, and turned their attention to the rope. I was wracking my brain for an explanation that wouldn't sound crazy when Barbie swung down the side of the building like Tarzan.

Landing like she does this every day, Barbie tossed her hair like a shampoo commercial, hit them with a megawatt smile, winked, and then purred, "Hi boys!"

The officers looked as mystified as I felt. Except they probably weren't wondering how she could swing gracefully down the side of an apartment building and land looking like a movie star, when I came away with a scraped cheek, bruised knee, and frizzed hair. If I had ever truly believed we were all created equal, this moment unequivocally disputed that theory.

"What is going on here?" The older of the two officers found his voice.

"We were just rappelling down from my apartment," Barbie explained.

The other officer looked at our gym bags, and asked, "Rappelling?"

I nodded, explaining, "We're heading to Aruba." What? Why did I say that? Now I sounded like a moron.

"Aruba?" The older officer repeated.

Barbie nodded, adding, "You wouldn't want to give us a ride to the airport would you?"

"What's in the bags?" He ignored Barbie.

"Passport, change of clothes, make-up, swimsuits." Barbie unzipped her bag, tilting it open to show the officers while she spoke.

I was pretty sure we were going to jail, but I showed them my bag of borrowed items as well.

Trading bemused expressions, the younger one asked, "Why didn't you use the elevator?"

"My ex is camped out at the door. He's been drinking, and he's violent," Barbie sniffed, producing an artful tear.

"We decided we'd avoid him this way. We didn't think it would cause a problem," I added.

"No problem," the younger officer assured us.

"It was just out of the ordinary," his partner added. "Do you want us to get rid of your ex?"

"That would be great, but it will take a while, and we have a plane to catch," Barbie said, hefting her bag.

"What floor do you live on? We'll check it out," the younger officer offered.

"The tenth." Barbie smiled sweetly. "He'll be the big guy, camped out in the hall."

"We'll take care of him. You girls just enjoy your trip," the older man assured us while leading us to a waiting taxi.

"Thank you so much!" We called from the cab.

As we headed to the airport, I said, "Eric is never going to speak to me again."

"You could be so lucky," Barbie offered.

"I thought you liked him," I reminded her.

"That was before he sent his merry men after me, and tried to keep me out of my own apartment," she explained.

"Us," I corrected.

"What?" She asked.

"He sent them after us, not just you," I clarified. "And, I don't think he was trying to keep you out of your apartment," I added. "He just thought we would go to the apartment…" I trialed off, realizing that Barbie was glaring at me.

"Whose side are you on?" Barbie demanded.

"Yours. Ours. I was just… never mind," I sighed, turning to look out the window.

Nineteen

Expecting to run into Eric's men at the airport added even more stress to what was always a taxing experience for me. By the time it was my turn at security, I had what I thought was a realistic sounding apology worked out. It hadn't been that difficult to come up with, seeing as I actually did feel like an apology was in order. I mean, we had stolen the man's plane and gotten two innocent men thrown in jail. If that didn't deserve an apology, I didn't know what did.

Barbie, of course, thought the apology should come from the other end. "I'm disappointed that we haven't run into Batman. I was hoping to get the chance to talk to him," Barbie announced as we waited to board our plane.

"What do you want to talk to him about?" I asked suspiciously.

"Off the top of my head… kidnapping, false imprisonment, stalking." She ticked off each offense with a perfectly manicured finger. "Give me a minute with a good lawyer and I'm sure I can come up with a few more."

"You just like lawyers," I taunted.

"I like them all." Barbie grinned. "If you hadn't seen him first, I'd consider letting the Wolfman make it up to me. But, I won't, because I'm a good friend."

"You'd be doing me a favor. As soon as you touch a guy, he becomes repulsive to me." I sighed wistfully.

"Really? You didn't seem repulsed at dinner last night." Barbie snickered. "I saw you staring. Not that anyone could blame you."

"Not that I'd ever date him, but Muscles isn't like your other guys. He's a really nice guy, under all that hotness," I pointed out. "It's hard for such a nice guy to be repulsive."

"I know," she agreed. "It's too bad he's so dumb. I could probably make that one stick, but I get bored halfway through his sentences. Oh good, we're up!" Barbie stood up, grabbing her bag.

"We're not up," I insisted.

"Of course we are. They just called first class," she insisted. "Come on. I could really use a drink."

"First class?" I asked calmly, but in my mind was panic. *Crap! Was I supposed to book first class?*

"You didn't book us first class?!" Barbie frowned, staring at her ticket. "Coach!" She turned to me in disbelief, then said, "Does this," she gestured to herself, "look like the kind of person who flies coach?"

I bit my lip, refusing to answer.

185

"Does it?" She insisted angrily.

"You didn't specify first class, and…" Where was all of this anger coming from? I stared at my petite cousin in disbelief.

"I shouldn't have to specify. You are the worst assistant," she fumed. "I can't believe you're making me travel coach. I'd be better off doing it myself," she continued her tirade.

"Think of all the money you're saving," I offered. "First class is so much more expensive, and for what? To sit in the front of the plane, in a slightly more comfortable chair?"

"Stop talking," she demanded.

"What?" I blinked at her.

"You heard me. I cannot listen to your voice say another syllable right now," she raged.

"What?" I asked again.

Staring daggers at me, she snarled, "Are you stupid?"

"No!"

"Then I shouldn't have to repeat myself. Face the wall. I don't want to see your face or hear your voice," she said, waving her hand to dismiss me.

"Is this really how you talk to people?" I asked.

My eyes widened as Barbie grabbed her bag, and walked up to the flight attendant. After a heated exchange, Barbie came back over to me, flouncing into a nearby chair. Not wanting to deal with her temper tantrum, I chose to ignore her presence.

"I need you to understand that, as my personal assistant, it is your responsibility to make me happy," Barbie informed me after a few minutes of silence.

"I need you to understand that I am not your personal assistant," I rebutted.

"Yes, you are," she countered. "Otherwise, you'd still be in Oklahoma, looking for a job to pay off your credit cards that are surely maxed out by now."

"I don't have any credit cards," I protested. "I paid them off with the money from Jim's ring, then cut them up."

"You did?" Barbie turned questioning eyes toward me, asking, "Why?"

"Because, I can't afford them." I sighed, knowing I had just walked into the trap Barbie was laying.

"So, you need a job?" Barbie smirked at me.

"Yes." I regretted the word even as it left my lips.

"Fine. I'll give you another chance. But, you've got to do better," she insisted. "Honestly, I don't know how you expect to ever keep a job with your attitude."

Slinking into my chair, I didn't even try to suppress the groan her words produced.

Ignoring me, she asked, "Where are we staying?"

"I don't know." I shrugged her off.

"You didn't make reservations?" She turned on me.

"Well, no. I mean, I guess I should have," I cringed, adding, "but I didn't really know where we were going other than somewhere in Aruba. You aren't the best communicator."

"You, cousin, are having an exceptionally bad first week on the job," Barbie remarked.

"Especially since I don't actually work for you," I agreed,

187

grabbing my bag and heading for the flight attendant as she called our boarding group.

I had hoped to get some peace from Barbie during the flight. Unfortunately, I had to listen to her complain about my incompetence the entire flight. By the time the plane landed in Aruba, we were barely speaking, and I had developed a nervous tic above my left eye. My only consolation was that Barbie didn't have her army of pink luggage to demand that I lug around.

"I'm sure there are any number of hotel rooms available on the beach," I offered, in an attempt to make peace.

"I've already taken care of it," Barbie said. "But, I shouldn't have to. It is your job as my assistant to take care of travel details."

"Okay." I yawned.

"I shouldn't have had to," she repeated.

"Of course not. We can't have your highness doing such menial tasks," I quipped.

Barbie placed a cold stare on me. "I shouldn't have to. That is what I pay you to do."

"You're not paying me to do anything! I don't work for you!" I shrieked, unable to take it anymore. "Why can't you understand that?"

"Why can't you just admit that you are my personal assistant?" She threw her hands up in frustration.

I opened my mouth to speak, thought better of it, and said instead, "If I agree to work for you, will you cut the attitude?"

"What attitude?" She asked.

Rolling my eyes, I explained, "The 'I am the boss, worship

me' attitude."

"I have no such…" she denied.

I narrowed my brows at her, my gaze daring her to finish her sentence.

"Fine. I'll adjust my attitude," her voice was cold, betraying her irritation.

"Good, because I'm beginning to see why you go through assistants the way you do," I said testily.

"You are the snarkiest PA I have ever had," she complained.

"If you don't like it, fire me," I offered.

"I should," she threatened.

"Please do," I begged.

She pursed her lips, and said, "If you don't want the job, why don't you quit?"

"Because you won't let me," I insisted, "even though I never actually agreed to be your personal assistant!"

"Sure you did, back at your parent's. We were in the attic and you told your brother you were my PA," her tones revealed her hurt feelings.

"No, you did." I softened my voice, "I didn't think you meant it. I thought we were creating a cover story, so I went along with it. How was I supposed to know that you meant it?"

"Well, this is awkward." Barbie fidgeted. "Oh look, an empty cab!"

Before I could respond, Barbie opened a door in the still moving vehicle. Tossing a handful of bills into the front seat, she jumped into the backseat. I shrugged to myself. For some reason, it was important for Barbie to have an assistant. She did so much for me, asking nothing in return. I could do this one thing for her.

"How hard could it be?" I asked the sun, just to have it retreat behind the only cloud in the sky. "Great." I sighed. Sliding into the seat next to my petulant cousin, I offered, "It might be fun to be your PA."

Letting out an unladylike huff, she ignored me while digging through her purse.

"Come on." I smiled at her, trying to look eager. "Can I please be your personal assistant?"

"You don't want the job." Her attention was still focused on the contents of her purse.

"I do want it," I said, a little too eagerly.

She glanced up from her purse, looking doubtful.

"I thought about it. It'll be fun, working for you, together, just me and you." I really hoped my face looked eager, because I wasn't at all sure about working for Barbie. She had a reputation as a horrible boss, glamorized by the extreme acts committed by her past assistants.

"Fine," she acquiesced. "But, you have to try. At this rate, you're just an embarrassment to your career field."

Resisting the urge to roll my eyes, I forced a smile, and said, "I'll try."

As the cab rolled to a stop in front of a shining white villa, I had to wonder once again how things had gotten so far out of control. "I graduated from college. I can get a job. Why doesn't she think I can get a job? I just need the right opportunity," I mumbled to myself. I was still contemplating how things had gone this far when Barbie exited the cab, leaving me to follow.

"Grab our bags and meet me around back," she barked.

"The servant's entrance, really?" I wanted to object, instead I did as she commanded. "WOW!" I gasped, rounding the corner.

The ocean view was stunning. I could feel the stress leave my body as I stood watching the waves race back and forth on the empty beach. By the time Barbie opened the door, I was completely relaxed.

"Sorry it took so long," she apologized, devoid of the attitude of the past twenty-four hours.

"Couldn't find the hide-a-key?" I wondered aloud.

"Something like that." Barbie shrugged noncommittally.

"Whose house is this?" I asked, stepping inside.

"A friend," she answered evasively, heading for the bar. He always leaves the bar stocked. "Do you want a drink?"

"Where is he?" I looked around, noticing the ambient lack of use pervading the area.

"He got picked up on smuggling charges, months ago." Barbie pulled a bottle from behind the bar. "I was afraid the government might have seized the house. That's why I was insisting on a hotel reservation, as a backup plan. Lucky for us, they didn't. Knowing him, he buried the real owner under a mountain of fake paperwork so complex they'll never link the place to him. I know I won't tell."

I know I should have been surprised to find out her friend was locked up, and we weren't exactly invited guests, but it was Barbie. She knew so many people serving jail sentences that I just assumed all of her friends were involved in some sort of criminal activity. "What kind of smuggling?" I couldn't help but ask.

"Jewels," she replied.

"Jewels," I gave her a questioning look, "from Aruba?"

"Of course not." Barbie waved the idea off. "He was part of an international ring. They concentrated mostly on embargoed countries."

Taking in my lavish surroundings, I let out a low whistle. "Business must be good."

She nodded. "This is just one of his homes."

"And they say crime doesn't pay," I remarked, sinking into a blissfully soft couch and covering myself with a Chenille throw. "I could get used to this."

"He's spending his days in a maximum security prison, don't think he isn't paying," Barbie warned.

"It's a good thing he keeps a hide-a-key," I offered sleepily.

"That SOB doesn't trust anyone, and he would never leave a hide-a-key." Barbie handed me a glass filled with liquid. "I overrode the security codes."

"What?" I sat up, spilling my glass. "We're trespassing!"

"It's not like he's going to show up, all pissed off," Barbie reminded me, adding, "at least not for twenty more years."

"Someday, we need to have a talk about your moral compass." I shook my head.

"My moral compass?" Barbie raised an eyebrow at me. "Yours isn't as straight as you'd like to pretend."

Changing the subject, I asked, "So, this guy is why you wanted to come to Aruba to start our search?"

"Sort of." Barbie sank into an opposing chair. "Just before he was arrested, Chester told me about a guy he met on the beach."

"Chester?" I asked.

"He was named after his grandfather." Barbie dismissed my question. "I thought he had been snorting too much coke when he told me the story, so I didn't pay much attention."

"Coke?" I asked, my eyes wide.

"I told you, he's a dirt bag. Anyway," she continued, "Chester was convinced that this old man he met on the beach was Father Christmas in disguise. For months, he went on and on about how he needed to get out of the smuggling business and go legit because he was a disappointment to Father Christmas, and if he ever had kids they would have to pay for living in luxury that was acquired immorally."

"You mean he was arrested after he stopped smuggling?" I asked, feeling bad for Chester.

"Unfortunately for him, he made one more run." Barbie shook her head, adding, "His last."

"That's so sad." I frowned.

Barbie looked at me as if I was crazy. "For years, he knowingly committed crimes against humanity, and the jewel industry. Suddenly he grows a conscience, not because it's wrong, but because some overweight, undertanned do-gooder, flouncing around the beach in a bright red banana hammock told him he was disappointed in him, and because of that his not yet conceived offspring wouldn't get toys for Christmas." Finishing her drink in one gulp, Barbie concluded, "Delusional prick belongs where he is."

"You have a way with mental pictures," I said, frowning. "I need to scrub that one out of my brain."

193

"If I'm right, you'll get to see the real thing soon enough," Barbie claimed, smiling at her own brilliance.

"I sure hope he's gotten a little sun," I cringed at the image stuck in my head, "or at least picked up more modest swim trunks, in the week since he went missing."

"You and me both," Barbie agreed, yawning. "I'm beat. I think I'll take a nap, right here."

"That is the best idea you've had in days," I agreed, snuggling deeper into the couch.

Barbie was soon asleep, leaving me to contemplate my life. With a sigh, I promised God that I wouldn't steal anymore planes. I thought about Chester, adding that I wouldn't squat in any more abandoned houses after this trip. Then a mental picture of Eric's men in jail on trumped up abuse charges popped into my head. I should probably add having people falsely imprisoned to that list, and blowing up Santa's power source. Unfortunately, I seemed to be the only one of us with an operational grasp on right and wrong, making it difficult to control the lies that were taking over my life, or was I just as delusional as Chester. I drifted off to fitful dreams where the bad decisions of my past became my future.

Twenty

I woke to a luminous moon reflecting its twin into gentle ocean swells. Wiping the sleep from my eyes, I looked for a clock. Ten. We had slept the day away. I was in the middle of my stretch when I realized that the house was a little too quiet. A quick search of the house revealed my suspicions to be true. Barbie was gone.

"It's just like Barbie to wander off," I fumed to the emptiness. Calming myself, I decided to check the beach. "She probably just went for a swim," I reasoned.

After a quick look around outside, I had to admit that she had left without me.

With a sigh, I went back inside to find my phone. After a quick search produced the borrowed contraption, I dialed Barbie's number. A muffled sound came from under a cushion. Sliding my hands under the pillow revealed Barbie's hot pink phone.

"You're kidding me!" I grumbled. "Surely, she wouldn't have gone far on foot and without her phone."

With a frustrated sigh, I ran a brush through my hair and headed outside to search for my errant cousin. Unable to enjoy the water tickling my toes, I gazed up and down the shore. Anger swelled within my breast. Barbie was nowhere to be found. The only evidence that she had been here was her phone, a bag of clothes, and sporadic footprints in the sand that had been partially obliterated by the rising tide. Out of options, I followed the footprints towards the sound of an island cover band.

Minutes later, the footprints stopped at a beachside bar. Judging from the crowd, it was happy hour. Strangely enough, Barbie was nowhere to be seen.

"Excuse me." I gave the bartender my best smile. "Have you seen a blonde, about this tall?" I held my hand even with my boobs as a reference.

He motioned to the busy bar, noncommittally.

"Big hair, movie star looks, huge boobs…" I continued, refusing to be blown off.

"Oh, her!" He nodded. "She left about half an hour ago, with Amador."

I gave him a confused look, asking, "Who is Amador?"

"He's a regular." With a smile, he asked, "Are you Jessie?"

"Yes," I answered, eagerly. "Did she leave me something?"

Nodding, he stepped over to the register, picked up a piece of paper and handed it to me.

"What is this?" I asked, holding up the paper.

"Her bar tab. She said you'd take care of it," he answered.

"She said what?" I closed my eyes, trying to dispel the

irritation surging through my thoughts. First she bails on me. Then she leaves me a fifty dollar bar tab to pay, knowing that my purse is somewhere in the states and I don't have so much as a credit card on me. Taking another deep breath, I replied, "Put it on Amador's tab. If he's gonna spend time with Barbie, he might as well get used to sharing his wealth."

Chuckling, he gave me a genuine smile, then asked, "You want something?"

"A new life." I sighed.

"It's on the house." He handed me a fruity drink, with an umbrella tucked inside.

"Thanks." I attempted a smile.

"You look like you could use it." Smiling again, he said, "Take a breath, and mellow down. You're in paradise."

It was difficult to be mellow when I was in an unfamiliar country, broke, hungry, and forced to chase after Barbie's ghosts. Things weren't going as planned. I sighed, asking the bartender, "Do you have any pretzels?"

He shook his head.

"Nuts?" I asked hopefully. He had already moved to the other side of the bar to serve yummy looking fruity slushy drinks to two blonds who barely looked old enough to drive. "Just as well," I said to my drink. "I don't like pretzels that much."

"You're too pretty to look so glum," a deep voice whispered into my ear, just before an unfamiliar shirtless man took the seat next to me.

"I've been wearing someone else's clothes for so long that it's starting to feel normal, stole a plane, had two innocent men falsely arrested, squatted in an imprisoned jewel smuggler's abandoned villa, lost my best friend, have no money, and those are just the highlights. On top of everything else, I've got to find Santa and I'm sitting at a bar in Aruba talking to a strange shirtless man," I muttered. "Why shouldn't I be glum?"

The man next to me cocked his head, and smiled. "You had me going, until you threw in that part about Santa. Bartender, two more!" He shouted above the noise. Flashing me a crooked smile, he introduced himself, "Neik."

His grin told me that he didn't believe anything I'd just said, probably for the best. I didn't need to get arrested.

"Jessie," I shrugged, not in the mood to be hit on.

The bartender placed a twin to my drink on the counter, gave me a wink, and walked away.

"Jessie, I'm accepting your challenge," Neik announced.

I raised my head, meeting sparkling ice-blue eyes. Unable to resist, I asked, "Challenge?"

"I'm going to make you smile. If it takes me all night," he vowed.

"Listen Neik, you seem like a nice guy. And, I'm sure you're a catch, but I'm not really in a social mood." I motioned to the glass that the waiter had set down, adding, "Why don't you take this to," I looked around the bar, spotting an easy looking blonde, and pointed, "to her."

"I can cheer you up, and make you forget all of your problems," he promised handing me the glass.

There didn't seem to be any getting rid of him, so I shrugged my shoulders, and asked, "Have you seen Santa Claus lately?"

"If I say no, will you dress up like him and come down my chimney?" he asked provocatively.

"I would," I said, ignoring the heat on my cheeks, "but I already did that this week."

"Two more!" Neik called out to the bartender.

Twenty One

I woke with cotton in my mouth, and a freight train running through my head. Gingerly, I opened my eyes. I was in an unfamiliar apartment, lying next to the shirtless guy from last night. From the looks of things, he hadn't put on any clothes since we'd met.

"Really Jessie?" I whispered to myself.

One limb at a time, I eased off of the edge of the bed. The last thing I wanted to do was have an awkward conversation about what may or may not have happened last night. Looking down, I was surprised to find myself partially clothed.

"That's a good sign," I commented to the silent room.

My bedmate moaned, convincing me it was time to leave. First, I needed my shoes and clothes. I turned my attention to the room. It was a disaster area of takeout, and dirty clothes. At first glance, nothing appeared to belong to me, although there was an enviable left shoe under a table. I wondered where its mate was, not that it mattered. It was much too small to be of any use to me. I tried to remember what had happened to the shoes that I had been wearing last night, but I wasn't one hundred percent sure that I'd worn any. Snagging an unfamiliar pair of flip-flops and a men's button-up from the floor, I tiptoed to the door. Holding my breath, I slowly eased it open.

Looking back at the still sleeping stranger, I whispered to myself, "Maybe nothing happened. I hope nothing happened." Things were complicated enough in my life, without adding random hookups.

"Neik?" The voice of an older man resonated down the hall, stopping my flight. "You're up early. You want some eggs?"

"Shit!" I whispered.

At the sound of the strange voice, my heart began pounding so loud that I was pretty sure the whole block could hear it. I sank to the floor, on the verge of panic. Hooking up with a random stranger was bad enough, but I had to pick one who lived with his parents. What would he say? What would I say? How could I have let myself go home with a complete stranger?

"You're just going to have to own your mistake," I told myself. "You aren't an intruder. You were invited."

"By a man I'd never met before," I reminded myself.

"That doesn't make you a criminal. It makes you a whore," I reasoned.

"Maybe, I'm not a whore. I woke up with some of my clothes on, the ones I could find," I reasoned to myself. "Where's your shirt?" I asked the empty hallway, while fingering the unfamiliar men's t-shirt I had picked up from the floor.

"What about it? Eggs?" The deep voice came from around

the corner.

"Yeah," I deepened my voice, so much that it caused me to cough.

"I'll put some green tea on for you," the voice offered. "You sound terrible."

Blood pounded in my brain like steel drums, making it difficult to think. With no plan, and an urgent need to get out of wherever I was, I tiptoed down the hall. Confident that the voice was busy in the kitchen, I scrambled into the living room, where I immediately tripped over a misplaced garden gnome. My eyes widened in fear that I would be discovered as the gnome clattered across the hard floor.

"Vixen, leave that poor elf alone," the voice commanded.

"I guess he knows I'm here," I whispered to the gnome.

"Here kitty kitty," called the voice. "I have a nice big bowl of cream for you if you stop tormenting that poor gnome."

A coal black streak raced from under a chair, into the next room.

"Or he has a cat." I nodded, heading for a set of French doors on the other side of the room.

Thankfully, there was no one in the small yard. Seconds later, I found myself on an unfamiliar street, unsure which way led to my borrowed home. I tried, unsuccessfully, to remember anything from the night before that could help me. Sighing my displeasure, I randomly picked a direction.

"It can't be far." My voice sounded strangely loud on the quiet morning air. "A block would be far, dressed like a one night stand on her walk of shame," I berated myself, tugging the shirt down to cover my partially exposed cheeks.

Hoping not to draw any unwanted attention to myself, I hurried down the street, looking for the beach. Instead, I found a kind old woman standing outside of a cute little house watering her plants. After much confusion and gesturing, I was finally on my way in the right direction. Three turns later, the beach stretched before me. Fortunately, it was much easier to find my way this time. The house was on the end of the beach away from the hotels.

Breaking into a run, I began racing the sunrise. It had been awhile since I'd run on the beach. I was tempted to slow down and enjoy it, but I was focused on getting as far away from the little bungalow, and my one night stand, as I could. I needed to forget that last night had ever happened.

Slowing down to an out of shape jog, I passed the bar that I had tracked Barbie to the previous night. Finger combing my hair, I walked barefoot in the sand towards our illegally inhabited villa. Hopefully, Barbie was there, alone. Between the steel drums in my head, nausea, and the fact that I hadn't showered or eaten in two days; I didn't want to deal with people right now. I wasn't entirely sure I wanted to deal with Barbie.

The house was eerily quiet in a way that only large empty houses are. I felt like the intruder I was as I wondered from empty room to empty room. Standing at the top of the stairs, I debated taking a shower, raiding the fridge, or hightailing it out of there. With no way to contact Barbie, leaving was not an option. Heaving a loud sigh, I lowered my right foot. An unfamiliar noise echoed through the silence, freezing my foot in midair. Someone was pounding on the door. My heart leapt into my throat, gagging me with visions of being arrested for trespassing. Slowly, I backed down the hall, just in case they came around the back, where the wall of windows concealed nothing. Reaching the master bedroom, I crawled across the room, peering outside. Peeking past the closed curtain, my breath caught. A dark blue sedan sat out front.

"Is that the owner? Did he get out of jail? Is it the government? What if they find out we're not supposed to be here? What if they think I'm part of Chester's team and I get arrested?"

Cold panic shot through my veins, as the banging continued.

"Shit!" I exclaimed to no one. "Our bags are still downstairs."

The banging stopped.

Peeking out the window at the car, I wondered aloud, "Are they leaving?"

I watched as two menacing toughs walked around the car, just to turn towards the back of the house. My heart was beating so fast it felt like it was about to pop out of my chest.

"Did I lock the backdoor?" I whispered to the empty room.

"Why would I lock the back door? Barbie is still out there." My words seemed to echo ominously through the empty house.

I could hear my unwelcome visitors come in the back door. They were speaking too softly for their words to travel, but not softly enough to mask the sound.

"What if they're good guys?" I asked myself.

"They didn't look like good guys," I disagreed, remembering their unsmiling faces.

"Maybe, they're undercover. Undercover cops don't always look like good guys, especially when they're checking out a known smuggler's vacation home," I reasoned.

"Whoever they are, they shouldn't be here or they wouldn't be coming in the back way." I took a deep breath. "Where is Barbie? If she were here, she'd have some brilliant plan to just sashay down the stairs like she owns the place." Crap, it sounded like they were coming up the stairs! "Wherever Barbie is, she's better off than you are right now." I told myself, trying not to panic. I needed to focus. I needed a place to hide.

It was just a matter of time before I was discovered, arrested, and thrown into a drafty jail that I would undoubtedly have to share with the coffee grounds of society. I'd been in college the last time I was arrested for being in the wrong place, at the wrong time, with the wrong guy. It wasn't an experience I wanted to repeat.

I wasn't sure how much trouble trespassing would get me into in Aruba, probably not as much trouble as coming into the country on a counterfeit passport. Sure, it got me through security, but the TSA had paid more attention to Barbie's DD's than my passport. Was it good enough to stand up to the scrutiny of an arrest? I was sure that I didn't want to find out. I was equally sure that I didn't want to have to call my dad to bail me out of an Aruban jail. He got cranky enough when he had to come across town to bail me out.

Rejecting under the bed, I decided on the closet. Moving as quietly as possible, I closed myself into the dark space that was overly full of men's clothes. Delving deep into a pile of silk shirts, I searched for a safe spot to wait out the intruders. Voices, muffled through the closed door, sent me burrowing as far back in the dark space as I could get. Having no place else to go, I nervously strived to remember the Guardian Angel Prayer, hoping that the goons outside would overlook my hiding spot.

There I sat, in the soundproofed darkness, tucked into a small space behind a stack of suitcases, suspended in time. Long after my limbs stopped tingling, I dared not move. Fear of making a noise that would lead the intruders to my hiding space keeping me unnaturally still. Even my stomach stopped making loud gurgling noises. How long had it been: minutes, hours, days? I listened for noises telling me that the intruders were still there, still searching. Was that a noise, a voice? Unable to tell if they had left or not, I stayed put until I began to doubt that I could move. Even then, all I had the nerve to do was slightly rearrange. My fear of what may be waiting outside of my sanctuary was greater than myself. At some point, I slept.

Twenty Two

I looked at the clock, for the hundredth time, watching the second hand stumble across the eight, nine, ten... My eyes shifted toward the blinds covering the glass wall, and hiding the view of the beach. After my visitors left, I had decided to keep a low profile while I waited for Barbie. I looked at the clock again. I was officially worried. Barbie had now been missing for twenty-four hours, with no clue to her whereabouts.

"I should call the police," I said to the empty house.

"Where will you tell them you're staying?" I played devil's advocate, knowing that I couldn't tell them the truth.

I just didn't see the local police being okay with the idea that we had broken into an abandoned beach house. I pictured the look on their faces while they listened to me explain that Barbie said it was okay. After all, she knows the owner, who is by the way incarcerated for smuggling stolen jewels from countries that aren't legally allowed to sell their precious stones.

"That's one way to get yourself arrested," I muttered to myself.

Looking at the clock again, I hoped to see a tiny blonde waltz through the door, solving my legal dilemma, and staving off my worry. My stomach took that moment to growl, interrupting my fantasy. I knew better than to look for food in the kitchen. I had already ransacked it, without much luck. I reached for my borrowed purse. Except for the fake passport that Barbie had given me and a lip gloss, it was empty, and therefore useless.

"I should go to the embassy. I can file for a lost passport to make me legal, then report Barbie as missing," I reasoned.

"The embassy is probably miles away," I countered.

There was no car at the villa, and cabs and buses cost money. I didn't even know what town the embassy might be in. Closing my eyes in defeat, I shook my head. I needed a better plan. I needed help. I couldn't call my parents. They didn't even know I'd left the state. Knowing I was alone in a foreign country, and that Barbie was missing, would upset them. I could call Greg, but he'd just yell at me for being here in the first place. I hesitated. There was one person I could call, who wouldn't worry, or yell at me. He may not talk to me at all.

I sighed, not seeing any clear answers. Staring at the phone in my hand, not for the first time, I willed it to ring. It hadn't rung in hours. That in itself seemed strange. Barbie's phone always seemed to be buzzing.

I knew who I wanted to call, but the number I needed wasn't

programmed into this phone. I hadn't bothered to memorize it, and google wasn't any help.

"I've got to do something!" I exclaimed irritably to the empty house.

Without a better plan, I headed to the bar where Barbie was last seen. Maybe the bartender could tell me more about the guy Barbie left with. I was almost there when my hopes were dashed. The police were in the process of arresting what had to be half the patrons, and sending the rest away. Not wanting to join the party, I wondered up and down the beach, asking everyone I saw if they had seen my cousin, while keeping one eye open for a bearded old man in a red speedo.

The moon was high when I reached the door to the beach house. I hadn't learned anything and, in my scattered state of mind, I had locked myself out. Tired, hungry, and feeling like a failure, I let out a loud shriek of frustration.

"Now what?" I asked the empty beach. "I'll figure it out tomorrow," I insisted, curling up in a corner lounge chair, with a towel for a blanket.

Twenty Three

"Jessie!" Barbie's voice seemed to come from a long way away.

"Barbie!" My eyes shot open. "Where are you?"

No one answered, because there was no one other than myself there. It was just a dream. Yawning, I rolled over, closed my eyes, and hoped Barbie would be back for real when I awoke.

"Jessie," a deep voice reverberated next to me.

"What?" I asked, sleepily

"Get up," the voice insisted impatiently.

"I'm sleeping," I murmured, keeping my eyes closed.

"I can see that," he said.

"Then, go away. You people kept me up all night, jumping in and out of my dreams," I grouched. "Go haunt someone else's dream, and leave mine alone."

The familiar voice spoke softly into my ear, "I'm not in your dream."

"That's what you said the last time," I said, refusing to open my eyes.

"Do you really want me to leave?" Warm breath touched my cheek, leaving chills up and down my body.

Slowly, I opened one eye. Coffee colored eyes bored into mine. I closed my eye, took a deep breath, and then opened it again.

Perfectly shaped lips shaped sounds inches from my face. "Still here," Eric said.

"You're not a dream?" I blinked disbelievingly.

"Not this time." Eric shook his head. "Now, get up."

"Definitely not a dream," I said to myself. If it was a dream, he wouldn't have looked so cranky. "What are you doing here?"

"Looking for you," he said, in a tired voice.

"How did you find me?" I wondered aloud.

"I got a message from your cousin," he shrugged.

"A message from Barbie?" I jumping up. "When?! What did she say?!"

"The other day. She said you found Santa, and needed help bringing him in. I passed the info on to your brother, and headed out here to check it out." He glanced expectantly around the patio, asking, "Is he here?"

"Who?" I squirmed, suddenly very conscious of the fact that I was still wearing Neik's shirt and not much else.

"Santa." He sighed impatiently.

"No. No one's here." I shook my head. "How did you get

here?"

"Cab." He glanced around the patio.

"No." I shook my head. "I meant, how did you find me?"

"Barbie gave me the address," he explained.

"Of course she did." I frowned, deep in thought. "She knew I'd be hanging around, waiting for her to come back, because I'm that easy."

Eric chuckled.

Realizing what I'd just said, I looked down, and bit my lower lip, willing myself not to turn bright red. Neik's shirt seemed to flap in the breeze singing *'Easy. Easy. Easy.'* Why was I still wearing his shirt?

Unaware of my internal conflict, Erik asked, "What were we doing in your dream, alone?"

I could feel my face flush. Trying to ignore it, I denied, "I don't dream about you."

"Then what was all that talk about dreams?" He grinned. "And, why do you look like you fell asleep in the sun?"

"I… I dreamt about a lot of people last night," I stuttered, feeling my body temperature continue to raise. "Barbie, Greg, the weird guy who lives down the hall from Greg…"

"Let's get you out of the sun," he suggested, heading toward the door. After a moment wrestling with the patio door, he said, "The door is locked."

"I locked myself out. That's why I was sleeping out here," I admitted, wishing he hadn't shown up just in time to see me at my most inept.

"Whose house is this?" He stepped back, studying the walls.

"A friend of Barbie's, who is in jail," I admitted. "I'm not sure we actually have his permission to stay here."

"Anyone know you're staying here?" He leaned closer to look at the lock.

"I think so, maybe. A couple of guys came by yesterday, they searched the house." I shrugged.

"Two guys searched the house?" He turned his attention back to me. "Where were you?"

"Hiding. I'm a good hider." I nodded.

Fortunately Eric had turned his attention back to the door. "That's something," he murmured. Pulling something from his utility belt, he shoved it into the lock, and pushed the door open. "This place is as good as any to stay, now that we can get in," he announced, stepping through the doors.

"A good hider, Jessie? What are you five? You have got to get over this school girl crush!" I chastised myself, following him inside.

Dropping his bag on the floor, he asked, "Is there anything to eat?"

"I ate the last of what was left, yesterday," I answered. "A can of peas, and some freezer burned bread."

He gave me a confused look.

"No money." I shrugged. "Doesn't it bother you to stay in someone's house without permission?" I couldn't help but ask.

"You're staying here," he pointed out.

"That's because of Barbie. I'm not sure it's right," I admitted.

213

"Where is Goldie?" he asked, as if he'd just noticed that she wasn't there.

"She's kind of...," I hesitated, not wanting to say the words out loud, "missing."

He did that eyebrow thing, while looking me in the eye. It was unnerving.

"I was gonna call someone, but I don't know she's not missing on purpose," I explained.

"Would she do that?" Erik asked.

Not having an answer, I shrugged.

Silently, Eric stared at me, as if he was waiting for something.

I couldn't decide if he was agreeing with me, disagreeing with me, or waiting for me to say something more. Choosing the latter, I admitted, "I don't have my phone, or even know who to call, except maybe the embassy, and I came into the country on a fake passport. I was gonna check the bar she disappeared from, but it was crawling with cops last night, and I probably should have said something to one of them, but... I don't know." I paused. "I guess I expected her to come back by now," I finished guiltily.

He was still staring at me.

"I've got no money," I defended myself. "I'm living in a stolen house. All I have to prove I'm not a vagrant is a fake passport. I was afraid I'd get arrested. Then, who would find Barbie and Santa? What if they're missing together?!" I rambled.

Reaching into the black duffel bag at his feet, he handed me the purse that I had left in the car with his goons back in New York.

"My purse!" I exclaimed, digging inside it. "My phone! My

passport! I'm legal!" I held up the small blue book in triumph.

He looked around the room, as if he was seeing more than the furniture. "How long did you say Barbie has been missing?"

"Since yesterday, actually the night before." I followed him, trying to see what he saw.

"She isn't answering her phone?" He gave me an expectant look.

I held up Barbie's phone, explaining, "She didn't take her phone."

Taking the pink rectangle from me, he asked, "Is that like her?"

"It was under a couch cushion. She probably couldn't find it, so it's not unlike her." I took a deep breath, wondering how much I should tell him. "I spent all yesterday asking around. She met a guy at a bar down the beach. That's the last anyone's seen of her," the words erupted out of my mouth.

Quietly, he stared at Barbie's phone. When he finally spoke, all he said was, "You've been busy, since you stole my plane."

"Your plane," I whispered, my heart sinking. I was so happy to see him, I had forgotten about stealing his plane. He wasn't acting upset, but why else would he follow me halfway across the world? "Are you mad?" I asked, cringing.

"Yes," his tones held no emotion.

"I'm sorry," I offered. "I didn't plan any of this. Everything just happened so fast."

Giving me a disbelieving look, he asked, "You didn't plan to shut down Santa's Workshop's power systems in the middle of the night?"

"No, well, it kind of just happened," I stumbled over my words.

He stared at me, taking it all in.

"We had to stop the Santa monsters," I mumbled, painfully aware of just how crazy I sounded.

Tilting his head to the side, he asked, "How much sun have you had?"

"Forget it." I waved him off, knowing that if I tried to explain about the Santa monsters it would make me sound even crazier. "Will you help me find Barbie? I'm worried about her."

"It depends."

"I said I was sorry, and we handed over your keys as soon as we landed. I'm sure they had your plane back to you before you even needed it," I rationalized.

He stared at me, saying nothing.

Taking a deep breath, I found the nerve to ask, "What do you want?"

"I want to know whose shirt you're wearing," he said.

I looked down at Neik's shirt, bit my lip, and said truthfully, "I found it on the floor."

"You found it on the floor?" Erik repeated.

I nodded.

"Where are your clothes?" He looked around the room.

I gave him a hard look, then said, "You left them the middle of the terminal, when you kidnapped me."

"In Dallas? That was days ago." He gave me a confused look.

"Whose clothes have you been wearing since then?"

"I was wearing the elves castoffs, then Barbie's fat clothes, and well… I'm an Amazon. I don't fit." A solitary tear snuck out of the corner of my eye.

"I like Amazons," he said, wiping the tear from my cheek.

Twenty Four

I was back at the beachfront bar, getting nowhere with the bartender, while Eric sat in the back of the bar, all Rambo'd up. Half an hour ago, it had sounded like a good plan. I'd work the bar while he worked the crowd. Thirty minutes into our plan, all I'd learned was that my bartender's name was Bruno. I was pretty sure that wasn't his given name.

"Who comes to the beach like that?" Bruno stared across the room.

"Huh?" He'd caught me off guard.

"Look at that guy." He gestured to Eric. "Who's he trying to be?"

My gaze followed his hand across the room. I couldn't help but notice that we weren't the only ones looking. My bartender may not have been impressed with Eric, but there were plenty of others who were.

"Sure, he looks tough. Even you'd look tough dressed like that," he ranted.

"I would?" I smiled.

"Anyone would," he insisted. "He's probably an accountant or somebody's secretary. I'll bet he's never even held a real gun."

I turned my full attention back to Bruno, insisting, "He has."

"No way. He's just trying to look tough." Bruno flicked jealous eyes toward Eric.

"Is your girlfriend checking him out or something?" I couldn't help but ask.

"What?" He looked at me.

"She is!" I nodded my head in triumph.

We both watched as a waiter brought Eric his drink. After they exchanged words, Eric motioned to an empty chair. The waiter gave the room a quick once over before sitting. Did he know where Barbie was? I fidgeted nervously, fighting the impulse to join them.

"I don't… Forget it," Bruno mumbled, irritably tossing half a lime into the trash.

"Oh! That's your boyfriend!" I gasped in sudden comprehension. No wonder my best moves were getting me nowhere. He batted for the other team. It was time to switch tactics.

"He was, until Rambo showed up." Bruno slammed down a glass. "I work out. Eat right. I'm hot, aren't I?"

"Yeah, you're hot," I agreed.

"No, I'm not." He frowned down at himself. "I've got a gut! How am I supposed to compete with that guy with this gut?" Angrily he poured a drink that no one had ordered. "Look at this!" He pointed despondently toward his near perfect midsection.

Not seeing what he saw, and hating to see him torture himself, I said, "You have nothing to worry about."

"Do you see them?" He shrieked.

"That guy over there. He's not gay," I reassured him.

"You mean, he's been lying to me all these months?" He turned crazy eyes on me.

"Not him! The other guy, Rambo," I clarified.

Staring daggers toward Eric, he asked, "How do you know?"

"I know. Okay," I insisted.

"A good looking guy, dresses well. He could be gay." Frowning at the glass he was washing, he admitted, "I can't compete with that."

"He's not gay," I insisted. "Trust me. I know. He's a friend of mine."

"Really?" He peered hopefully across the room.

"Yes! He's helping me to find my cousin. The one that disappeared the other night," I explained. "I'm sure he's just asking your friend about her."

"Truth?" His eyes bored into mine, daring me to lie.

I smiled. "Truth."

With a shrug, he said, "We don't know where your cousin is. But, the guy she left with comes in here all the time, with his friend."

"Do you know his friend?" I asked, suddenly hopeful.

Shaking his head, he said, "Comes in a few times a week, picks up a new girl, pays his bill with cash. He never stays long. You met him."

"I did?" I looked around the room for a familiar face.

"He bought you a couple of drinks." He gave me an expectant look. "You left with him," he prompted.

"Why didn't you say something?!" I chastised.

"You never asked about his friends." He shrugged. "They're coming this way. Act like we weren't talking about them."

A hand grasped my arm, tight. "Trouble." Eric's voice was calm, but his grip said *'we need to talk'*.

"I just learned something interesting," I offered.

"So did I," he said through clenched teeth, practically dragging me off of the bar stool.

I froze, realizing what he must have learned. In a silent panic, I tried to think of what to say. Coming up with nothing. I took a deep breath and opened my mouth, just to hear the waiter say, "That's him, coming in."

Eric let go of my arm, moving away from me. I closed my eyes. I couldn't look. I couldn't not look. Holding my breath. I opening my eyes just far enough to see him knock someone through the door with one punch.

"You were right," the bartender agreed. "He doesn't just look tough."

My mouth was open in shock. I wanted to race outside, but I was rooted to the spot. Was this really happening? Was Eric beating up my one night stand? Taking a deep breath, I looked around at a suddenly empty bar. Pushing my way through the crowd, I could see Eric standing over a still form. The crash of ocean waves interspersed

221

with sirens wailing through the air added to the surrealism of the moment. The crowd began to dissipate, enticing me to move forward for a better look.

"Is he dead?" Someone asked, echoing my thoughts.

Taking a good look at the man lying on the sand, I asked, "Who is that?"

"You tell me," Eric growled.

"I've never seen him before." I shrugged.

"That's Amador, the guy your friend left with," Bruno offered from behind me.

"That's the guy Barbie left with?" Eric asked the waiter.

"Who did you think it was," the waiter asked.

Eric looked at me.

"Ohhhh!" The waiter nodded. "That guy hasn't been in since they hooked up the other night."

I could feel my face turn crimson. Eric knew about my one night stand, and he just beat up the wrong guy over it.

The scarcely conscious man moaned as if to confirm his identity, bringing everyone's attention back to him. Wincing he asked, "What was that about, Man?"

Eric grabbed him by the shirt, pulling him off of the ground. "What did you do with Barbie?"

"Barbie? Doesn't ring a bell," Amador smirked.

Suddenly filled with rage of my own, I lunged forward yelling, "Where is my cousin!"

Mid-leap, strong arms grabbed me from behind, lifting me off of my feet. "Let me handle this," Eric said, setting me down behind him.

"Tiny blonde, big boobs, left with you the other night. No one's heard from her since," Eric said.

"I have many women. I don't remember this Barbie." Amador smiled.

Without saying a word, Eric hit Amador, with his fist, in the face. A tooth fell out of Amador's mouth just before he sank into the sand.

I stared at the tooth. "Wh... What did you do that for?"

"He was lying," Eric replied, calmly.

"Now, we'll never find out about Barbie!" I screeched. "What did you do to my cousin you sorry piece of beach shit!" I yelled, throwing myself at the unconscious man.

Arms grabbed me around the waist, pulling me off of Amador. "Take her," Eric's voice commanded, just before I was unceremoniously dropped in the sand.

Held back by Bruno and his boyfriend, I watched Eric carelessly throw the semi-conscious man over his shoulder and head down the beach. Realizing that the entertainment was over, the patrons went back to their drinks.

"He's so hot, I'm on fire!" The waiter murmured, staring off after Eric.

"That's what you want? A Neanderthal?" Bruno turned, storming back into the bar.

"Wait! I'm not interested in hot. You're all I need," the waiter cried after Bruno.

I stood on the beach alone, staring after Eric, not sure what to say or do. It wasn't as if I'd cheated. We weren't together. If you thought about it, it was more like I'd cheated on Mike than Eric. Just days ago we'd at least been an item, engaged. But, I hadn't cheated on him either. We'd broken up, too. I took a deep breath, realizing that in less than a week I'd been engaged to Mike, broken up with Mike, kissed and kind of made up with Eric, and slept with some guy I didn't even know.

"I'm a slut!" I kicked the sand.

Eric didn't make a sound as he trudged off across the beach with the unconscious man over his shoulder. I stood alone, contemplating my options until they disappeared from sight. Not knowing what else to do, I followed.

Twenty Five

I walked through the door to our borrowed villa just in time to see Eric unceremoniously tossing Amador on the floor.

"You could have put him on the couch!" I admonished.

As if I hadn't spoken, Eric rolled the unconscious man over with his foot. I wanted to believe his silence was due to the hike up the beach, carrying a two hundred pound man. It would have been easier to convince myself he was winded if he had been breathing heavy. He was breathing normally. He wasn't winded. He was angry.

I leaned down to check Amador's pulse. He had one, but he wasn't looking good. His face was puffy and red from hanging over Eric's back. He had a huge bluish purple knot where Eric had hit him, and one eye looked like it had turned inside out.

"He's going to hurt when he wakes up," I commented.

"What do you care?" Eric demanded.

"I don't. I was just saying," I answered, not that he stuck around to listen.

Not sure what to do now, I looked down at the unconscious man. He let out a low moan, causing me to jump. I looked around, hoping Eric hadn't taken that moment to come back into the room. He had, of course.

He didn't say anything, crack a smile, or even make eye contact. He just flipped the man over, squatted, and proceeded to tie his arms and legs with strips of blue material that he was angrily tearing from a bedsheet. Once he finished, he stood up, picked the man up, and tossed him in an empty closet by the front door.

"You're just going to leave him in there?" I accused.

"Yes," he answered, shoving a chair under the door handle.

"He's beat up, tied up, and unconscious," I pointed out. "Do you really think that's necessary?"

"Yes," he insisted.

Irritably, I asked, "What now?"

"You do whatever you want. I'm going to bed," he said, heading for the stairs.

"But," I protested.

Turning from the stairs, he placed cold dark eyes on me, and asked, "But?"

"What about him?" I pointed to the unconscious man. "And, Barbie?"

"Don't open that door," he barked, ignoring my questions.

Glaring at him, I demanded, "What's your problem?"

"I don't have a problem," he denied.

Stubbornly, I asked, "If you *don't have a problem*, then why are you being so mean to him?"

"Am I being mean?" His took a step toward me.

"Yes." I folded my arms across my chest.

"And, why do you care? Are you looking to make this guy your next one night stand? Perhaps you'd like something more." He stared down at me. "A three nighter?"

I jumped at the ferocity in his voice. "What?"

Our eyes locked in heavy silence.

"You're such an ass," I whispered.

"At least I didn't hop into bed with the first guy I met on the island," he said pointedly.

"That's because the first guy you met has a boyfriend," I said snarkily. "I don't."

He opened his mouth as if to speak, took a deep breath, and said, "No. I guess you don't."

A strange look crossed his face as he said, "I'll talk to him in the morning. Right now, I need some sleep."

He was half the way up the stairs when I asked, "Is this your first kidnapping?"

He paused, one foot in the air.

"I mean, it's my first kidnapping. I'm not sure if I'm doing it right," I admitted.

He sighed, continuing up the stairs.

Not sure what else to do, I curled up on the coach to wait for what? Amador to wake up? Eric to come back downstairs and apologize? I was afraid neither of those things would happen.

"I've really screwed things up this time," I said to the empty room.

Twenty Six

The morning sun was just beginning to peak through the window when a door opened, startling me awake. Scenarios of bad guys coming to do bad things flashed through my mind. Forcing my heart rate down from stroke to mild panic, I searched the dim room with my eyes for an intruder. All I found was Amador, eyes open, still bound, gagged, and laying on the floor in front of me. How had he gotten out of the closet? Cautiously, I sat up, looking around for Eric. We were alone.

A door closed somewhere behind me, followed by heavy footsteps. My eyes rested on those of our trussed up prisoner. Cringing, I realized that I now had Amador's undivided attention. I wasn't ready for this. I still hadn't figured out what to do about him lying in the middle of the floor. I mean, I couldn't move him. He was too heavy. But, I couldn't leave him there. He looked pathetic lying on the floor, bound by the limbs like a Christmas turkey, with his face black and blue, and one eye mostly swollen shut. He looked worse than he had the night before, and he hadn't looked good then.

As if in response to my thoughts, his eyes softened, silently pleading with me. I turned away, hoping that ignoring him would remove the guilt from my soul. Unwilling to be ignored, he began making loud grunting noises. Biting my lip, I reminded myself that he may have done something terrible to Barbie. He may have killed her. I closed my eyes so that I wouldn't feel guilty about not helping him.

I opened my eyes to see Eric glaring at Amador. Jerking Amador into an upright position, he growled, "I didn't say you could speak."

"Where did you come from?" I asked Eric, hoping to distract him from the man on the floor.

Eric turned to me, and said, "I'm sorry, did I interrupt?"

"What is that supposed to mean?" I demanded, hands on my hips.

"You tell me," Eric answered grumpily.

Tilting his head defiantly, Amador began making loud garbled noises.

Eric's foot swung through the air, knocking Amador back over. "You'll speak when I tell you to, and only then."

My mouth fell open in surprise.

Amador groaned quietly, as blood trickled down his cheek.

Eric stood in front of him, looked down, and said, "I'm taking off the gag. You will not make a noise, except to answer my questions. If you give me the right answers, I might not kill you.

Understood?"

Amador nodded silently.

Sinking further into the couch, I slowly closed my mouth. I wasn't sure what to think of this side of Eric. He was brutal, unpredictable, someone I didn't want to meet in a dark alley, or on the wrong side of the street in broad daylight. It was kind of a turn on. Too bad he hated me.

"Who are you working for?" Eric demanded of Amador.

Amador very purposefully spat at Eric.

Calmly, Eric reached over, grabbed Amador's right ear, and gave it a twist, hard enough to turn his head, bringing tears of pain to his eyes.

"I asked you a question," Eric's voice was deadly quiet.

"I work only for me," Amador growled.

"What did you do to Barbie?" Eric scowled at Amador.

"Nothing. I never met her," Amador insisted. "The barmen are lying!"

"You're kidding me!" I mumbled to myself.

"What?" Eric asked. He dipped his head, allowing his dark eyes to meet mine and a lock of hair to dip over his right eye.

Taking a quick breath, I fought the urge to brush the stray hair away from Eric's face. Crap! He saw me staring at him. Desperately trying not to think about the parts of Eric that weren't on display, and some that were, I focused my thoughts on Barbie, and what the scumbag in front of me did to her. Jumping up from the couch, my feet got tangled up in our prisoner, throwing me off balance. Somehow I managed to keep myself upright.

Ignoring my extreme act of clumsiness, I growled at Amador, "You're not leaving here until you tell us what you did to my cousin."

Raising an eyebrow, Eric's eyes mocked my feeble attempt to play the tough guy. His gaze had the unwelcome effect of sending a shiver rushing through me as his eyes dipped below my face.

Why was he checking out my boobs? Didn't he hate me for having low morals or something like that? I watched as he moved towards me, causing his t-shirt to tighten up in all the right spots. I sucked in my breath. Why did he have to be so sexy hot, while I'm such a spaz?

Was that a smile? It was! God he had a great smile. Was I drooling? I lowered my head to, hopefully unobtrusively, wipe the drool from my mouth. Dipping my head, my eyes widened, not wanting to believe what I was seeing. Cursing Barbie's huge boobs for stretching out the tank top that I was wearing, I turned away and shoved my left boob back where it belonged. Could things get any more embarrassing?

"I think I can find out what we need to know without you exposing yourself," Eric murmured.

Heat rushed to my face. Having nothing enlightening to say, I bit my lip to keep from shrieking my embarrassment. Finally gaining my composure, I stood up, announcing, "I'm going to take a shower."

"Don't forget to shut the door. I think he's seen enough skin for one day," Eric growled.

Twenty Seven

Thirty minutes later, I looked and felt like a new person. Unfortunately, there were two men in the other room with fresh memories of more of me than I was comfortable sharing. After weighing my few options, I decided to pretend that it had never happened. Determined not to flash anyone again, I pulled one of the homeowner's t-shirts on over a sports bra and shorts.

With my head held high and my shoulders pushed back, I headed downstairs to an unexpectedly empty living room. Cautiously, I opened the little closet where Eric had stowed our guest the night before. It was empty. Confused, I listened for voices or movement to indicate where Eric had taken our guest. Following the sound of running water to the master bedroom, I stood outside the door, imagining all sorts of horrible things that Eric might be doing to that poor guy to get information.

"That poor guy?" I said to the empty room. "That poor guy did something to Barbie, so don't feel sorry for him."

"But, what if he didn't?" I played devil's advocate. "What if he was just an innocent one night stand?"

"Shit! We just kidnapped an innocent man!" I turned to the girl in the mirror. "We're going to jail! Worse, we're going to Hell!"

Panic surged through my veins, draining my brain of all of rational thought. A noise brought my attention back to the bathroom. I had to do something, before it was too late! Grabbing the door handle, I yanked open the unlocked door.

A surprised, and freshly out of the shower, Eric stood facing me. Not even attempting to cover himself, he ran a hand through his dripping hair, pushing it away from his eyes. We stood facing each other, without either of us speaking, for what seemed like an eternity, but was probably only seconds. Shaking his head, he brushed past me to the bed, grabbing a towel on the way.

"I um... uh...," I stuttered. The sight of his perfect body sent heat rushing through my veins. My mind was blank. Slowly coming back to the moment, I became uncomfortably aware of how naked he was, and the fact that I was staring. "I mean, I didn't... um," I floundered.

"Of course you didn't," he offered, pulling on a fresh pair of black cargo pants.

"No underwear? I mean, I uh...," I floundered as he took a step toward me.

"I don't get you." His low voice vibrated huskily.

I looked up into his coffee colored eyes. When had he moved

so close? His scent enveloped me, causing a shiver to race into my lady parts. "You don't?" I squeaked.

"I don't think you want me to." He brushed a hair from my face, leaving a trail of fire across my forehead.

"I don't?" I whispered, caught in the spell of the moment.

"No," he murmured.

My pulse raced as he dipped his head. Was he going to kiss me? He was! He was going to kiss me! A low moan slipped through my lips in anticipation.

As his lips brushed mine, a loud noise echoed throughout the house. Pulling a black t-shirt over his head, Eric vaulted for the door.

"Stay here," he barked, disappearing down the hall.

Shaking off the fog of my near encounter with Eric, I stared into the empty room. Another loud noise echoed through the house. "Barbie!" I shrieked, heading toward the door.

Before I reached the doorway, a black clad blur raced in, slamming the door behind him. Surprise coated my features as I attempted to think of something intelligent to say. Instead, I stared at him in open mouthed surprise. Fortunately, Eric was too busy shoving a chair under the door to notice my lack of brain activity.

I was just about to ask who he was blockading us from when he grabbed a gun from the bedside table, his duffle bag from the bed, flung the window open, shoved me towards the open window, and roared, "Go!"

Without thinking, I jumped through the window, scrabbling to hang onto the roof tiles. A hand grabbed mine, just as my body slid over the side of the roof. Trying not to look down, I used my free hand to grasp the broken edge of a roof tile.

"Hold on," Eric growled, easing himself to the roof's edge. With catlike grace, Eric slid down the tiles next to me.

Nervously, I glanced down.

"Hold on?!" I yelled. What did he think I was going to do? Let go?

The broken tile was cutting into my hand. My fingers slipped, dropping me another inch closer to falling. When I glanced back at Eric, he was sliding over the edge of the roof. I looked down, hoping he had landed safely. That was a mistake! It was still a long way down!

"SHIT!" My fingers were slipping. What was that safety prayer again? "Lord grant me..." No, that was the serenity prayer. This was no time for serenity!

"I can't... hold on!" Panic made my voice unnaturally high.

"Let go!" Eric yelled, just as I lost my grip.

Strong arms caught me mid-fall, tilting me upright to a standing position. Warm breath caressed my ear. "Stay low, and head to the dunes. I'm right behind you."

I gave Eric a dazed look. I wasn't dead? I looked down at my limbs, other than a few scratches, I was unhurt. Hearing a gunshot, I looked up. A dark form was in the window that we had leaped from pointing the wrong end of a pistol at us, prompting me to run.

Raising his gun, Eric fired at the shape, yelling, "Go! I'll catch up."

My brain was still trying to figure out why someone was shooting at me. My feet didn't care. I was halfway to the dunes before the next shot rang out. I started to look back, to make sure Eric was with me, when a bullet pierced the sand at my feet. Two more drilled the sand around me, a little too close for comfort. Seeing a dune ahead of me, I dove over it.

Gunshots rang out behind me as I scrambled down the beach, staying close to the dunes for shelter. I wanted to stop, but adrenaline and the trail of bullets behind me kept me from slowing. Reaching a path through the dunes, I left the beach, desperately searching for cover. Hoping it was unlocked, I sprinted towards the nearest house backing up to the beach. Finding the back door locked, I veered around the side of the house. My heart was pounding, my side was hurting, and my knees were covered with sand filled scrapes.

"I really need to get in shape!" I gasped to the endless blue sky.

Leaning against a wall to catch my breath, I listened for sounds of pursuit, hoping that whomever our assailants were, they had lost interest. Just as I started to relax, footsteps echoed heavily behind me.

"Crap!" I gasped, heading toward the street.

I was so focused on the sounds of footsteps overtaking me, I didn't see the school bus yellow jeep barreling down the road toward me. Big arms enveloped me, heaving me to the side of the road, just as four tires and a loud horn screeched their dismay at the interruption of their task. Black fabric protected my face as I rolled across the street in a jumble of arms and legs, some belonging to me, the rest belonging to a faceless mass that smelled of comfort.

Wincing, I tried to hold back a moan of pain.

"You alright?" A deep voice rumbled.

"I think so," I replied.

"Good." Eric nodded, releasing me from his hold.

"What about you?" I asked. "Is that blood?"

"Nope," he answered, not even looking at his scraped arm.

"Yes, it is. You're hurt." I pointed at the spot where his arm had been two seconds ago. "Where did he go?" I asked the empty street. Turning, I saw him shoving his way into the driver's side of the Jeep that had almost hit us.

"Trouble! Get in!" He commanded, as a new volley of slugs drilled into the other side of the Jeep.

Diving headfirst into the backseat, I flattened myself to the floor, hoping that one of the bullets didn't find me. Instead of bullets, I found myself face to face with a snarling tea cup Chihuahua. Tires squealed, and the Jeep made a one-eighty knocking the small dog into a pile of clothes.

As we sped away from the volley of bullets, an unnaturally high pitched voice accused, "You're upsetting Ajax!"

"Ajax?" Eric asked.

"My dog!" The voice explained.

"Dog?" Eric repeated, glancing around the Jeep.

Hands reached in front of me, lifting up the Chihuahua just as it lunged for my nose. Laying my head on a pile of what I hoped were clean clothes, I breathed a sigh of relief at the near miss.

"Ajax!" The voice insisted, holding the startled Chihuahua inches from Eric's face.

With a dismissive glance, Eric said, "That's not a dog."

"Yes, he is!"

Where had I heard that voice before? I cautiously pulled myself onto the seat, taking a look at the man sitting next to Eric.

"I know you!" I pointed. "You're the waiter!"

"I was a waiter," he sniveled, hiding his face in Ajax's fur.

"Was?" Hadn't we just met him yesterday? I couldn't help but wonder what had happened since yesterday.

Nodding, he explained, "Bruno fired me, and kicked us out."

"Why?" I wondered aloud.

"Because of him!" He pointed an accusing finger at Eric.

"Me?" Eric asked.

"You! You ruined my life!" He accused.

"Now is probably a bad time to bring this up, but you do have insurance, I hope," I said.

"What?" Crazed eyes turned toward me, daring me to say anything else.

Shrugging apologetically, I fingered a bullet hole in the side of the driver's seat. Pointing his finger rapidly back and forth between me and Eric, he began to speak in an agitated tone in a language that I couldn't follow. I watched, mesmerized, as his hands danced along with the words tumbling out of his lips. Eric ignored him.

Twenty Eight

"Holes! Holes!" Our passenger wiggled his fingers through a bullet hole in the side of the once pristine Jeep.

"How long is he going to do this?" Eric grumbled.

"He's having a rough day," I defended.

"He needs to get over it," Eric stated. "You," he said, gesturing to our passenger.

"Waiter?" I suggested.

"I'm not a waiter. I'm not a boyfriend. I'm not a student. I'm nothing! Nothing but a '*you with the Swiss cheese Jeep*!'" Our reluctant companion wailed.

"What is your name?" Eric demanded.

"Huh?" The guy stared uncomprehendingly at Eric.

"Your name," Eric reiterated, not even trying to hide his impatience.

"Stelios. Stelios Stephanopoulos," he replied, absently fondling a hole in the dashboard.

"Stelios, enough," Eric stated.

"Enough? Enough! Look at this!" Stelios gestured to the holes lining the side of the Jeep. "This," he made an encompassing gesture to the Jeep and its contents, "is all I have. I'm jobless, homeless, friendless, and you say enough!"

Eric grumbled something unintelligible.

"You still have Ajax," I reminded him.

"Ajax!" Stelios cradled the small dog close to his chest. "We're all we have now."

"I'm sure you have family or friends, somewhere," I added.

Stelios sniffled, and said something that I couldn't distinguish, followed by, "Sadly, I can never return home."

"Why not?" I asked.

He loudly blew his nose on a shirt from the backseat, before throwing it back on the pile. "I've made a mess of things."

Pushing the pile of semi-clean clothes away from me, I offered, "It can't be that bad. I make a mess of things all the time, and my parents always let me come home."

"You spent thousands of Euros on law school, just to drop out before your exams, because you met a guy, moved halfway across the world to be with him, and became a waiter, crushing your father's dreams for you, and your mother's heart?" Stelios stared at me hopefully.

"Not exactly," I hesitated.

"You dropped out of law school to be a waiter?" Eric asked incredulously.

"Just like my abba!" Stelios wailed. "That was his dream! I

241

never wanted to go into civil service."

"You wanted to be a waiter?" I tried to understand.

"Who dreams of being a waiter?" Stelios waved the thought away. "I wish to be the next Konstantinos Maleas."

"Who?" I looked at Eric, wondering if anything Stelios said made sense to him.

"He was a painter," Eric offered.

"A painter!" Stelios exclaimed. "Was Shakespeare a mere writer? Was Michelangelo a mere clay worker? Is Waterford merely glass?"

"So, you want to be an artist?" I interjected.

"Yes," Stelios answered. "I came to Aruba to find my muse, and I found Bruno. But, now… now I've lost him!"

"Were you together a long time?" I laid a comforting hand on his shoulder.

Stelios nodded. "Six months."

Eric made a noise that sounded suspiciously like a snort.

Giving him a dirty look, not that he noticed, I said, "I'm sorry."

Wiping a tear, Stelios nodded. "Thank you."

"What will you do now? Go home?" I asked.

"Go home… to what? My family is poor. Greece is broke. I am a disgrace to all who know me, without the ability to take care of even my most basic needs." He reached into a bag by his feet, took out a dog treat and fed it to Ajax. "Here before you is all that I own!" He gestured to the bullet laden Jeep filled with a haphazard assortment of shoes and clothes.

"Um… things will get better?" I offered, unsure of what to say, and not wanting to upset him further.

"You really think so?" Stelios looked hopeful.

"They can't get much worse," I offered.

Stelios nodded his head slowly. "I've been driving in circles for hours, looking for a ray of hope. I should take this as a sign. A sign to move on."

"That's right! You don't need him. You'll get a better job, and a new apartment," I encouraged.

"Wait," Eric interjected. "You're giving him advice?"

I rolled my eyes, and said, "Yes."

"Have you ever had a relationship that lasted longer than two months?" Eric asked.

"Not recently." Did it have to be consecutive? I wondered silently.

"Have you gone more than six months without moving back in with your parents?" Eric asked, pointedly.

"Um…" Surely I had! I just couldn't think of when right now.

"Here's an easy one, when was the last time you had a job?" He pressed.

"I have a job!" I yelled, excited to be able to answer a question without sounding like a loser.

"You do?" He gave me a disbelieving look.

"Yes." I glared at him. "I'm Barbie's personal assistant."

"How convenient," he said, his voice dripping with sarcasm. "So tell me, how long were you employed before you lost your new boss?"

"It was, a few days… hours…" I frowned. "That is beside the point!"

Eric raised a condescending eyebrow at me.

Who was he to judge me? I raged inside, saying aloud, "What business is it of yours how I live my life?"

"It's not." He tightened his hands on the wheel.

"Thank you!" I angrily exclaimed.

"But, you may want to consider getting your own life in order before you give Stelios, or anyone else, advice," Eric advised.

"I didn't mean to start a lover's quarrel," Stelios said uncomfortably.

"You didn't," I said. "We're not… anything."

"You're not?" Stelios asked, surprise coloring his words.

"We're not?" Eric tightened his grip on the wheel again, speeding up dangerously.

"No," I said, defiantly.

"So, that's how you want it?" Eric took a turn so hard that I fell backwards and Stelios was forced to grab ahold of his seat to keep from falling out.

"You can let me out here," Stelios pleaded, in a high pitched voice.

"Yes," I answered Eric, as the Jeep zoomed around slower moving traffic.

"Keep the Jeep as long as you need it," Stelios squeaked.

"Fine." Eric stopped the Jeep suddenly. "If that's how you want it. Let's go rescue your boss, so that I can get back to work."

"Fine!" I yelled, joining Stelios and Ajax on the sidewalk.

"Where do we start?"

"In there." Eric gestured to a large, rundown building down the street. "Ladies first," he said, pointing the way.

Twenty Nine

Leaning over my shoulder, Stelios whispered, "What would your cousin be doing in there?"

My heart sank, it definitely wasn't the kind of place that Barbie would willingly frequent. One of her ex-husbands, sure, but not Barbie. She preferred higher class establishments.

I turned skeptically toward Eric, "Are you sure she's in there?"

"That's what our friend said," he affirmed.

"Our friend?" I asked, unwilling to believe that Barbie was anywhere near us.

"Amador," Eric answered. "After you went to bed he told me everything."

"When were you going to share?" I glared at him.

"After I verified his information. People will tell you many things to stop the pain," he answered.

Stelios looked at Eric, and said, "You are a scary guy."

Ignoring him, Eric gestured to the abandoned looking building.

Trying to look unruffled, I studied the area. No overly sure of himself, egomaniac was going to say I wasn't prepared. Not this time. Squinting as if it would help me see through the dirty brick walls, I wondered what kind of mess Barbie had gotten herself into, and if it could be my fault. Giving myself a mental slap, I forced myself to focus.

Trash and city dirt lined the block, adding to the abandoned look of the building. The doors and windows had long ago been boarded up in a half-hearted attempt to keep people out. The dark clouds forming overhead and lack of people out front only added to the derelict feel of the area. If Barbie was in there, it wasn't by choice.

Taking a deep breath, I muttered, "None of that matters." Pushing back my shoulders, I steeled my nerve, and resolutely stepped off of the curb. Before my feet scraped the pavement, an arm wrapped around my waist, leaving me dangling in the air like an errant child. "What now?" I turned my head toward Eric.

Eric's dark eyes bored into mine, making me very aware of just how close we were. His eyes flickered to the right. Curiosity overcoming my baser senses, my gaze followed. He seemed to be indicating the dirt crusted windows watching over the street. Did he actually see anything, or was he just messing with me?

Frustration surged through me. "What?" I snapped. "I don't see anything."

"Nothing is there," Stelios agreed, peering intently across the street.

Eric released me. Turning my head, I strained my eyes, trying to see what he saw. All I saw were walls and windows, coated in decade's worth of soot and grime.

Taking a step back, I looked at Eric, and asked, "You wanna go first?"

He sighed, making it clear that I was once again missing something. "Stelios, wait here," he ordered.

Dejectedly closing the door and sliding back into the jeep, Stelios clutched Ajax to his chest.

Without looking at Stelios, Eric said, "Honk if you see anyone coming our way."

Stelios nodded.

Stepping into the street, Eric called, "Come on, Trouble."

Apprehensively, I followed, wishing that I could take back the things that I'd said earlier. Bumping into a suddenly still Eric on the other side of the street, I whispered, "I'm sorry."

Wordlessly, he put a finger to his lips.

"I shouldn't have said..." I attempted to apologize.

A large finger touched my lips, silencing me.

"I guess he doesn't want to hear it," I muttered to myself. Following the dark clad figure around the block, I wondered why it was so important to me. It wasn't like we were dating, or even likely to pick up where we'd left off. Since we'd met, our lives had bumped elbows, never intertwining. At best, we would continue to run into each other at the most inopportune times. At worst, we wouldn't.

In the shadow of the building, Eric stopped in front of a broken window. Reaching out, he quickly ripped away the board that partially covered the window out of the way. I tried not to stare as he pulled off his shirt, wrapped it around his fist, and began knocking the remaining glass shards out of the frame. After clearing off the broken shards, he shook out his shirt, sliding it back over his head.

I turned away, with the guise of checking the alley. What I was really doing was catching my breath. "Why does he have to be so frickin' sexy at everything?" I asked the dumpster.

Rain drops caught my attention. Peering up at the sky, all I could see were heavy dark clouds. The storm that had been threatening all day was bearing down on us. A strong wind swept through the alley, almost taking me with it. The darkening skies painting ominous shadows on the wall.

"As if this place weren't creepy enough," I said to myself. Unsure of what to do next, I turned toward the broken window. Eric was gone! "You have GOT to be kidding me!" I stepped up to the window, peering into the silent darkness. There was no one there.

"He left me out here, without a word," I fumed. I stood in the ally, wondering if I should keep watch, or go in after him. "Calm down, it makes sense for someone to keep watch." I nodded to myself. "But, Stelios is keeping watch," I reminded myself. I let out a frustrated sigh, telling the wind, "He could have said something. What if bad guys come around the building?" I crouched to the left, hefting the gun Eric had handed me minutes ago. A shiver of fear ran up my neck as I listened to hurried footsteps behind me. I closed my eyes, afraid to look. With a deep breath, I turned. There was no one.

"It was just the wind," I told myself.

A hand grasped my shoulder. Startled, I dropped the gun. Without thinking, I spun around, raising my knee and getting my hand ready to strike.

"Who are you talking to?" Stelios stood behind me, Ajax cradled in his arms.

"No one," I said, all too aware that I had almost attacked a man who was already having the worst day of his life.

Stelios looked at my odd pose, and then back to me, confusion clouding his face.

Straightening out of my attack position, I shrugged, then said, "I do that, talk to myself."

"You talk to yourself?" Stelios gave me a cautious look.

"Not in a bad way," I insisted. "I'm not crazy or anything. There just isn't always someone else around, so I just talk to whatever...," I trailed off. Biting my lip, I asked, "Does that make me crazy?"

"No." Stelios shook his head. "It makes you human, in a lonely world. We are the same!" Stelios reached out, grasping me tightly in a one armed hug.

Suddenly, water poured from the heavens in heavy sheets, followed by thunder and lightning loud enough to shake the ground beneath our feet. Startled, the little dog jumped from Stelios's arms through the broken window, disappearing in the darkness of the old building.

"Ajax!" Stelios wailed, letting go of my shoulders just as suddenly as he had taken hold.

Without another word, Stelios followed the little dog through the window. Standing alone in an eerie alley, in the wrong part of town, and drenched with rain; I had to wonder where my life had gone wrong. Lightning struck again, close enough for me to smell the burnt earth.

"That's it!" I muttered. Picking up the gun, I followed Stelios through the window.

Once inside, I could just make out Stelios crouched in a corner and peering into the dark, whispering, "Ajax!"

I decided to go the other direction.

Once my eyes adjusted to the low light, I could see that the building wasn't as empty as it appeared. It was full of obsolete machinery, long forgotten equipment, and boxes stacked in no discernable order. Something skittered in the dark, causing me to shudder. Something more than dust and rusty metal must be making this long forgotten place home.

After several minutes of gingerly watching my step, and wishing that I was wearing my red cowboy boots, I heard a sound. Pausing, I slowly lowered my foot to the floor. It seemed to be coming from somewhere above me. Craning my head, I searched the rafters. Sure enough, there were steps leading to what must have been an office in another life. I could see slivers of light through the broken window blinds.

"That must be where they're holding Barbie," I reasoned. Trying to walk silently, I headed for the stairs. I had almost reached the staircase, after slowly inching my way around the poorly stacked boxes that seemed to be everywhere, when I heard a familiar sound.

"Ajax!" The words echoed through the deathly quiet, followed by a litany of Greek expletives.

A door opened above me.

"Stelios!" I whispered fearfully, as I searched the darkness for my new friend.

I was still searching for Stelios when a dark mass of bodies raced out of the small office, and down the stairs. I was staring right at them when a flashlight clicked on in front of me, bathing the area in golden beams, and effectively blinding me.

Clumsily, I edged into the darkness, desperate to avoid the gilded torches. Backing as far as I could go, I tried moving to the side, but something had me by the shirt. Panic surged through my veins before I realized that I had been captured by an iron sentinel. Frantically, working to free my shirt, I shoved the strange machine holding the fabric in its bolts. It was no good. I was stuck. I took a deep breath, willing the men to move to the other side of the building. Uninterested in my well-being, the light slowly edged closer to my hiding place.

Knowing that I couldn't help Barbie if I was caught, I freed myself by slipping out of the borrowed t-shirt. Quickly ducking behind some nearby boxes, I held my breath in fear of being caught. The light raced across the spot where I had been standing moments before, pausing on the oversized shirt that dangled from the sentinel's grasp. Beams of light danced around the shirt as I slunk deeper into the darkness.

"Another shirt!" A voice rang out.

"We'll put it with the others. Kids!" Another voice muttered.

Footsteps turned away from me, taking the light back toward the stairs. I sank against a pile of boxes, silently congratulating myself on not getting caught. Staring up at the door, illuminated by a single yellow light, I wondered how I would get up there to rescue Barbie.

"She's got to be up there," I whispered into the darkness.

Something skittered across my foot. "Mmph!" I bit my lip to keep from crying out.

"Who's there?" Someone called out as light rays raced around the dark building.

Cringing, I held my breath, afraid to breathe. It was still on my foot! Closing my eyes, I focused on not moving, afraid of being rat bit, and then shot by Barbie's kidnappers.

Something bumped my leg, startling me. I looked down, just in time to see Stelios' dark form snatch the rodent from my foot.

Standing next to me, he said, "You found him!"

A whimper escaped my lips, heralding the light rays back in our direction. Paralyzed with fear, I stood frozen. A large hand firmly covered my mouth, preventing more sound from escaping, then jerked me further into the darkness.

"Trouble, what are you doing?" Eric whispered in my ear, as he hauled me and Stelios deeper into the darkness and away from the approaching footsteps.

"You're safe now." Stelios crowed, cradling the little dog.

With a disapproving glare, Eric growled at Stelios, "I told you and that to wait in the car."

"We did, but…" Stelios cradled Ajax in his arms. "It started to rain, and I don't have the top to the Jeep. I was in such a hurry, I left it with him." Stelios frowned. "Now, what will I do when it rains? Do you know how often it rains here?!"

Beams of light moved closer to our hiding spot. I looked for a way out. We were trapped between rusting equipment, boxes, and a wall. Stelios's wide eyes met mine as the danger closed in on us.

"You." Eric pointed at Stelios. "Go to the other side of the building, making as much noise as you can. If they catch you, tell them you were looking for that." He pointed to the quivering Chihuahua.

Before Stelios could protest, strong arms pushed him away from our hiding place. Eric and I stood rooted in the safety of the darkness, leaving Stelios to stumble around making enough noise for three people, grumbling in a mixture of Greek and English, and taking the golden beams with him.

With the immediate danger averted, I let out the breath that I'd been holding, relaxing into the familiar warmth that seemed closer than was necessary.

"We haven't broken into a building together since the night we met. It's nice." Eric's sultry voice whispered into my ear as a thumb lightly traced up my side, edging toward my sports bra.

"This is not the time to get handsy," I admonished.

"It's never the time," he grumbled. "I miss those days when we first met."

"You mean, when I was being stalked by a homicidal mobster?" My voice did nothing to hide the surprise in my voice.

"We always had plenty of time to fool around," he reasoned.

"You are a sick person," I told him.

"You're the one who's basically topless." He fingered the edge of my sports bra. "Is that for me? It's not my birthday, but I still appreciate it."

"Let's just find Barbie, and get out of here," I mumbled, trying to ignore the heat surging from his touch.

"Don't be in such a hurry," Eric said, brushing my hair back.

"Barbie…" I started.

"Can take care of herself for a few more minutes. Now, what was it that you were sorry about?" His lips brushed mine, taking all rational thought with them.

"Ummmm…" I murmured. "We need to find Barbie."

"After you," he said, panderingly patting my rear.

I could just see Stelios near the door, cradling Ajax, and talking to Barbie's captors. After a tense moment, he stepped through the doorway. I breathed a sigh of relief as Stelios made his way out of the building. A hand grabbed me. It was Eric motioning for me to follow him up the steps. Sneaking up the stairs brought my focus back to the plan. Well, my plan. As usual, Eric hadn't bothered to share his plan.

I took a deep breath. "It's simple. Surprise anyone who was left behind, get Barbie, and don't get shot."

"Just open the door," Eric grumbled impatiently.

Thirty

At my touch, the door swung open, revealing a round kitchen table, cluttered with cards and clothes, surrounded by six mismatched chairs. Perched on one of the chairs was a half-dressed Barbie. A midget dressed in just his boxers sat next to her. The other chairs were empty.

Eric raised an eyebrow, as if to ask if he was interrupting something.

"Damn it! Your timing sucks. I was winning," Barbie groaned, tossing her cards on the table.

My mouth dropped open. I hadn't expected to find Barbie playing strip poker with a midget. Not sure what I had expected to find her doing, I shrugged. I had to admit that it wasn't the strangest situation I'd ever found her in. To be honest, I would have been more surprised to see her playing the role of model prisoner.

Footsteps sounded on the stairs, reminding me that this wasn't poker night. When the door opened, letting in the rest of Snow White's grumbling roommates, Eric and I motioned them to a corner with our guns, taking the remainder of Barbie's minuscule captors by surprise.

"Get your clothes on," Eric barked at Barbie, once he had her half-dressed captors huddled in a corner.

"That's not the reaction I normally get. Are you sure he's straight?" Barbie goaded.

"Pretty sure." I slid back into the overly large t-shirt that I had just liberated from one of the old men. "So, um don't take this wrong but, were you kidnapped by midgets?" I asked Barbie.

"No, these guys are just my guards," she explained.

Buzz ... Buzz ...

"What is that?" I asked, looking around for the source of the noise.

"Pizza Bob's," one of our prisoners answered.

"Pizza?" My eyes lit up.

"No," Eric growled.

"But, I'm hungry," I pleaded.

"I'll feed you later," he promised.

"It's already paid for," the tall one said, matter of factly.

Eric narrowed his eyes, in a way that immediately silenced the old men.

"It is," Barbie agreed.

I gave Eric a pleading look.

"No," he barked.

"Why not?" Barbie asked, heading for the door.

"This is a rescue," he stated.

Barbie glanced around at her half-dressed guards, and said, "Please, I could have escaped anytime I wanted."

"Hey! No need to be insulting," the shortest guy grouched.

"You don't even have real guns." She pointed to the weapons, piled on top of the table.

"Just because it's tiny, doesn't mean it's not real." One the men lunged for the pile, grabbing a gun.

"Click." The sound of the safety being released echoed ominously through the small space.

I looked up to see Eric standing by the door with his gun cocked, staring the little man in the eye. Slowly, the little man lowered his weapon, keeping his eyes on Eric. Kicking the gun away, he raised his hands in a symbol of surrender. Eric gestured with his gun for the man to move back to the corner.

Keeping his eyes on the group, Eric asked Barbie, "Is there rope around here?"

With a nod, she said, "Downstairs."

"Get it," he commanded, keeping his gun on the group of aged dwarfs.

"Throw us our clothes, will ya?" One of the men gestured to the pile of clothes on the table.

Eric stood stoically, ignoring the request.

Surprise registered on the gray bearded face. Looking past Eric, he asked me, "What kind of pervert are you girls hanging out with?"

"Can't we just give them their clothes?" I asked Eric, not wanting to stare at naked old man butt any longer than I had to.

Eric shook his head. "Can't see their hands that way."

Sounds of disbelief met his words.

"Give them their clothes. I've seen enough old man dwarf butt to last me a lifetime," Barbie chimed in from the doorway. After setting four steaming pizza boxes on the table, she handed Eric a pile of rope.

"Pizza! I'm starved!" A familiar voice called out from behind us.

Eric closed his eyes, took a deep breath, and said, "I told you to wait in the car."

"I saw the pizza guy." Stelios held up Ajax. "We're hungry."

"Yeah, we're hungry!" The corner of dwarfs agreed.

"What a cute little doggy!" Barbie cooed, holding out a piece of pizza to Ajax.

Ignoring everyone, Eric took the rope over to the corner. "Jessie, grab his hands," he commanded.

The dwarf in front of me held up a hand, and said, "We surrender."

"What?" I looked at Eric in confusion.

"We never wanted to keep anyone here against their will," one of the dwarfs said.

"Yeah, we're sorry you got all worried about your friend," another said.

"It's our boss. The guy is a total nut job," the tall one explained, as the rest nodded.

"Who is your boss?" I asked.

"Calls himself Mr. Claus," the tall dwarf answered. "He's got a real Santa complex." The other's nodded their agreement, as he explained. "He wears this threadbare Santa coat and boots, and calls this dump his workshop." He gestured to the warehouse. "He pays us real good, to be his elves and pretend to make toys. He originally wanted us to make the toys, but we don't know nothin' about toy making. So, he has them shipped in a couple times a month. A couple of days ago, he brings this broad in, and says to keep her on ice. We don't argue with the paycheck. You know what I mean?"

Barbie, Eric, and I traded glances.

"That's it? You just give up?" I asked the dwarves.

"That's right, you win. We won't try to run away or nothin'." The men nodded in unison.

Shaking his head as if to say 'none of this makes sense', Eric reached for the closest dwarf.

"You don't need to do this big guy," he said, pulling away from Eric.

Unbidden, a chuckle escaped me.

Eric shot me an unamused glare.

"Give it up Batman," Barbie admonished. "They're harmless."

"How do you figure?" Eric grabbed the dwarf's arms, tying him to his friend.

"If they're harmless, then why have you been missing the past couple of days?" I demanded. "You had better have been adultnapped. I've been worried sick." I glared.

Barbie shrugged. "Yes and no. Grab a slice, and I'll explain."

Eric made a groaning noise, as if he was in pain.

Shrugging, I reached for a slice of pizza, causing him to shake his head again. I couldn't blame him. None of this made sense to me, and I've spent enough time with Barbie to not be surprised at anything that she gets involved in.

Thirty One

"What are we doing here, again?" Stelios clutched Ajax to his chest.

We were downstairs in the warehouse, waiting for the dwarves' employer to arrive for his nightly check on the place.

"Why is he still here?" Eric growled.

"He's going through a tough time. He just got dumped," I defended Stelios.

"You want to help him? Dress him up and take him to the bar, just get him away from me," Eric grumbled.

"I can't believe I thought you were a nice guy," Stelios glared at Eric.

"You were wrong." Eric discounted Stelios's complaint.

Barbie raised an eyebrow, suddenly interested.

"We met him at that beach bar, down from the house, while we were looking for you," I explained.

"Never trust a guy you met in a bar," Barbie cautioned Stelios, with a meaningful glance towards Eric.

"I just saved your ass," Eric growled at Barbie.

Barbie shrugged. "I could've left anytime. I hung around hoping to catch the big guy."

"You could have called or something," I scolded Barbie. "I was worried sick!"

"Yes, Aunt Claire," Barbie sneered.

"Ugg! I'm turning into my mother!" I moaned.

"Ajax hears something!" Stelios whispered dramatically.

Eric held up a hand for silence.

The silence was deafening, as all eyes focused on the little dog's pointy ears. The right ear twitched, then Ajax slowly turned his head to the East entrance.

Ajax let out a low growl. I turned to see what he was growling about. When I turned back, Eric was gone. I exchanged looks with Barbie. She shrugged, moving the opposite direction.

A door clanged open.

"Stelios?" A voice echoed through the darkened warehouse. "Are you in here? I saw your Jeep out front."

Ajax jumped from Stelios's arms, racing through the darkness. I looked over at Stelios, he was ghost white, and looked as if he'd turned to stone. His frozen face wore an expression that made me happy he didn't have a weapon. I half expected to see steam coming out of his ears, like in old cartoons.

"Are you okay?" I whispered.

"What is HE doing here?" Stelios hissed.

"Um…" I didn't have an answer.

"Ajax! I missed you!" A vaguely familiar voice called out.

"It isn't enough that he kicked us out of our home, and workplace, now he's come for Ajax!" Stelios muttered.

Heading up the dark staircase, Bruno continued chattering to the little dog. In a rage, Stelios stood up. A new, more sinister sound echoed through the cavernous building. I grabbed Stelios, pulling him back down.

Stelios pushed me away.

"Someone else is here!" I whispered, pointing in the direction the sound had come from.

Stelios shot an alarmed look towards the stairs, where Bruno and Ajax stood looking out over the warehouse.

"Stelios!" Bruno called again. When no one answered, he turned towards the office.

"They'll be safe up there." I nodded, as if I was trying to convince myself.

"What the Hell!" The words echoed through the air above us.

"I think Bruno found the dwarfs." I cringed.

Stelios giggled beside me. "I'll bet that gave him a shock."

"At least we know he isn't the bad Santa," I offered.

Stelios nodded his agreement.

As if on cue, heavy footsteps echoed through the building. The footsteps stopped. I held my breath, not sure what to expect. Cheap yellow overhead lights, haphazardly burnt out and broken, flickered on throughout the large space, bathing the warehouse in a pallid glow. The light above me buzzed just before flickering out, plunging our corner back into darkness. The overall effect was spine-chilling.

Holding my breath, I peered around the boxes, with Stelios over my shoulder. All I could see was the back of a bright red coat, and black boots. Slowly, I released my breath. Was it him? Had we found Santa?!

"What is that man whore doing here?" Stelios snarled.

"Santa?" I turned to Stelios in surprise.

Before he could answer, seven tiny men, in various stages of dress, came running down the stairs, beards flying behind them. Behind them trailed Bruno, wearing what looked like a mermaid tail and holding a teacup Chihuahua. Stelios and I traded wide eyed glances. Just as Bruno reached the bottom of the stairs, Barbie and Eric emerged from different sides of the warehouse with their guns drawn.

"Hands up," Barbie roared. "Everyone!"

Surprised, Santa, and the dwarves threw their hands up in the air. Bruno struggled to put his hands up while holding onto the squirming little dog. The silence was disrupted by the front door banging open. All eyes turned to the door as a too familiar blonde agent with a gun, and six similarly clad friends rushed through it.

"Greg?" I asked Stelios. "What is Greg doing here?"

Shaking off the fog of surprise, Stelios shrieked, "He's wearing my tail!"

"He's... what?" I asked, thinking I had heard him wrong.

"My tail!" Stelios repeated, standing up. "That's it!" He

charged the room.

"Is this happening?" I asked the boxes around me as I watched a startled Ajax jump from Bruno's arms and run to Stelios.

"Stelios!" Bruno cried, running to Stelios. "You're alright!"

"Jessie! Take Ajax," Stelios demanded.

Dutifully, I ran over to the frightened Chihuahua and attempted to snatch him out of the path of the enraged man in front of me. Taking advantage of the moment, the dwarfs charged Barbie and Eric. Barbie and Eric fired at the dwarfs. Diving for cover, Santa fired at Greg and his agents. Before anyone knew what was happening, bullets were flying in all directions. Dog in hand, I grabbed Stelios and ran for safety. When the shooting stopped, Santa and the dwarves were gone, leaving behind them a trail of blood, bullets, and questions. I turned wide eyes to Stelios, then everything went dark.

Thirty Two

I woke up in a small dark space that smelled like dirty gym shoes. The first thing I noticed was that my head felt like it was about to split in two. I attempted to move, managing only to bang my already aching head into the carpet. At least it's soft, I winced to myself. Worried that I might be bleeding, I moved to touch my head, and couldn't. My hands and feet were tightly secured by a thin piece of plastic that dug deeper into my skin with the slightest movement, and something sticky was covering my mouth, forcing me to breathe out my nose. Panic flooded my brain at the realization that I was completely incapacitated, in a bad way.

Knowing that panic wouldn't get me out of this jam, I forced myself to take a deep breath, and calm down. After four more breaths, I felt calm enough to take stock of my situation. I couldn't remember how I got here, or where I was. The last thing that I remembered was all hell breaking loose between the dwarves, agents, merman, Santa, Eric, and Barbie. All of that was completely unhelpful. I peered through the darkness, hoping to see something. A long sliver of light appeared in front of me. I quickly came to the conclusion that I was on the floor of a closet. That would explain the dirty gym shoe smell.

Ignoring the pain in my wrists, ankles, and head, I wriggled closer to the light. I couldn't get my face low enough to see anything on the other side of the door. It was frustrating! I listened, hoping to get a clue to my whereabouts. Faintly, I could hear snoring. Snoring! I was lying in a smelly closet, trussed up like the holiday turkey, and whoever was out there was sleeping! Life is not fair.

I could feel the panic swell inside me. Closing my eyes, I took a deep nose full of air, immediately regretting it. Where were those gym shoes! I wriggled onto my back, trying to escape the smell. I needed to focus. I needed a plan to get out of wherever I was. Unable to concentrate, all I managed was to make my wrist pain more intense by laying on my arms. Giving up, I tried wedging myself into a more comfortable position.

I had no way of knowing how long I lay there, long enough to fantasize about shoving a thick rag into the snorer. Eventually, a new noise interrupted my thoughts. I held my breath, listening as hard as I could. There it was again, footsteps, and was that Christmas music? There was someone else here, other than the snorer, who was most probably the person who had tied me up. I should make some noise. But, what if the snorer wasn't my abductor, just the person on watch duty? What if the Christmas jingler was my abductor?

My stomach growled, telling me to hurry up with my

reasoning. The sound of a door opening caught my attention. Was that bacon? My stomach growled again. It was bacon! My thoughts were interrupted by words floating under the door in a language that I'd never heard. The snoring stopped. More foreign sounds were exchanged. My head sank deeper into the carpet, they were in this together.

"Is that bacon?" A woman's voice asked.

"Would you like some? I can make you some eggs and hot cocoa as well," a jolly voice offered.

"Coffee?" She countered.

"Um..." a male voice moaned.

Had I heard that voice before? Barely daring to breathe, I listened to the conversation on the other side of the door, hoping for some indication of where I might be and why.

"Jasmine," she offered.

"Jasmine has to get going. Don't you?" The snorer prompted.

"But, what about breakfast?" The jolly voice insisted.

"Jasmine is on a diet. Don't want to put on another ten, now do we love?" The snorer sneered.

"If you change your mind..." The jolly voice trailed off, hidden in the sound of a door closing.

"Right, I'd better go." Jasmine's voice faltered, "Can I get a ride? I'm not sure where I am."

"Get dressed," the snorer commanded. "You can catch a cab outside."

Where had I heard that voice before?

"Thanks. Um... I don't usually. I mean...," she faltered,

embarrassment heavy in her voice.

"Relax." I could hear him smile. "You were a porn star."

"Really? I don't remember... I must have had a lot to drink," the woman apologized.

It was such an awkward conversation, I forgot to make some noise. I realized my mistake when the door clicked shut, followed by silence. Just like that, the moment had passed. I was mentally berating myself for missing my opportunity for salvation, when I heard a groaning noise coming from inside my blackened prison.

Forgetting that I was gagged, I tried to speak, "Umm hmm gmnh!"

The blackness responded, "Umhhhmg Hmnmy!"

I was not alone.

Thirty Three

It had taken incalculable minutes, a massive amount of effort, and an extraordinary amount of pain, but my fellow prisoner and I were now free of our tape gags. We lay covered in sweat, back to front, gulping in the pungent air, as our bodies succumbed to the pain of the cords wrapped too tightly around our limbs.

"How did we get here?" Stelios whispered.

I shook my head, forgetting that we were cloaked in darkness.

"Where are we?" Impending panic coated Stelios's words.

"A closet," I answered frankly.

"What's going to happen to us?" he asked. "Are they going to kill us?" His body vibrated with panic as it surged to the surface.

"We're going to stay calm, and get out of this," I responded, keeping my voice calmer than I felt.

"How?" Desperation clouded his words.

"When Barbie was kidnapped, she got to play strip poker and eat pizza," I reminded him.

"They didn't tie her up and lock her in a closet," he stated morosely.

"Feel around," I interjected. "There's got to be something we can break these things with."

"You're right. I'm not going out without a fight," Stelios rallied, throwing himself headfirst into the far corner.

"Bang!" Something hit our door.

"Knock it off in there!" The snorer demanded.

My eyes widened as I heard the door handle turning. Biting my lip, I held my breath as the door opened, flooding the darkness with violent light. Reflexively, my eyes slammed shut.

A demonic chuckle assaulted my ears. "You like that?" The light was shoved into my face, boring pain through my closed lids. "I got the idea from that stupid cat." Rough hands grabbed my head, slapping something sticky onto my mouth, and wrapping it around my head. Slamming the door, he said, "Keep it on this time. If you make too much noise, I'll shoot you."

Stelios gasped.

"If he was going to shoot us, he would have already done it," I whispered, more to myself than Stelios. Unfortunately, my words sounded less comforting through the tape covering my mouth.

"The hot guy will save us, Nai?" Stelios whispered in the dark.

"If he can find us," I whispered.

Thirty Four

Stelios had been unusually quiet since the threat of being shot, allowing me to focus on the sounds of the house. Not able to speak or hardly move, I had spent the time eating a hole through my gag. It gave me something to focus on, and was better than giving in to the fear. Now that I could almost move my lips, I had nothing else to keep me occupied.

"Stelios," I whispered.

"Jessie!" He softly elated.

"I'm gonna be tasting tape glue for the rest of my life," I grumbled.

"I'm sorry." His voice was like a hug in the dark.

We sat quietly, listening to the darkness.

"Stelios." I broke the silence.

"Yes," he answered softly.

I hesitated, then asked, "Do you think you can turn the knob with your mouth?"

"I can try," his voice lacked confidence.

"Try." I forced confidence into my voice. "It's time for us to get out of here."

"What if we get shot?" He sounded scared.

"I've been shot before. It isn't nearly as bad as sitting in a dark closet worrying about getting shot," I admitted.

Stelios didn't respond. For a minute, I was worried, then I heard him move. Hope swelled inside me. He was going to try it! We were going to get out of here.

Minutes passed, with Stelios hard at work edging himself into position. I put my body behind his for support as he worked his head and neck to open the door. Finally, the door gave the faintest click, throwing us into a heap in a familiar room.

"You've GOT to be kidding me!" I grumbled.

"We're free!" Stelios sang his victory.

"God hates me," I sighed.

"What?" Confusion laced Stelios's voice.

"This is not good," I warned.

"It's not?" Stelios looked around the messy bedroom. "So, where are we?"

"I have no idea," I answered truthfully.

Before Stelios could ask another question, the door in front of us opened. Standing in the doorway stood an overweight, pasty white, sixty something, dressed in a loud Hawaiian shirt, Bermuda shorts, and Jesus sandals. He sported a large spare tire, thick head of white dreads, matching beard, and shocked expression. It all made sense now. The jolly laughter, Christmas music, elf statues… I just hoped he was the Santa Barbie's friend met on the beach all those years ago, and not the deranged Santa wanna be who had recently held Barbie hostage.

Breaking the stunned silence in the room, the Santa in the doorway said, "I heard a noise."

We watched, wide eyed, as he reached into his pocket, slowly pulling out a large knife. Stelios and I screamed as if on cue, trying to flop away from the deranged beach front Santa in front of us. A door banged open somewhere down the hall, and footsteps pounded our direction. My hopes of a happy ending faded when a face that I had hoped never to see again peered past the old man.

"Shit." I closed my eyes, praying not to be recognized.

"Look who's tied up this time." Amador ran his tongue across the empty socket where a tooth had been just days before.

Of course, he remembered me. If I was him, I'd remember me. "Your face looks… better," I offered, hoping to establish some good will.

"I hate you," he said calmly.

Of course he did. "I get that. I totally do." I nodded. "And, under the circumstances, I can't blame you for tying me up and stuffing me in a closet. But, this guy," I motioned my head towards Stelios, "he isn't a part of this. He just, literally, was in the wrong place at the wrong time. Being the Christmas season and all, maybe you could let him go?"

"I hate him, too," Amador said.

"You do?" I asked.

275

"I hated him first," Amador answered.

"You know each other?" I asked Stelios.

Stelios shrugged non-committally, then said, "We've met."

"He slept with my boyfriend, then outed me to my parents," Amador said stiffly.

"You did that?" I asked Stelios.

Stelios shrugged again, obviously unrepentant. "That was months ago. Are you going to kill me over it?"

Amador looked like he'd gladly kill over it.

"Amador," Santa chided. "That is no way to talk. You don't want to end up on the naughty list now, do you?"

"No," Amador protested.

"It's time to take care of these two," Santa insisted, taking out his knife.

Somewhere in the house, a door closed.

"They were out of the brand of soy milk you like, so I bought almond milk instead," a voice called out. "I hear it's better for you than cow milk. I'm excited to try it."

No one said anything. I thought about it, but I was afraid it was another bad guy.

"Dad? Am? Are you…" The voice stopped talking. From the hallway, he said, "Dad, I can explain."

"I don't think you can," the older man replied, bending down on one knee.

My eyes widened, as the old man raised his knife. Giving me a sympathetic look he took my head in his hands, and skillfully cut at the tape on my face. Once he had two ends free, he ripped off the tape from my face.

Fighting tears of pain, I somehow managed to choke out, "Are you Santa? I mean the real one?" I pursed my lips, hoping he wasn't about to slit my throat.

"No. I am." A familiar face stepped past Amador.

"Neik," the Santa crouched in front of me admonished.

"I'm a Claus." Neik stared him down.

"Son…" He sighed. "You can't just go around calling yourself Santa."

"I know my destiny. And, I'm ready. I've been practicing," Neik insisted. "I even have my own elves."

Santa shook his head sadly. "Son, being Santa isn't something you can practice. It's something you are. This," he waved his hands at me and Stelios, "this isn't the kind of thing that a Santa does."

"I know," Neik agreed. "But, it had to be done. They wanted to take you away from me, to undo everything that we planned. We can't let that happen."

"Son." Santa shook his head sadly. "The world doesn't need the Claus' anymore."

"It does!" Neik protested. "Can't you see? I'll make a great Santa."

Santa frowned. "When you were little, I wanted nothing more than to work the sleigh with you. I gave you the best education, the best presents, ignoring the elves when they said you'd been bad. I had such high hopes for you, my only son. I guess I should have raised you myself after your mother died, but I wanted you to have what I never did, friends your own size, and a life outside of the workshop. I thought it was for the best. I guess sometimes love and good intentions just aren't enough."

"What are you saying?" Neik asked.

"You're not good enough to take over." Santa gestured to mine and Stelios's bonds.

"I'll never be good enough for you!" Neik cried.

"No, no." The old man shook his head. "I mean you're not good. You do bad things. Santa has to be good. It's his most prevalent trait. It's not about me, boy. I love you, no matter who you choose to be. Sure, I'd like you to be more... well... good. The rest, I don't care. Honestly, I don't even care that you're gay. I think I've always known you were gay."

"What?" Neik and Amador said at once.

"I talked to some of the parents in my support group, and I've accepted it." Santa nodded.

"So, if I'm good, then I can be Santa?" Neik asked.

"Technically, yes. But, eventually Santa has to have a wife. One that can bear him children." Sadly, Santa explained, "Santa has to have an heir."

"I'm not gay. I had a girl here last night, and her the other night." Neik winked at me, adding, "You were a rock star."

"You're not fooling anyone," Santa said. "The whole town knows you and Amador are a couple. You two drug these women, drag them home, and make them think they slept with you."

"You mean," relief flooded my face, "we didn't?"

"You knew? Then why didn't you say something?" Neik demanded.

"I didn't want to upset you. You were so worried about what I thought," he said.

"I knew if you thought that I was gay, you'd never make me Santa. But, that's wrong. Amador and I would make the best Mr. and Mr. Claus," Neik pleaded.

"I don't care that you're gay. But, the world will expect an heir," Santa reminded him.

"There are options. We can adopt," Neik reasoned.

"If that were the case, don't you think the Missus and I would have adopted? To inherit, you have to be a blood relative. That's why she started growing those damned clones," Santa shuddered.

"We can do invitro. There are options," Neik countered.

"I hadn't thought of that. The times are different than they used to be," Santa acknowledged.

"So, you'll make me Santa?" Neik pushed.

"No." Santa shook his head sadly. "You're a monster. Drugging women and taking them to bed, kidnapping," he gestured to me and Stelios, "lying, theft, conspiracy... The list is exhausting."

"So, that's how it is then?" Neik's voice was dangerous.

"It's how it has to be," Santa agreed, leaning down to cut my bonds.

The knife slid across my arm, cutting me lengthwise, as Amador jerked it from Santa's hands. Moments later, Santa joined us on the floor, bound and gagged. Amador gleefully slapped another piece of tape on our mouths before leaving the room.

I tried to move say something, anything, but it was no use. I wasn't sure I had it in me to chew through another tape gag. At least

Jenn Brink

we were out of the closet.

Thirty Five

I awoke with a killer headache, in the trunk of a car, next to Stelios. The car wasn't moving, and the trunk was open. Unfortunately, I had no idea where I was. I couldn't see anything except the night sky, and that wasn't giving me any clues. I tried to piece together the events leading up to now, but all I could remember was Neik holding a small towel with a sweet odor against my nose and mouth.

I could hear voices. Listening closely, I tried to piece together what was happening, where we were, and where Santa might be. Suddenly, Amador leered into the trunk. With an alarming grin, he reached in, manhandling me out of the trunk. Amador roughly dropped me on the ground, as close to head first as he could.

My head exploded again. As he leaned back into the trunk, I lay on the dock, listening to what sounded like ocean waves. Amador and the dwarves carried an unconscious Stelios past me. Forcing myself to roll over, I watched them walk down a deserted dock, to a small boat.

The sound of a car door closing came from the distance, followed by an almost imperceptible thunk. I knew it wasn't Stelios, he had just disappeared over the side of a boat. It must be Santa. I had come to save him. Instead, I had gotten him tied up, and carried onto a boat in the middle of the night, on his way to a fate that wasn't looking good.

Desperate to free myself, I pulled at the ropes holding my hands and feet, succeeding only in banging my head against the hard ground. I kicked the side of the car in frustration. Forcing myself to calm down, I focused on wriggling away from the car. If I could just find help, I could still save us all.

I was still trying to wriggle away from the car, when a dark figure scooped up an all too familiar looking dwarf and tossed him into the still open trunk. I watched as two others were disposed of just as quickly. I was still trying to get a look at what I hoped was my rescuer when a lithe figure reached through the darkness, expertly cutting my hands and feet free of their bonds. Gingerly, I sat up, reaching for the tape covering my mouth. I pulled, was it supposed to hurt that much? I closed my eyes, steeling myself to yank the tape off.

"Let me do it," Barbie's voice came from behind me. "Don't scream. We still have the element of surprise on our side," she added. Before I could react, she ripped the tape from my mouth, taking half of my face with it.

I held my palm over my mouth, trying not to cry. Once the pain had subsided, I whispered a weak, "Thanks."

"My pleasure. Now, let's go rescue Santa," she said, running soundlessly down the dock.

I got to the boat just in time to see Barbie, Greg, and Eric, handcuffing Neik and Amador to the same group of dwarfs that had held Barbie captive in the warehouse. Santa and Stelios, also freed of their bonds, stood in the center of the boat, looking just as dazed as I felt.

"What happened?" Santa asked.

"These elf impersonators, along with their associates in the car, just admitted to planning to drop you all about thirty miles out, without a life jacket," Greg attested. Looking at me, he said, "You've got to get a nice quiet job somewhere. Mom and dad would have a heart attack if I had to go back and tell them that you'd drowned in Aruba. And, they'd blame me. They always blame me."

Rubbing the raw spots where my wrists had been tied for so long, I had to agree with him. A nice quiet job, in a nice quiet apartment, on a nice quiet street, sounded fabulous. Fabulous, and dull, very dull. Avoiding the subject, I said, "Neik wanted to be Santa."

"We know. He told us everything." Greg nodded. "Mrs. Claus was in on it. She knew all along where Santa was."

"She knew about Neik?" Santa looked up in surprise.

Greg nodded. "They've been in contact for years."

Neik sneered, "She told me all about how you were keeping me from my destiny as a Claus. She's always had faith in me, unlike you."

"She was using you." Santa shook his head sadly. "That woman was so busy with her clones, I never thought she'd look elsewhere for an heir. What happened to her clones?"

Greg looked accusingly at Barbie, and said, "Terrorists broke into the lab and power unit. They shut down the central power station, effectively destroying the existing clones, and all chances of creating future clones."

"The power core! What about the elves?" Santa asked.

"The elves are fine. Everything went offline, but they were able to get it repaired and running before we left. It was just a little darker, and colder than most of them liked for a few days. Not much different than a power outage after an icy storm," Greg explained.

"All you care about is your elves and your lists!" Neik shrieked. "What about your only son? You should care more about me. You were supposed to make me the heir! Instead, you left it all with her." Neik stared accusingly as his father.

"I'm sorry son. She made my life miserable for twenty-two years." Santa shook his head. "I couldn't do it any longer. I only have so many years left, I want them to be happy years. So, yes, I was getting ready to leave. I told you all of that last week, after I came to bail you out of jail again. As soon as I could work out the details, I was ready to move here, to my favorite place, with my only son." He looked at Neik with sad eyes. "But, my son betrayed me." Wiping a tear from his eye, Santa looked at us, and explained, "I had planned to go back days ago, but my wallet and passport disappeared. I tried to call the Missus and have her send a sleigh, but she hasn't been picking up. You wouldn't believe how hard it is to get back home without the proper ID."

We all nodded our understanding.

Eric tossed Santa what looked like a man's wallet and passport. "We found these in the warehouse where Neik and Amador were holding Barbie."

Santa turned questioning eyes to Neik.

Neik turned his face away, refusing to meet Santa's gaze.

Greg explained, "With the Santa monsters out of the picture, Mrs. Claus called Neik. Knowing you would never make him Santa, he made a deal with her. She would help him become Santa, and he would keep her on as the widowed Mrs. Claus. All he had to do was dispose of you, and he'd have it all."

Santa shook his head in disappointment, and sadly said, "My own son. My flesh and blood."

Neik gave him a hard look, and said, "You never cared for anything except your precious workshop."

Greg turned to Santa, and said, "Don't worry. She's being arrested for conspiracy to commit murder. She'll be long gone by the time you return."

"Return?" Mr. Claus frowned.

"The workshop must have a Santa." Barbie smiled encouragingly.

"I suppose it must." With a sigh, he added, "I'll have find a proper heir, now." Looking at the group standing around him, Santa attempted a smile, and said, "Thank you all, for saving me, for saving Christmas. I, the workshop, we are in your debt."

"How did you find us?" Stelios asked Barbie.

"We tracked down Santa's boat, just as Amador came to gas it up this afternoon. We decided to stake it out, just in case. When they drove up and started pulling bodies from the trunk, we thought the worst, but it looks like you're all just fine. More or less," Barbie explained, gently touching the tape stuck to the ends of my hair.

285

"Mr. Claus, are you ready to go home?" Eric asked.

"I guess I'll have to," he answered. "The workshop has to have a Claus. The only reason I planned to leave was that woman. I couldn't stand the thought of living out what years I have left with her. Now, I just need an heir," Santa said, winking at Barbie.

"I don't think so, big guy." Barbie shook her head, saying, "Don't get me wrong. I have as much Santa fetish as the next girl, but in my scenarios, Santa is about twenty-five with a washboard stomach. Of course, enough vodka and I could be persuaded to loosen my standards."

"Ewwww!" I moaned.

"You never cease to disgust me," Greg said to Barbie.

"It's a gift." Barbie smirked. "Sorry Santa."

"I'm too old to be a father again anyway. Too set in my ways to change diapers, and I need my sleep. Neik was supposed to be my heir. I gave him everything I never had. The best that money can buy... toys, a nice home, friends, education in an exclusive school in the Netherlands." He turned sad eyes to Neik. "I wanted him to grow up normal. I didn't want him to have to wonder if his friends liked him for him, or because he was the heir. I didn't want him to feel awkward about his height, like I always did. Instead, I turned him into a self-centered twat."

"What will you do for an heir?" I asked. "Doesn't Santa have to have one?"

He gave me a thoughtful look, scratched his head, and said, "I have a second cousin who lives in Minsk. Good man, we get together a couple times a year and go ice fishing. His youngest boy has always seemed like good Santa Claus material. I think I'll go talk to my cousin," he stroked his beard absently.

"First, we need to get you back to the workshop," Eric stated.

"Yes. My visit can wait until after Christmas," Santa agreed. "Just give me a minute to look over the boat. I want her ready for a long vacation after Christmas is over," Santa answered.

"After the stunt you just pulled, you may find it difficult to slip away for vacations," Greg said.

"I just wanted to spend some time with my son. He needed me," Santa explained.

"Why didn't you tell anyone where you were going?" Greg asked.

"And let her know that I have an illegitimate son? I've worked too hard to hide him from her all of these years." Santa frowned, adding, "I've wanted to tell everyone for years. I was just waiting for the right time."

"Hey, Santa." Barbie winked. "I've got a proposition for you."

"Oh my God!" I wailed.

"Why do you hang out with that amoral train wreck?" Greg asked.

"I don't know," I said, tripping over a rope on the boat and falling headfirst onto the dock.

Blinking slowly, I worked to focus my eyes. I was laying on my back, with Eric staring deep into my eyes. My headache had moved up a notch on the pain scale to *'cut if off please'*.

Eric gave me a concerned look, asking, "Trouble, how many

fingers am I holding up?"

"Which hand?" I asked, blinking again.

Eric and Greg traded worried looks.

"I didn't sleep with Neik," I explained. "He drugged my drink and I woke up in his room. I couldn't remember anything. I thought maybe I must have, but I didn't. He's gay," I trailed off, not sure why it mattered so much to me that Eric didn't think I was a ho bag.

Eric smiled, helping me to my feet. The water under the dock was causing it to shift and sway, affecting my balance. I started to fall, Eric pulled me up, securing me with his arm as I stepped forward.

It felt nice, wrapped securely in Eric's arms. I wondered if we could get past all of the misunderstandings of the last few months. I wondered if we could have a future together. I wondered what day it was.

"So, we saved Christmas?" I leaned against him, enjoying the moment.

Eric gave me an odd look. After feeling around my scalp, he asked, "How many times did you get hit on the head, Trouble?"

"Did I?" I asked.

"Someone needs to watch her for a concussion," Barbie suggested. "I did it last time."

"I got her," Eric offered.

"It's not my first concussion, not even my second. I'll be fine," I protested, knowing that no one was listening.

Thirty Six

It had been a long flight back to Santa's Workshop. Every time I dozed off, Barbie would wake me up with a new issue that required my immediate attention. I was starting to understand why all of her assistants go crazy. Barbie doesn't do well in confined spaces, especially when she's not in charge. Knowing it would give her something else to focus on, I couldn't wait to get to Santa's workshop. Then the doors opened, and I remembered we hadn't brought any clothes.

I frowned.

"Déjà vu?" Barbie asked.

"Yeah," I answered.

"Boss said to give you these." Eric's pilot handed us snow gear.

"What?" I fingered the snowsuit I'd just been handed.

"He says you are to put them on, and exit the plane," he replied, heading toward the cockpit.

I looked up to see Eric, dressed in white snow clothes that matched ours, heading our way.

"What's the deal, Batman?" Barbie asked.

Eric looked her in the eyes, after a long pause, he said, "I don't trust you with my plane."

"Fair enough." Barbie shrugged.

"Where are you headed next?" Eric asked me.

"New York," Barbie answered for me.

I bit my lip. The last few hours had been a constant barrage of get me this, get me that, this drink is too cold, and this drink needs ice. I was expected to make phone calls, travel plans, itineraries, and run her schedule, which was a lot more complicated than it seemed when we were together. At one point, she even insisted that I taste her food for her, because she was afraid she would scald her tongue leaving her unable to kiss properly when the opportunity arose. She told me how I was to dress, and wear my hair and makeup, how to speak, who to speak to... The micromanaging insistence of her ideas of perfection was constant. I wasn't sure how much more of being Barbie's assistant I could take.

"Jessie, while we're here, I need you to see if Amanda's boyfriend is interested in getting together. From what I heard, he's a horn dog and I've never done it with a midget," Barbie commanded. "And, make an appointment with Santa. I want to continue our discussion about repealing the workshop's ban on alcohol. I'd like to open a liquor store and a bar. Since we saved his ass and all, he should be grateful enough to share a piece of his pie."

"That's it!" I threw my hands up in frustration.

"What?" Barbie stared at me in surprise.

"I can't. I love you like the sister that Greg will never be, but I cannot work for you," I said.

"Well, not with your hair like that," Barbie fingered the strands of my hair, still caked with leftover duct tape.

"It won't come out," I cried. "My hair is ruined."

"We'll have Amanda show us to the beauty shop. She has great hair," Barbie reasoned.

"Yeah, okay. But, I quit. You know that, right?" I asked.

"It's for the best. You suck as a personal assistant," Barbie admitted. "At this rate, I'd have to fire you in a week."

"Now that's settled, what's next for you?" Eric asked me.

"Christmas, and then, I don't know," I answered. "I need to figure some things out."

"I have the best present this year, too!" Barbie squealed with anticipation.

"What is it?" I asked.

"You'll see," she crowed, following everyone out into the cold.

A strong arm caught me by the waist, pulling me back into the plane.

"Trouble," Eric's voice was strained, "I've been trying to ask, wondering if you would…," dropping something, he bent down on one knee. Picking it up, he looked up at me.

My blood ran cold. Was he about to propose? Did I want him to propose? My mouth went dry, my brain slowed down to a crawl. I didn't know if I wanted him to keep going, or stop, like it had never happened.

"Would what?" I asked softly, my heart in my mouth.

Looking up into my eyes, he nervously asked, "Trouble, now

that you're not working for your cousin, would you come to Boston, and work for me?"

"Work for you?" I asked slowly.

He stood up. "You would have your own apartment at Wolf Inc. headquarters, salary, medical, and dental. You can pick out paint, and furniture, whatever you want, or I can have my housekeeper do it for you."

"Dental?" I asked dumbstruck. I looked around. Was anyone else hearing this? They had all left. It was just me, and Eric. Was this my Disney moment? It couldn't be. I looked back at Erik. Had he really just offered me a job?

"That way I could keep you out of trouble." He smiled at me.

Staring at Erik, I somehow managed to mask my disappointment. "It's a great offer, for a girl like me," I said, "but, I... I have a wedding to attend."

"After Stelios and Bruno's wedding," he clarified.

"After that, I think I need to go home." I nodded to myself.

"If you change your mind..." He stopped, mid-sentence.

Not sure what else to say, I turned towards the open door.

"You're not going back to that guy?" he asked.

I turned around, wondering if I was missing something. "Mike?"

He gave me a questioning look.

"We do have unfinished business," I evaded, stepping through the door, and into the cold.

Epilogue

The twinkling pine tree seemed to float on a cushion of torn paper. Gramma Hart, mom, dad, Greg, Barbie, and I sat in a circle around it, eating homemade cinnamon rolls, and smelling the slow roasting Christmas ham wafting in from the kitchen. It was Christmas morning at the Hart's.

I held my breath as Mom pulled the paper off of a carefully wrapped box. Shock raced across her face, and a tear formed in her eye. "Jessica? How? Where?" Speechless, she stared in awe at the wooden box.

"What is it?" My dad asked, craning his head to see.

Turning the box, with the lid lifted, mom showed him. Dad and Greg turned surprised glances my way.

"I swear, I will never touch them. I won't even go near them. I mean, this is as close as I'll ever get," I stammered.

"I've looked everywhere." Mom stared adoringly at the box of handcrafted ornaments. "Where did you find them?"

"I know a guy." I winked at Greg.

"A guy?" Mom perked up. "Is he married?"

"Yes, he's married," I answered. Under my breath, I added, "for now."

Barbie rolled her eyes, and asked, "Are you going to open that?"

I looked down at the box mom had handed me several minutes ago. It was the last present. Turning it over in my hands, I searched in vain for a tag, finally asking, "Who is it from?"

Everyone looked at each other. Then dad offered, "It came certified mail, yesterday."

"Certified mail?" Mom made a clicking noise. "Well, open it."

I reached for the ribbon, just as the door opened, causing the dogs to go crazy. A moment later, Bubba, Junior, and Mike came in with Junior's kids in tow. Conversation stopped, as we looked from one to the other. I looked at Junior. Beaming from ear to ear, he produced a sleeve of papers form his coat.

"I got my kids fer Christmas! I woked up, and there they was, sleepin' under the tree, like little angels. And this, this was next to them," he shouted, waving the papers in the air.

"What do you have there?" My dad held out a hand demanding the papers.

"Signed and legal, divorce and custody papers!" Junior waved the stack in the air. "She said she'd get my kids back, and she did.

This woman is an angel." He kissed Barbie, surprising everyone. "I'd marry you in a New York minute."

"I'm not the marrying kind," Barbie declined.

"Well what do you know, it is a Christmas miracle!" Gramma Hart snarked.

"Oh my! I just can't believe it!" Mom gushed. "Let's get you kids some cinnamon rolls and juice!" Mom hurried into the kitchen with Junior's kids in tow.

I raised an eyebrow at Barbie.

She winked.

Stepping closer, I asked, "YOU did this?"

"Let's just say, I asked Santa for a favor. It turns out, I was VERY good this year," Barbie drawled.

"Oh god no!" I choked.

"What's that?" Mike interrupted, pointing at the small box in my hand.

I shrugged, "I hadn't finished opening it."

"Well, finish up. I want you to open my gift," he said, holding out a small delicately wrapped box.

All eyes were on me as I slowly unwrapped the mystery gift. Opening the box, I stared at the contents, unable to speak. Taped inside the top, was a note that said, *'Think about it'*.

Barbie looked over my shoulder, asking, "Keys? Did someone get you a car? It's about time. What kind is it? There's no emblem on it." Barbie looked around, everyone just shrugged.

"They aren't car keys," I said. I knew what they were, and who they were from. They were from him. The keys to my new apartment in Boston, and a job at Wolf Inc. I frowned, recalling his words, *'Think about it'*. I wasn't sure what I wanted from Eric, but employer and landlord had never crossed my mind.

"Who would buy you a car?" My dad asked suspiciously.

"He's too late," Mike said. Taking the keys from my hand, he added, "I'll buy you a car, house, whatever you want."

Before I could say anything, he knelt in front of me, popping open a small square. My eyes bulged, as I struggled to catch my breath. Inside the box was the freshly shined engagement ring that he had offered me what seemed like a lifetime ago.

"Mike?" His name was all I managed to squeak out, and it seemed to echo through the group of stunned adults.

I looked around, unsure if this was really happening, at Christmas, in front of my family. Stunned faces held their breath, waiting for the pageant in front of them to play out. The only sound came from the jingling of Mom's silver bells.

Staring into my eyes as if I were the only one in the room, Mike said, "I know we've had our ups and downs, but there is no one else that I'd rather be with." He swallowed loudly, then continued, "I promise to be the man you want me to be, for the rest of our lives." Mike paused. Taking a deep breath, his voice full of emotion, he asked, "Jessica Katie Hart, will you marry me?"

Silver Bells

About the Author

Jenn Brink spent the first half of her life going to school with the goal of working with some of the most interesting people you could never imagine. After a few years in the trenches, she retired to live a life of ease changing diapers, picking up Legos, and learning to use a crockpot. These days, she uses her knowledge and experience of people, personalities, and stranger than fiction events in her writing.

Follow Jenn on social media and her page.
https://www.jennbrinkauthor.com/

www.ingramcontent.com/pod-product-compliance
Lightning Source LLC
Chambersburg PA
CBHW031254170626
46807CB00001B/135